THE HEART OF DEATH

A NOVEL BY

L. RYAN STORMS

Published by RaineStorms Press, 2020.

The paperback edition has been catalogued as follows:
Name: Storms, L. Ryan, author
Title: The Heart of Death / by L. Ryan Storms
Description: Electronic file (eService)
Series: The Tarrowburn Prophecies; Volume 2
Summary: Reina and Quinn expected a happily-ever-after. Instead they've been thrust into the center of another prophecy. To stop the Chaos Wielder's madness from turning the world into the living dead, they'll have to journey through enchanted lands, make untold sacrifices, and retake control of the talisman's unexpectedly volatile magic.
ISBN 978-1-7328492-2-8 (paperback)
ISBN 978-1-7328492-3-5 (ebook)
Subjects: | YFC: Children's / Teenage fiction: Action & adventure stories | YFH: Children's / Teenage fiction: Fantasy & magical realism | YFB: Children's /Teenage: general interest | BISAC: YOUNG ADULT FICTION / Fantasy / General | YOUNG ADULT FICTION / Action & Adventure / General | YOUNG ADULT FICTION / General

www.lryanstorms.com
Cover art by Jess Bieber, more at www.entertheglow.com

For Nate, also known as "He Who Does Not Read"
Thanks for reading my books.
I'll always look forward to our adventures together.
Reina and Quinn have nothing on us.

CHAPTER ONE

Unfinished Business
Quinn

Marrying Reina was not my first act as king.

Oh, I wanted it to be, but stepping into the role of ruler in a kingdom ruined by chaos over the last few years meant there was little that didn't demand my immediate attention in one way or another.

No, my first act was to direct the surrender of the King's Army to the Resistance forces. Officers were to be tried for war crimes based on their actions under Bruenner, and foot soldiers—all twelve-thousand of them—were given the opportunity to appeal for clemency and return to their lives, their penance in helping restore order in one way or another.

I'd seen enough death to last ten lifetimes. I wasn't about to steal men's lives for being on the wrong side of a war.

Mercy, Reina says, defines a king.

And if I *must* rule, I intended to do it properly. Especially since my grandmother would have my head if I didn't.

I smiled. Grandma Elle had a ring to it. She hadn't arrived at the capital yet, but I expected her any day. Kelford had sent word weeks ago. Once the news traveled to Gillesmere, it took everything in his power to keep Madam Bonverno from leaving that very night. He'd somehow managed to convince her to wait and travel with McElson's party. Or so his letters proclaimed. I pictured it easily enough, though. She'd fight anyone standing in her way to get to family.

Governor McElson of Gathlin was a member of the High Council who had played a pivotal role in helping us get Reina's message to the Resistance forces. Without him and his messengers, our army never would have made it to Reina's side in time to help take control of the King's Army once Bruenner was dead. I would be glad to see him again, but I'd be far gladder to see my grandmother.

If someone told me a year ago what kind of turn my life was going to take, I would have brushed it off as pure hogwash.

I'd gained a grandmother—and a kingdom—almost overnight. The grandmother was worth a thousand kingdoms in my humble opinion, but even so, I vowed to do what was best for the hundreds of thousands of citizens of Castilles who deserved better than they'd received over the last several years.

Marrying Reina wasn't even my second or third or fourth act as king. Actually, I hadn't yet married Reina. Since the rushed coronation, I'd been up to my neck in trying to restore some semblance of a peaceful, prospering land, but Castilles would need more than a few weeks to recover. It would need years.

Which was acceptable. I was familiar with waiting and well versed in throwing everything into my work to ensure the end results were what needed to be. I was no stranger to giving up everything for the *right* thing. And if that's what needed to happen to bring Castilles and her people back to prosperity, that's what I would do.

How many times had I done so before?

I lay awake in the ridiculously enormous bed in the outrageously enormous bedroom that once belonged to my mother and father—my biological mother and father—and stared at the ornate, painted ceiling, contemplating my life choices and how I'd come to be the king of one of the biggest nations on Liron.

I rubbed my eyes. Kings probably weren't supposed to debate the wisdom of such things. Surely they were supposed to accept their destiny as it had been handed to them. But then I hadn't exactly been brought up with the wisdom of kings past. My destiny had come as a surprise—even to me.

I almost didn't hear the tap at the door. If I'd been asleep, I would have missed it entirely, but that was probably intentional on her part.

"Come in, Reina," I said. The massive door opened a crack, revealing a sliver of Reina's profile. "I'm not sleeping," I told her.

She slipped into the room, closing the door with the smallest of clicks and leaned against it, a sly smile on her face. She viewed me from across the room.

"How did you know it was me?" she asked softly, her inquisitive eyes narrowed. I could watch her brain work all day—or all night—and never get tired.

I knew because I always knew, but instead I answered, "Who else would dare wake a slumbering king?"

"You just said you weren't sleeping."

I fought a smile. "I'm awake either way, aye?"

She glared at me with raised brows, amusement tugging at the corners of her lips again.

"I'll go," she threatened, but the smile on her face widened in contrast to her words.

I rolled onto my side and patted the mattress beside me. "Sit."

She made no sound as she crossed the carpet to the bed. Truth be told, a herd of horses could probably cross this carpet without a sound given the thickness of the pile. The coin sunk into every corner of the castle reminded me of the wealth of the royal family of the Southern Plains. Other than the Plains, I'd never seen anything remotely comparable.

Reina crawled onto the bed beside me, her nightgown half held in one hand so she wouldn't pin it down as she moved forward on her knees. She let it go, lay down, and curled against my side, resting her head on my arm, careful to keep the talisman she wore around her neck from hitting my skin. The bloody pendant had shocked me more times than I could count in the past few weeks. I'd learned to cover it with a hand when I leaned in to steal a kiss lest it shock my chest and stop my heart. Hands absorbed a shock better than a heart would.

"There was a time you would have died of mortification at the thought of lying beside me in bed," I said.

I enjoyed the feel of her thick hair resting on my skin, her face close to mine, her breath on my bare chest. My words were true. A mere few months ago, she would have turned beet red at the thought of lying beside me in a bed. Not that I wasn't glad for the change.

I was.

"Are you complaining, Quinn D'Arturio?" She tilted her head to look at me.

"I wouldn't dream of it." I looked back at her and smiled, loving that she still called me by my name—my real name. Eron Alexandre Morel of Brenwyn didn't exist here. Not between us.

"Good," she replied, nestling down again.

I breathed her scent in and closed my eyes. Something lemony with a hint of an herb I couldn't identify. Intoxicating nonetheless. She was mine, and I was hers, in a dream I never could have imagined turned reality. But it had. We were here in Irzan, and despite the messy business of rebuilding a kingdom, despite the fact that I rarely saw her throughout my days, we were in this together. Our future would be built together. I hadn't ever thought to be handed such a gift.

"Why are you awake?" I tucked her closer to my side. I wanted to inhale her, to kiss the spot behind her ear, and nibble her neck. I wanted to kiss her perfect mouth silly and chew her bottom lip.

She sighed.

"I was in the library today."

The library. She was thinking about the library and I was thinking about kissing. It figured, really. I didn't think it would take Reina this long to find the royal library, but the coronation preparations had kept her busy, too.

"He wasn't lying when he said there were more

Tarrowburn Prophecies," she said, and she didn't need to tell me who she was talking about. General Bruenner.

The mere mention of him darkened my mood and in the space of a single sentence, I no longer thought about nibbling Reina's neck or chewing her bottom lip. The imposter was still ruining my life. Bruenner was gone, dead—thanks to Reina, but even so, I didn't like to think about him, about the lives he destroyed, the kingdom he ruined.

"Are you about to tell me something to keep me from sleeping tonight?" I asked with a cringe.

She gave a light tap on my chest. "You were already awake, remember?"

"Right."

I waited for her words, my mind reeling with the possibilities. Every facet of dread gleamed like the side of some jeweler-cut stone.

"There's more to the prophecy. A lot more." She paused, either gathering her thoughts or gathering the courage to tell them to me. Finally, she blurted, "We don't have much time."

I withdrew my arm from beneath her head and pulled myself into a sitting position, leaning against the gilded headboard and angling to get a more direct look at her in the dark. Enough moonlight shone through the window to highlight the worry in her brow, the concern in her eyes. Whatever she had read, it disturbed her.

Reina wasn't one to worry without reason. If something bothered her, it would bother me, too.

"Out with it," I said, hoping, praying it was not as bad as I feared.

"Joseph Faranzine made…morethanonetalisman." The last words tumbled from her mouth so quickly it took me a moment to decipher them.

"Joseph Faranzine—"

"Made more than one talisman," she finished for me.

I breathed a small sigh. For a second, I thought the unknown prophecies were going to predict some new horror. A few life-bringing talismans weren't much to be worried about. Unless…

"How many?" I asked.

"Three total."

"And?"

I waited for the remainder of the bad news to fall from Reina's mouth. She hesitated a moment, biting a lip before continuing.

"The power of the three talismans acts to channel the natural abilities in three individuals at any one time. I wear the talisman that brings life, but there are two others…and if I interpreted things correctly, they reflect the other two aspects of our existence."

She paused a moment to look up at me, trying to gauge if I was following. I was. Neither of the other two aspects of our existence were pleasant, nor so benign, as life itself. Of course, Reina had managed to kill even with the power of life, proving nothing was what it seemed.

"The other two aspects. Death and chaos," I said.

She nodded.

"You're telling me out there, somewhere, are two more talisman necklaces with the potential to bring death and chaos on the kingdom?"

She wrinkled her nose. "The world."

"Fiermi," I breathed with a sigh. I ran a hand along my neck, massaging the tightness there. "Why do I feel you're not yet done delivering the bad news?"

She took a breath and held it, regarding me, before letting it out. "It's up to us. You and I…we have to make this right."

I let my head fall back, my skull clunking against the headboard with a dull thud. It was up to us. Again. Why should I think that Reina and I would ever get a semblance of normal life? Who was I to hope for such things? I reined in the errant thoughts, pulling them tight, stopping them short.

My time with the Order prepared me for this. It prepared me for everything. I don't know why I thought things would be different once the White Sorceress—Reina—was discovered.

I sighed, resigned myself to the inevitable, then pulled myself out of the bed and began to pull a pair of pants over my nightclothes. I wasn't sleeping anyway.

Reina leaned on an elbow. Her hair cascaded over her hand in a dark waterfall I wished I could drown in. It was shorter than she used to keep it, but I suspected she used the talisman to grow it since her recent cut. The locks seemed to have gotten longer again quickly.

"What are you doing?" she asked, her eyes falling on my chest. I hoped she was admiring the muscles there and not the smooth scar near the center of my abdomen. The scar was one more to add to the collection I'd earned. For the things I'd done, I deserved them all.

"Heading to the library." I shrugged a tunic over my head, concealing both my muscles and the scar. "Are you coming?"

"Why do *you* get to get dressed first?" She stood and gestured to her night gown.

I raised an eyebrow. "Because I don't go sneaking into other people's rooms in the middle of the night?"

She pressed her mouth into a line and issued me a cocked eyebrow of her own. "You don't normally have complaints when I sneak into your room in my nightclothes. Stay put. I'll be right back." With that, she leaped from the bed and disappeared from the room.

In another moment, she reappeared, wearing a deep blue silk robe tied at her waist. I followed Reina's lead through the stone hallways, past the flickering oil sconces on the walls and down several sets of large stone stairwells. I nodded at each set of guards stationed in various locations along the castle corridors. With peace only recently restored, the personal guard insisted on setting up watch, even though I had said it wasn't necessary. I suppose that's what I should expect for making Agent Brigantino Captain of the Guard. At least the guards we passed looked watchful and alert, each one holding a fist to his heart as I passed. I expected no less of former agents, but I wished they'd stop saluting me.

The library was in the castle's lowest level to keep the books safe from heat and humidity during the summer months. The cool air wasn't good for them either, but it was better than exposing the invaluable ancient texts to the sunlight and varied temperatures of the castle's upper levels.

As we entered the oldest section of the library, I brushed my fingers across the carvings in the dark stone archway mottled with lichen. IV3. It had been carved so long ago that the corners of the impression had rounded and dust and cobwebs nearly filled in the markings.

"What does IV3 mean, do you think?" I mused aloud.

She paused, looking up at the dark stone in the middle of the arch, keen eyes observing.

She was quiet a long moment, considering. "Irzan Verity."

Irzan's truth. A library *could* be labeled as such.

"Irzan's Vernacular, perhaps? Irzanian Vestibule? Irzan's Veranda?"

"Veranda?" I questioned with a laugh at the irony of comparing an underground library to an outdoor patio. Or a garden. Was a veranda a garden? I wasn't sure.

"Either way, it still doesn't address the three. I've no idea," she said.

We left the archway puzzle behind and traveled through the stacks. The library itself looked more like a dungeon than a fountain of knowledge, the dark stone walls seeming to press inward the farther back we ventured. Reina grabbed a low-burning oil lantern from the wall before we pressed into the narrowest of the passageways between the stacks.

"It gets darker back here," she explained.

"Tighter, too," I commented.

She didn't reply, but trailed her fingers across the books until she found what she was looking for. She pulled a leather-bound tome from its place on a dusty shelf before turning back the way we'd come. Once we reached a small table, she placed the book down, sending plumes of dust into the air that tickled my nose. I suppressed the urge to sneeze. I'd have to task someone with cleaning the library soon. 'Twas a crime for a place so important to have fallen into disarray.

"Why didn't you leave the book out?" I asked, wondering what made her put it back into the library's darkest corners.

"Hm?" she asked distractedly, flipping the yellowed pages.

"Earlier. If you looked at it earlier, why not just leave it out to return to later?"

"Oh, I didn't want anyone else coming across it."

As though anyone else would be spending time in the darkest corners of the dungeonesque library.

She ran a finger across the words on pages before finding what she was looking for.

"Here!" she said, sliding the book toward me.

I took a moment to center myself before reading the bad news that awaited. *Here. I am here. Here and now.* Then I let my eyes scan the page.

The true king sits
On the throne at last
A short-lived peace
Which passes fast

Months at best
'Til the scale tips
The kingdom has
Until the first eclipse

What's dead is alive
What's alive is dead
The veil has thinned
In places shred

To mend what's broken
Three must travel
Scour the Plains
Or worlds unravel

The Bringer of Life, the King,
The One Who Failed
Find the Heart of Death
Through much travail

Only in Death
Can balance restore
For a time at least
'Til the next great war

For the Chaos Wielder
Has allowed
The balance to slip
Too long, too proud

That Liron may fall
To darkness and mayhem
When the power rests
In the stone of the diadem

To fix forever
Chaos bound
Only then
Balance found

Fiermi. Reina was right.

The horse's hooves pounded the earth beneath me, the rhythm beating itself into my very bones, soothing my thoughts in a way nothing else had in the past few weeks.

I wasn't running away.

I didn't know how to run.

Even if I wanted to.

The life of a king and ruler wasn't meant for a hermit like me. Oh, I recognized the irony. I accused Reina of being a hermit once. Maybe it was because I could see so much of myself in her.

With the coming and going of what seemed like a hundred advisors every day, the forming of the Guard under Brigantino's command, and reassigning agents from the Order as they arrived in the capital, my head was spinning. Most days I couldn't even hear my own thoughts. Add to all of it the weight of another prophecy and I'd lost my balance entirely.

But here, crouched low on Chiron's neck, galloping across the nearby plains, the wind in my ears, for once I could breathe. We approached the small stream that wound its way in coils back and forth across the land and rather than splashing through it, I shortened the reins, stood in my stirrups, hunched over Chiron, and gave him the signal to jump.

He was more than ready to oblige, and we sailed through

the air, landing on the other side of the stream with hardly a thump, as though the horse had been born with wings. Then I felt myself doing something I hadn't done in a long time. I laughed.

This horse could jump.

I slowed him down a bit, intending to circle around and jump again just for the hell of it, but I was greeted with a surprise.

Reina.

She charged across the fields on Aeros, not slowing a whit, heading straight for the widest portion of the stream. Before I could open my mouth to warn her, she and the horse flew through the air, a blur of dappled gray and flying green cloak.

After arriving in Irzan, I'd sent a courier for Aeros, and I'd made it clear the horse was needed quickly. Reina and Aeros rode together like a single being. I'd never seen anything like it. I could ride any horse for any task on any given day and feel no bond with the creature, but Reina… Reina and Aeros were of one mind.

As if to prove my point, Reina hollered as they landed perfectly, then led the horse to where Chiron and I had stopped, winded and heaving. Amazingly, neither she nor Aeros seemed out of breath.

"That was dangerous," I said.

She let the reins fall to Aeros's neck and allowed the mare to drop her head and relax.

"If the king can do it, so can I," she responded with a shrug. "Where are you running to?"

"I'm not running."

She gave me a flat stare, round, dark eyes unamused. "You think I don't know running when I see it? Should I remind you of my own expertise in the area?"

"Fine. I'm not running *away*, though. Just running."

She was quiet for a moment before commenting, "It was pretty bad."

The prophecy.

"It was."

My eyes scanned the swaying high grasses of the plain. Habit, I supposed. Always in motion, always moving, always scanning for danger. Even when there was none.

But that wasn't exactly true, was it? There was danger aplenty. Just not visible.

"So what are we going to do about it?" Reina asked, her eyes never leaving my face even when I looked elsewhere.

"What we do best," I answered, turning my gaze to meet hers. "Meet the danger head on. Are you ready?"

She tilted her head and offered a small smile, but there was fire in her eyes.

"Always."

CHAPTER TWO

False Promises
Quinn

Slipping away wasn't going to be easy. I'd become a public figure wherever I went and going unnoticed wasn't an option. Not to mention, the daily reports needed to go to someone for review and action.

Luckily, *someone* arrived just in time. I waited impatiently for my newfound grandmother, Reina standing beside me in the high-ceilinged receiving room. In the weeks we'd spent in Gillesmere, I'd developed a soft spot for Madam Bonverno. The old woman had become like family. And now…now she *was* family. Reina grabbed my hand and squeezed it once to stop me from pacing the floor again. I swallowed and stood beside her, quieting my thoughts.

"She'll be here soon," she murmured. "I doubt she'll let the carriage stop before flinging open the door."

The image of the silver-haired woman in a high-necked gown of satin and lace leaping from the carriage in excitement formed itself in my mind, and, before I could stop it, a smile spread across my lips.

"That's better," Reina said.

"Are you the keeper of my emotions now?" I asked,

amused.

She nodded earnestly, dark eyes dancing. "I am. I must ensure all emotions are in the positive spectrum at all times, particularly where I am concerned."

"Where *you* are concerned, my emotions are molten," I replied, leaning to kiss her while we enjoyed a rare moment alone together.

A giggle escaped her throat before I stole her breath away and deepened the kiss, weaving one hand through locks of her hair and placing the other in the small of her back, molding her body to my own. She leaned in willingly, standing tiptoe to kiss me back.

I wanted to devour her lips. Emotion I had suppressed for so many years overflowed in kisses I had waited too long to share. She tasted of mint and fuisberry and Reina, and, God, I wanted so much more. A pressure welled in my chest.

Was it because Reina kissed me back every bit as fervently, with matching desire, with equal emotion? This thing I had wanted for so long with Reina, it was real. If the rest of my life fell apart in every way, what Reina and I had never would. She was my forever.

"She's here," Reina said, pulling back, her eyes glittering with mischief. She composed herself, smoothing her gown, attempting to look as though I hadn't just kissed her senseless and wanted nothing more than to continue doing so. The sound of boots echoed across the highly-polished floors of the castle's corridors, and Reina's breath caught with excitement. With reluctant effort, I focused my attention on my grandmother and her escorts.

Madam Bonverno wasted no time on formalities when she entered the room. She rushed past McElson, almost knocking over one of Brigantino's guards stationed at the room's door in the process, then gripped me in a hug with a ferocity someone her age and size shouldn't have possessed.

"Glad to have your heir back," Governor McElson said with a laugh, his hand still against the wall he'd used to steady himself.

"Heir be damned," she said, her eyes shining with tears. "He's my grandson, blood of my blood. I've been too long without family and now, my dear boy"—she turned to me, tilting her head upward— "I have you."

Her voice cracked on the last word, betraying her emotion. I hugged her back tightly, a feeling I couldn't discern taking root in my chest. Family. Madam Laurelle Bonverno was family.

And she knew how to rule a kingdom.

"You can't know what it's like to find something you've lost when you thought it was gone forever," she said. "I thought my entire family had been taken from me. Losing Isobelle was bad enough, but when the baby—when *you* were taken, well I almost gave in. I wanted to, you know. Saints, how I wanted to."

"But it's all right," I said, stroking her back lightly. "You'll never be without me again, I promise."

Except that I was planning to leave her again…and soon. Guilt began to form in the base of my skull, and I brushed it away. There'd be time for guilt later. Not now. Now, I had gained family.

She wiped her eyes as she pulled away, nodding. "Foolish old woman am I."

"Nonsense," Reina said. "Family is everything."

Madam Bonverno snuck a sideways look at Reina, not releasing her from intense scrutiny for a moment. With a motion quicker than seemed possible for her many years, she released me, turned to Reina, and embraced her with just as much enthusiasm.

"Pah! Don't you get on about not having a family, child. I suspect you're part of this one already, and if you aren't"— she leaned outwards, holding Reina's arms, examining every inch of her face— "we'll remedy that shortly."

She returned a stern gaze to me, leaving little doubt of her implications. I almost had to bite back a smile. She'd known all along of my feelings for Reina. Unsurprising.

And further proof my gut was right about her from the start. My grandmother was a sharp woman. And she'd make an excellent ruler while I was away.

Naturally, there was still the matter of slipping away from Reina. She wouldn't make it easy, but there was no way I'd allow her to throw herself in danger's path yet again. After the last year, she, of all people, deserved the peace and luxury of a fully-staffed castle and a fully-stocked larder.

The new prophecy made it clear Reina would need to be involved, but the less I dragged her into it, the better. I'd let her get involved…eventually. But first, I'd do the legwork. Reina wasn't trained in the ways of death. She wasn't conditioned to ghost, to spy, to hide in the darkness. She shouldn't be pulled into another death-filled prophecy.

I saw what it did to her, the killing. She might not regret killing Bruenner, not really, but the memory of it lived on, tormenting her even in her sleep. She thought she could hide it, but deep in the night, she whimpered in her sleep beside me, and it wasn't hard to guess what horrors her dreams held.

I wouldn't let her throw herself back into that kind of life, not when I could keep her safe in Irzan, on the palace grounds, with at least a dozen people who would keep her from harm's way.

What's dead is alive, what's alive is dead.

What did that say about Reina? Reina was life itself.

And I wouldn't let her die.

"I'm thrilled to see the kingdom returning to her former glorious state, Your Majesty, but there are some… unsettling concerns that have been brought to my attention most recently." McElson cleared his throat and pushed his spectacles upwards on his nose.

I studied him closely. He was as direct in person as he'd been in his letters over the past weeks. An uncomfortable quiet fell over the dining table. So much for pleasant dinner conversation. I'd hoped to spend at least one night not discussing pressing issues, but since this was the first time my ears weren't being monopolized by citizens of the kingdom begging for help with matters of restoration, I couldn't blame McElson for seizing the opportunity. At least he'd waited until the dessert dishes had been cleared.

I leaned back in my seat, folded my arms across my chest and studied him, giving a slow nod. "Go on," I said, steeling myself for the worst.

McElson hesitated, at once nervous. Perhaps he hadn't expected a willing audience. His eloquence in speech suddenly lacking, he stuttered while trying to figure out where to begin.

I waited.

Finally, he cleared his throat again and began anew. "We've had word, reports from numerous sources. There's unrest in the south."

"Unrest?" I questioned, my eyes never leaving his.

My gaze made him uncomfortable, but I didn't let up. There was as much to be said from a man's body language as there was from the words he spoke. The way McElson played with the corners of his napkin while speaking, and the number of times he blinked while trying to pull together his thoughts told me all I needed to know about whatever was on his mind. It wasn't good.

My thoughts wandered back to the prophecy Reina found. Maybe I shouldn't have eaten dessert after all.

"Well, I don't quite know how to put it," McElson said.

Reina eyed me from her seat beside me, willing me to look her direction, but I resisted, unwilling to turn my attention from McElson. There was no need to confirm her suspicions anyway. McElson would do that soon enough on his own.

"There's unrest throughout the kingdom, Governor. There has been for years. It's going to take more than a few weeks to right what's gone wrong for so long," I said.

"Quinn…" Reina murmured, placing a hand on my arm.

I covered her hand with my own, firm pressure letting her know I had no intentions of letting McElson's concerns go ignored.

"You'll need to be more specific, I'm afraid," I said.

"Oh, just say it already, Rolf. You did nothing but talk my ear off on the way here and now suddenly, you're all 'ers' and 'ums.' On with it!" Grandmother Elle spat, throwing the scarlet napkin from her lap onto the table, where it sat in striking contrast to the starched white tablecloth. "The details, Governor."

McElson's face turned a fierce pink. My grandmother had called him out on his dawdling, something I suspected she did to anyone wasting her time . She would have been an intimidating woman to grow up with. For a moment, regret at being denied that opportunity welled within my chest. I pushed it down. Regret later.

"Right, well then. There's been reports of…monsters— er, creatures—prowling our southern borders."

I narrowed my eyes. "Monsters?"

"I don't know how else to explain it, I'm afraid."

Exasperated, Grandmother Elle took over, and McElson took the opportunity to hide behind his water glass. "Undead. McElson's people report seeing undead *things* in their fields at night."

McElson coughed on a misdirected sip of water. "At night, midday, it matters not! It started in the darkness, but they've been spotted now several times in the fields while the noon sun still shines." His voice echoed a desperation I hadn't heard in months.

I gritted my teeth. *What's dead is alive, what's alive is dead.* This time, I met Reina's gaze and nodded. *Yes,* I confirmed. *It's as we feared.*

"Can you describe these undead things?" I asked McElson, hoping for some rational explanation.

He shook his head. "I haven't seen one myself."

"It might just be a misunderstanding," Reina said, her voice thick with hope. "Perhaps nothing more than desperate farmers needing help with a wild animal?"

"Wild animals don't walk on two legs," Grandmother Elle said. "The Governor's reports describe instances of both four-legged *and* two-legged creatures."

McElson nodded, toying with the corner his napkin once more. "I have reports from two different residents who tried to approach one of the…things. They spoke of unseeing eyes and mindless wandering in these creatures."

I let the conversation lapse into silence a moment, knowing I needed to respond, knowing they waited for my thoughts. I allowed my gaze to wander over the far corner of the painted recessed ceiling with its gold trim and cornflower blue center.

"Has anyone tried to capture one?" I said finally, turning back to McElson. "Or kill one?" I added as an afterthought.

McElson's gaze dropped to his lap. "No one who has lived."

"They've killed! The undead creatures you speak of?" Reina cried. "Why didn't you say that from the start?"

"It's happened twice, so far as I know. The first time was in the middle of the night, and the farmer's son found him facedown in the fields the next day. It appeared he'd been… mauled."

"If he was alone in the middle of the night, and his son found him the next day, how do we know he wasn't killed by an animal?"

"We assumed it was a wild animal at first, too, Sibyl. A bear. A boar. We didn't yet know what was roaming the lands there. A week later, there was another death, this time a smith traveling home late at night. He met with local friends at a nearby pub after he closed shop, then ran into an undead on his way home. His friends…they said they begged him not to intervene, but he insisted he wouldn't see his town terrorized, that he wanted to protect them all. He was a big man, you understand.

"I don't know if he knew the scope of what he was up against. The witnesses say it was a person, but not. A human form, but no soul. Sightless eyes filled with blackness. They…saw it tear him apart much in the same way we'd found the first man. That's how we concluded the mystery of the first man's death."

Appalled, Reina sucked in a breath beside me.

"And the man's friends…they lived?" she asked.

"They did. One was injured when he tried to assist briefly. The other fled and was unharmed."

I'd hoped for more time. I ran a hand along my jaw, going over the options in my mind.

Finally, I said, "You brought these reports with you?"

McElson nodded.

"Meet me in the west wing study. Half-hour. Bring the papers," I said, standing. Reina rose to her feet beside me, her chair scraping along the polished floor.

"Where are you—"

"Library."

It was time to do what I warned Reina against doing the last time we relied on Tarrowburn's words—translate prophecy.

Where was my father when I needed him most?

A ridiculous question.

Being a governor, my father was still in Barnham, probably explaining to everyone in the town exactly how his son had become ruler of the entire kingdom. He and my mother planned to journey to Irzan eventually, but since Barnham was nearly as far from Irzan as one could get without boarding a ship, it was better for him to stay put to help restore order on the other side of the kingdom.

Now, in the cool, dark library, I stood over the book containing the prophecy. My hands gripped the edges of the thick wooden table, knuckles whitening under the pressure of each word read. Blasted prophecy. It was supposed to have ended with the finding of the White Sorceress. We were promised peace.

CHAPTER THREE

Where You Lead, I Will Follow
Reina

How could he?

As I stared at the empty bedroom chamber, I couldn't help but wonder what on Liron was going through the man's head. Quinn wasn't one for running away. He promised. I crossed the room, my bare feet falling across the thick indigo and gold carpet. I tried not to let the panic and betrayal sink in.

The sheer curtains on wide east-facing windows glowed golden with early morning sun, the light, gauzy fabric stretching from the ceiling downward and pooling on the floor. Grabbing hold, I ripped one of the curtains sideways to reveal the world outside, as though I might find Quinn standing with a smile just on the other side of the window. The metal rings holding the curtain in place screeched in protest as they slid across the bar, echoing my feelings better than any words might.

But Quinn was nowhere to be seen. Not that I expected to see him. Still, the serene view below made me want to scream in frustration. Manicured gardens sparkled with sun-kissed droplets of dew as if the greenery had been covered by a thick layer of glittering diamonds. Even through the closed window, the happy trill of morning sparrows' song carried to my ears in complete opposition to my spiraling mood.

With a huff, I let the curtain slide back in place, spun on my heel and headed back into the hall, fingers curling into fists at my sides. Just minutes ago, I'd thought to share a new idea with Quinn. Now, before the hustle and bustle of the day. Before the advisors came looking for him. Before the Guard came calling. Before even Elle could nab his ear and carry him away to other matters.

But Quinn wasn't here.

Quinn didn't run. He said he wouldn't run. He—

Fiermi.

He wouldn't run *away*. Quinn wouldn't run *away*.

No, but he *would* run directly *into* danger, *into* future prophecies, *into* the Southern Plains.

Without me? Without—I swallowed back my distaste— Niles? Even though the prophecy said he needed both of us?

"Dammit all, Quinn!" I muttered under my breath.

I dressed and headed to the stables to discover two horses already missing. That didn't necessarily mean Quinn was on one of them, but it was hard to imagine who else would have gone for a pre-dawn ride.

I knew. I knew last night something was off with him. I just didn't think he'd leave me behind. Rotten oaf.

Well, he wouldn't get far. I knew whom to call for help.

Brigantino was still a captain, but now he was Captain of the Royal Guard, a position that seemed tailor-made to fit his very personality. When I shared the news of what Quinn and I had learned and where Quinn was headed, he glowered.

"Of all the dumb ideas."

"He probably thinks he's saving us all the trouble by going himself," I said.

Brigantino uncrossed his folded arms and ran a hand across the cropped steel-colored hair on his head. "Undoubtedly."

I tapped my foot on the floor impatiently, disenchanted with Brigantino's lack of verbal outrage. "We're going, right?"

His gaze rose to meet mine. "Of course we are. I've just got to pull that weasel from the prison…if what you say is true."

I nodded and pressed my lips together. "I don't want to be in his company any more than you, trust me."

Brigantino sighed. "You handle provisions. I'll take care of the rest. Be ready to leave by noon."

I didn't relish telling Elle the news. She would be horrified to learn that her newfound grandson slipped away to try to solve another colossal riddle on his own…capable though he might be.

And Quinn was most certainly capable.

He was also hardheaded, and too smart to believe he could really solve this on his own. Part of me wondered if he wasn't just visiting the southern border to see the…*things*

McElson had mentioned. And yet, he would have told me if that were the case. No, he was headed to the Southern Plains. Even though the prophecy clearly said *three* were needed to fulfill it.

It was mid-morning by the time I entered the wing of the castle where Laurelle Bonverno once lived during her time as the Queen Mother before the king was killed, before the war came, before Bruenner and so many others chased her from her home and into hiding.

Like the rest of the building, this wing was ornately decorated with elaborately carved, gold-trimmed molding adorning the space where the ceiling met the walls and where the walls met the floor. The detailed carvings of birds with their outstretched wings was impeccable in its intricacies and left me wondering how long it had taken an artist to design, let alone to craft. How many feathers in those wings?

The ceilings in this room were high and painted a pale yellow with sprigs of tiny blue flowers and broken only by golden support beams that ran the length of the room. Why someone should pay such attention to a ceiling, I couldn't say. It seemed a terrible waste of money, even if it *was* eye-catching. Painted ivy trailed along the walls, melding into lush green ivy plants that grew from enormous clay pots all around the room. The room smelled clean and fresh, and mildly, not unpleasantly, like dirt.

Elle sat in a drawing room on the cushion of a large blue-trimmed sofa that dwarfed her body, book in hand, spectacles perched on her nose. Though I remembered my initial impression of her well, I found it difficult to believe

I'd ever been intimidated or afraid of the silver-haired woman before me. Regal, yes, but sharp and always, always authentic in every way. Laurelle Bonverno would never stand for falsehoods or drama. She would forever shine light on the truth and only ever stand for what was right. I hoped to someday be half as inspiring as she.

"Ah!" she said when she spotted me. "Reina, my love, good morning! It's so good to see you again. Come, sit." She placed the book in her lap and patted a place on the sofa beside her.

I obliged and sat, sinking into the plush cushion, wishing I had an easy way to break the news. She took my hand in hers and gave a squeeze. Her hands were cool and soft, the weathered skin proof of the many decades she'd seen, and though they were frail, they were not weak. There was a strength in these hands that mirrored the strength of her spirit. I wanted to crush her in a hug and never let go.

"I forgive you," she said.

Surprise must have shown on my face, but I didn't have time to reply.

"For leaving in the middle of the night and not telling me."

So, she intended to guilt me about last fall, when I left the safety of Gillesmere and set out on my own to figure out the secrets of the talisman. She *would*. I laughed, the sound a surprise to my own ears.

"Elle! You would have tried to go with me. I couldn't tell anyone, least of all you."

She smiled, the wrinkles around her eyes multiplying in

number. "And *that* is why I forgive you."

Warmth flooded my chest. Love for this woman who had become like a grandmother to me. She understood so very much.

"There's something I must tell you," I said to her before I lost my nerve. "I have to leave again."

She gave me a slow, knowing smile.

"To find Quinn? Yes, I figured."

"What? But how—"

Elle patted my knee. "He left a note. I have to say, though, I thought our conversation strange when he approached me last night to ask about every manner of kingdom management. The reasoning became clear enough when I read his words this morning. That boy. What *will* we do with him?"

I floundered for words. "Wait. You mean…I mean…he left a note?"

Elle nodded.

"May I…may I see it?"

I didn't want to encroach on private correspondence, but Quinn hadn't left me much of a choice. I needed to know what he'd told Elle. It might change what I needed to tell her in turn.

"Of course," Elle said. She pulled a folded piece of paper from the pocket of her skirts and handed it to me.

> *Dearest Grandmother Elle,*
>
> *I cannot emphasize how much joy the above statement brings me, knowing that you are my grandmother, that we are family,*

and that you are, in all things, knowing and capable.

I'm sure you wondered at the reasoning for our strange conversation last night, perhaps more so at my odd line of questioning of your knowledge of kingdom affairs. To relay all that has transpired would take too long, so I will remain brief. Another prophecy is unfolding before our eyes, one that requires my attention. I do not relish leaving Irzan— or you—behind, but I have not been given a choice in these matters.

I humbly ask that you take my place as head of Irzan, and of Castilles, until my return. You are perhaps the one person suited to such a monumental task. I have left notes with my advisors, informing them of my decision. They will not question your authority. With luck and Saints' protection, I will see you again soon and beg forgiveness at putting you in such a position.

Your Loving Grandson,
Quinn

The letter slipped from my fingers, falling to my lap.

"He left you a note," I said, almost in disbelief. "He left his advisors notes."

"I take that to mean he didn't leave one for you. It doesn't surprise me, child. He knows you too well. You're going after him, aren't you?"

I should have counted on not actually having to break the news to Elle. She was too smart for that. She'd known I was coming to say my farewell from the moment I walked through the door in my traveling clothes.

"I am," I said. "I must. I don't know what he hopes to achieve on his own. The prophecy was very specific—the king, the sorceress, and the one who failed. That doesn't leave much room for interpretation, does it?"

I stood and Elle stood as well, placing her open book on the arm of the sofa. I handed Quinn's note back to her.

"I shall miss you," I said to Elle, feeling the tears well against my lower lashes. Were they good-bye tears or tears of hurt at the fact that Quinn had left notes for everyone but me?

"And I you. Go, child. Catch up to that stubborn grandson of mine," she said, embracing me in a tight hug.

"And this is why I didn't say goodbye last time." I stepped back and wiped the tear stains from my cheeks with the back of my hand.

Elle squeezed my arm lightly. "Onward. Whatever this prophecy says, whatever it needs, you'll figure it out. You and Quinn have saved Castilles from horrors before. I have no doubt you'll do so again."

I wished I could be anywhere near as certain as Laurelle Bonverno.

"And you?" I asked.

"I'll do as my king has requested. I'll oversee the kingdom until he returns."

Niles didn't look thrilled to be seated on his horse, but maybe that was because his hands were tied to the pommel. He pressed his lips together tightly and watched me with narrowed eyes. I led Aeros to the paddock and cinched my bags to her saddle while Brigantino sat atop an enormous horse that must have been bred specifically to carry men like him.

The talisman hummed at my chest, and I tucked the aqua-hued cabochon beneath my tunic to rest against my skin. At least the stone negated the need to bring my medical bag. I could heal faster with its magic than I ever could with any of my remedies.

Diagnosing an illness or injury had become easier than ever with the talisman around my neck. It *knew* what needed to be fixed and did the work as I pushed the healing magic into the bodies of my patients. Add to it the fact that I'd sewn locks of Quinn's hair into the lining of every pair of shoes I owned, and we'd managed to avoid the need for him to be present for every healing. I imagined it was a relief for him, given the amount of his attention that was required elsewhere.

After the Resistance reclaimed the kingdom, the first person I healed was James Henley, a young soldier from the opposition who had burned his own hands beyond natural repair to get the talisman into my possession. While still raw, and forever scarred, the skin had healed, and he would regain full use of his hands—an asset considering his new occupation as a winemaker. Private Henley was the first of many I healed in the weeks since peace had been restored. Once finding the talisman's true source of power, I had little need of the medicines and tonics in my bag. It was a relief to have to prepare one less bag.

"I would've thought you'd be more excited to see daylight again, Niles." I finished readying Aeros, checking her hooves one last time.

Niles didn't look bad, given that he'd spent the last two weeks locked in a cell. His blond locks had been cut short, not long enough to be tied back. His skin was no longer the tanned gold it once was, and dark circles had taken residence beneath his eyes. I supposed being caught boarding a ship bound for Farthon and getting dragged back to Irzan hadn't been part of his big escape plan. And yet, all that was missing from his regular attire was his smirk.

No, that wasn't quite true, was it? I peered closer. Niles's eyes no longer sparkled the way their bright blue depths once did either.

"Should I care to see daylight, Moreina, when I've been tied like a hog, manhandled by a brute"—he motioned to Brigantino who looked amused with the description— "and made to sit on a horse with zero explanation of what's going on? Does it matter? Does it matter if I'm in a cell or in the sunshine if my hands are still tied? If I recall, you probably remember the feeling quite well."

The jab stung. He lifted his tied hands to emphasize his point, and my wrists burned thinking about the ropes that bound them together months ago…back when I thought I was going to die, when I was certain I'd failed everyone.

I let Aeros stand and crossed the distance to Niles and his mare. He looked surprised, shocked that I'd consider coming closer probably, but I didn't stop until I stood inches from him. I put a hand on his horse's neck, then tilted my head back to look upwards, viewing him through squinted eyes.

Chin lifted, I stood tall. Let him see no fear. Niles Ingram had done his worst, and I'd never again fear him or what he could do.

"There's a new prophecy," I said. "You're in it. Will you help?"

His smirk returning, Niles looked almost amused at my question.

"I'm captive. And you're asking if I'll help? Isn't it a little late to negotiate with the prisoner? Aren't you supposed to do that before you bind my hands?"

Brigantino huffed. "You're wasting your breath, Sibyl."

I ignored Brigantino, my eyes never leaving Niles's. I was better than Niles. Unlike when he'd taken me prisoner, I would give him a choice.

"Niles, I need to know. Will you help us? Can we trust you?"

His eyes narrowed for a second, the smirk falling from his mouth. "What's in it for me?"

"Not rotting in a prison cell, Ingram. I should think that'd be enough for anyone," Brigantino answered before I could reply.

"Help us fulfill whatever it is in this prophecy that will

save Castilles and you'll receive a full pardon," I said.

If possible, Niles looked both interested and wary. He hesitated before giving a soft, sad laugh. "Am I to believe Quinn—I'm sorry, *King Eron*—would really pardon *me*? After everything that happened? Moreina, you're not a fool and never have been. There's no pardon in this for me."

"I swear it. Saints as my witnesses, you will have a *full* pardon, Niles." My words were rushed. I glanced to Brigantino and back to Niles again. "And land and a pension. If you help us."

Brigantino coughed, expressing obvious dissatisfaction with my negotiation skills, but he'd read the prophecy. He knew what was at stake. He also knew Quinn would never oppose anything I asked, even if it *did* include appeasing Niles.

"Where is *King Eron* anyway?" Niles said, his eyes scanning our surroundings.

I hesitated. "He's taken a head start."

He sniffed. "Ah. He left without you. Interesting. I wouldn't have guessed."

I gritted my teeth. "Will you help or not?"

Niles observed me for a long moment. I almost thought he might say nothing at all. Finally, his eyes shifted, and he gave the subtlest of nods.

"Free my hands." His voice cracked with the words.

"Too far," Brigantino warned. "You overstep your bounds."

"A knife, Captain Brigantino," I said. His knife would cut the ropes much quicker than the small blade I carried in my boot.

He reluctantly guided his horse to where I stood, pulled a knife from his belt, and handed the blade to me. I took the hilt without a word and turned back to Niles.

Niles held his hands down, and I sliced through the layers of coarse fiber, letting the rope fall to the ground and kicking it aside. Let some animal take it piece by piece to line a nest or burrow. Once Niles was free of his bonds, he rubbed his wrists, wincing.

Up close, he was thinner than before, the tendons in his neck showing, hollows in his cheeks dark with lack of nourishment. Was I pleased to see he had not had an easy two months since Quinn had taken his place as king and the Royal Guard had been sent to hunt Niles down? I feared the answer might be yes and shoved the feelings deep inside. I met his stare with one of my own.

"Help us," I demanded, no longer leaving room for a 'no.'

Niles gave a thoughtful nod. "As I can," he replied.

"No." I grabbed his horse's reins, a show of power Niles was unprepared for.

Niles looked surprised at the force of my voice.

"Help us in *every* way you can, not just *as* you can, Niles. You think I don't remember how you manipulate words? I do. All too well. So, you will help us in *every* way we ask… or our deal is off." I paused before adding, "And when we're out there"—I motioned to the empty road that led from the stable— "there's no prison to return to."

"And you'll what—kill me?" he asked. In an echo of the

Niles I remembered, he blinked slowly as though bored with our conversation.

I pressed my lips into a scowl and dared him to cross me.

"She won't have to, Ingram. I'll be happy to do it for her." Brigantino's rough voice confirmed any thoughts Niles might have had about how he'd meet his end if he didn't aid us.

Realizing he was cornered, Niles curled a lip in disgust before answering. "Fine, Moreina. I'll help. And when I'm done, I want a pardon, land, and a pension, just as you've promised. Somewhere far from here. I don't care to see what Irzan has become."

"Done."

I released the reins and returned to Aeros. As I passed, Brigantino leaned down in his saddle.

"I don't trust his word," he said.

I mounted Aeros, then turned the mare to face him, my mind already made up. I met his eye, leaving no question about my own feelings on the matter.

"Then keep an eye on him."

CHAPTER FOUR

___

Inescapable History
Quinn

"You are here because you have been hand-selected to join one of the most elite forces in all of Castilles. This is the Order. THE Order. You know the one. You will learn things during your training here that you may wish never to have known. You will hurt others. You will be hurt. Some of you will die. If you can't handle these simple facts, you may leave now."

Two young men around my own age stepped out of the line and headed for the door. The man who'd spoken was Commander One. That was what we were to call him anyway. Until we were fully trained, our commanders were known by number only. Commander One didn't say a word about the two who left, only watched them with hooded eyes until they'd left the windowless gray-walled room where two dozen of us stood, somehow still willing to put our lives on the line for a chance at protecting Castilles's most important secrets. I wondered about the men who left and why they'd come at all. Commander One's words weren't unexpected.

One didn't seem like a very pleasant man, but that was to be expected. Every agent I'd encountered thus far looked like he had his mother's broomstick shoved up his arse. Was that my future, too?

"Anyone else?" Commander One said once the two were gone. His shrewd eyes shifted across the men in the room. Could he guess which of us were quaking in our boots?

Those of us remaining glanced between one another, waiting to see if anyone else would bow out before the training began.

"No? All right then. Let's get on with it. I want every single one of you to look at the man beside you. Examine him. Closely."

I did. He was shorter than me by several finger-lengths with shaggy, dark hair—scrappy in a sense. He looked like he'd been brought up in a rougher section of a larger city, judging by his frayed clothes and the way he held his shoulders as though the world couldn't deal him anything he couldn't manage to beat. He eyed me with close-set, beady eyes just the same, giving a half-smirk out of one side of his mouth. He was sure of himself. Solid. I wouldn't want to tangle with him.

I issued a curt nod. This was someone I hoped to be working with in the future. Might as well get on his good side now.

"Now," Commander One said. "Take him down."

The room stood still, uncertainty on every face. Doubt, disbelief. Was he...serious?

"We leave this room only when half of you remain standing, so the sooner you start the sooner we move on."

Eyes on confused faces darted from left to right, men

trying to figure out if Commander One was insane or if we'd perhaps gone insane in thinking to join the Order.

It took one pair of men to start throwing punches before the entire room transformed into grunting, sweating, bloody chaos.

I took the first punch to my mouth before I had time to consider hitting the scrappy guy next to me. He hit every bit as hard as I'd imagined. Hot blood dripped from a split lip, but I didn't have time to put a hand to my throbbing jaw before he was punching again, this time pummeling my stomach.

The air left my lungs. I struggled to draw a breath. What the hell was going on? This was the Order? This was how they drafted?

Then my opponent caught the arm of someone who stumbled toward him after being hit. With a growl, he swung the man into me, knocking us both to the ground. I only half-shoved him off so I could attempt to stand again. The man was eager to get back to his own fight. He bounced off the floor and back into the middle of the insanity with little help from me.

Then Scrappy hovered over me, pounding his fists into my face, my middle, anywhere he could reach, and I couldn't think straight except for the need to get myself off the ground. Had to get myself off the ground. I'd never felt so much pain at one time, not ever. Every part of my torso was on fire. I swung my arms blindly, finding his head and shoving my thumbs into his eyes with force. I felt my fingers sink into his eye sockets, pushing into a hot pulpy mess and yet I didn't stop. I pushed harder.

He screamed, shrieked in a bloodcurdling way I'd only ever heard from goats at the slaughter. I was so frightened by the sound from this human—this man—that I jerked my hands free and rolled to the side to be free from him.

I needn't have worried. He wasn't concerned with me any longer, instead holding his palms to his blind and bloodied eyes. I glanced frantically from him to Commander One, to the others still fighting, to the seasoned agents standing around the perimeter of the room.

In a fit of rage, Scrappy hurled his entire body at me. I didn't think about what I needed to do, I reacted on pure instinct. My fist hit his face and drops of blood sprayed from his nose and eyes, splattering my skin and clothes. A tooth fell from his mouth as he yelled in surprise. Then he dropped to the floor like a sack of flour.

Wide-eyed, I stared at his body in horror. Still alive, still breathing, but out cold. Before today, I'd never hit anyone. Now I'd just about taken a man's eyes from his head. Saints, I'd almost murdered. I stared at my bloodied hands. God, the blood. Would they ever be clean?

I looked to the rest of the room. Fights wound down one by one until a single pair of men were left grappling. I turned my gaze to the stone-faced agents at the walls. What were they thinking? Had they once done this? Were they remembering? Were they reminiscing fondly? For God's sake, would I become like them? Unfeeling, uncaring, blank-eyed, and indifferent?

The last man fell to the ground, moaning and holding

his side. Not all of the defeated opponents were knocked out like Scrappy, but a few were. More of them were like the one who'd just gone down, groaning in pain, one or two rolling on the floor while holding their sides.

Commander One stepped forward. "Those of you still standing, follow me," he said. No 'well-done,' no 'good job.' He gave no indication of whether or not the outcome was as he'd hoped.

I wiped the blood from my lip with a sleeve and followed the remaining agents-in-training through a different door than the one that led us there, leaving the fallen men behind.

Before I crossed the threshold, I turned to one of the agents who had already begun pulling bodies toward the other door.

"Where will they go?" I asked.

"Not your concern, Recruit."

"Will they receive medical attention before coming back to the barracks?"

My mind flashed to Reina, to how she would have stepped in to help the fallen, how disappointed she would have been that I was the cause of such injury. I brushed the thought away.

"They won't be coming back to the barracks. Now, march on."

I stumbled through the doorway, reconciling the meaning of their words. Were these men sent away? Left for dead? Did I even want to know?

I caught up to the survivors of the gory match and followed to the next portion of our testing, wondering all

*the while what kind of bloody violent cult I had been talked
into, and what kind of hell awaited people like me.*

Was he still alive? The man I fought three years ago?
Stumbling around this world, blind and angry with the man
who stole his chance to become an agent of the Order of the
Southern Cross? Did he know that same man was now his
king?

There wasn't a day gone by where I didn't think of him
at least once, but whenever I was traveling, whenever I was
by myself, the thoughts came more frequently. I clamped
down on the sickness that threatened. I would not repent for
what I had done, for what was necessary.

I'd gotten used to Reina's company, to being in a castle,
surrounded by people. I'd forgotten how the ghosts came
back to haunt.

Scrappy's memory was one of dozens. Maybe hundreds.
I stopped counting long ago.

I didn't deserve happiness. I didn't deserve Reina. If she
knew…

Sensing my unease, Chiron sidestepped beneath me. I
settled him, mumbling nonsense to him soothingly. Control
the anger. Control the fear. *Here. I am here. Here and now.*

It wouldn't do to have my horse spook because I let
myself get carried away with the past. I turned in the saddle,
checking the pack horse behind us. He plodded along
mindlessly, following Chiron's steps, unconcerned with the

load he carried. Would that my own load were as easy to bear as the one on his back.

Turning forward with a snort, I urged Chiron into a lazy canter, bringing the three of us that much closer to death with every step.

Wasn't that what waited? Death?

The prophecy mentioned it four times. What's dead is alive, what's alive is dead. Add in McElson's tales of undead things trolling the southern border and we had the perfect ingredients for disaster.

By myself, I could make it to South Trellington in three days' time. From there, I'd cross into the Southern Plains and see what more I could uncover about the Heart of Death. I hated leaving Reina behind, but I wouldn't drag her into this until I had to. The prophecy said she was needed, yes, but it didn't say I couldn't do investigative work on my own. Better to find out what we needed to do before launching ourselves headfirst into danger.

Maybe that's what had me on edge. This journey. South Trellington, the Plains. These places dredged up long-suppressed memories, memories I'd not dared to dwell on for the last three years. The Order made me who I am, turned me into the man who was able to protect Reina. Without the Order, Bruenner himself would have sat on Castilles's throne. Could I then begrudge the Order for also turning me into a killing machine?

The Heart of Death.

Was it me? Was I this bringer of death?

Blasted confusing prophecies.

I glanced at the sun, high in the afternoon sky. By now they'd all have realized I was gone. My grandmother would be seated in the throne room or with the council, conferring on whatever matters had cropped up today. And Reina would be…

Furious.

But safe.

I couldn't ask for more than that.

CHAPTER FIVE

Strange Weather
Reina

Brigantino, Niles, and I spent a quiet day riding the south road through the surrounding woods, the leaves of the towering oaks and elms rustling with the late spring breeze. Brigantino's silence was normal, but quiet from Niles? Almost unheard of. His sullenness threw me off, even though I didn't expect him to be in the best or brightest of moods.

I was relieved when it was time to camp for the night. We'd pushed hard today and with any luck, we'd catch Quinn tomorrow. Then our peace would be gone for sure.

I planned to give him an earful.

Still fuming at him while I grew something for our dinner that didn't have meat in it, I didn't immediately notice anything wrong with the fuisberry vine I coaxed from the ground. When the leaves withered and blackened, I blinked in confusion at the mess by my feet.

You killed it with your anger, Reina. Fantastic.

I shook my head, pushed the mess aside with my boot and focused again, feeling the comforting heat of the talisman glow at my chest. Then I watched with my *vision* through closed eyes, gently persuading a new vine to grow where the other had withered, satisfied as a healthy green sprig took root.

The sprig turned into a shoot, then a vine that began to twist and curl, but before it reached two feet in length, it folded in on itself, withered, then blackened just as before. My eyelids shot open and I stared at the spot on the ground and the small pile of ash quickly blowing away as if it had never been there at all.

Saints above, I *wish* it had never been there.

Something was wrong with the talisman. Or with my ability.

Or both.

Cold tendrils of fear crept along my spine. What would I do without the talisman? I'd become so used to using it, I hadn't thought the power would ever go away.

Not that it had gone away exactly.

There was still some sort of power involved. It just no longer seemed like the power of life. And if it wasn't the power of life…then what was it?

I wanted to believe the mishap was because the trick Quinn and I had devised didn't work the way we'd intended. Maybe it wasn't enough.

But even as the thought ran through my head, intuition insisted it wasn't correct, that it wasn't enough to explain what had just happened. Something was wrong with the magic.

The prophecy hadn't said anything about the magic being broken. Sure, chaos didn't imply anything good, but if I didn't have the magic of the talisman at my fingertips, what use was I in any of this?

"I thought you were growing something to eat with the meat and beans." Brigantino stirred the small pot over the fire and searched for the fuisberries I hadn't grown.

"Oh…I'm beat," I said with a wave of my hand. "I'll just eat around the meat. Beans are fine for one night. A piece of bread with it and I'll be plenty full."

This was a lie, really. After a long day of riding, I was starved. I'd been so worried about Quinn this morning that I hadn't eaten anything for breakfast, and when we stopped for lunch, I'd crammed my mouth with fruit, cheese, and dried callogh chips to keep our stop short.

Brigantino didn't reply to my lie, but his gaze followed me. I moved around the camp and spooned a ladleful of beans into my own bowl, pretending not to notice his stare. Damn Brigantino for being so observant. He knew…or at least suspected something was off.

Niles finished his bowl and wiped it clean with a chunk of hearty brown bread. "Mmm mmm," he said. "Nothing like questionable meat and tasteless beans to make the road feel like home."

Neither Brigantino nor I responded. With Niles, it was probably best not to.

He shook his head, then pulled a tiny book from the pocket of his tunic. He held it sideways so the fire would shine enough light on the pages for him to read.

"They let you have a book?" Brigantino said, surprised that Niles owned any belongings at this point.

Niles gave Brigantino a weary stare before blinking

once slowly. "Yes. Believe it or not, they didn't deem a book dangerous. Absurd, I know. I'm sure I could read poetry aloud until your ears bleed and you die of boredom. Dangerous, indeed."

Brigantino stared at Niles a long moment, his face an unreadable mask.

"I'm going to bed," he said, turning to me.

I nodded.

"Which means"—he stood with a stretch— "you're going to bed, too, weasel."

"Really, I'm quite capable of determining my own bedtime, Papa, thank you very much," Niles replied.

"You think I'm going to leave you untied overnight? No."

I hadn't thought about how we would spend the night, but clearly Brigantino had.

"Fine," Niles said, standing and shoving his book back into his pocket. He thrust his wrists forward, offering them to Brigantino who took the opportunity to bind them tightly, let out a couple feet of cord, then tied the end of the rope to his own wrist.

Niles's eyes bulged. When his shock wore off, he resorted to his normal antics.

"Naughty. I didn't figure you the sort."

Brigantino responded to the taunt by fixing him with a steely glare.

"If there's one way I know you'll stay put, it's this. Now, shut your hole, weasel, and go to sleep."

"As if there's anywhere to run…" Niles muttered. Yet he

followed Brigantino to where we'd set up the bedrolls.

I suppressed a smile and leaned closer to the fire, stoking it with a stick, coaxing the flames a little higher. Then I returned to my lukewarm beans and bread. What I wouldn't give for a few fuisberries…

I pulled my hand-written copy of the prophecy from my pocket again, studying the lines. They repeated a theme of chaos and balance, and balance slipping into chaos. The talisman hummed around my neck as though teasing me into trying again.

"No, thank you, bauble," I said quietly. "I gave you two chances already today. I won't risk a third. We'll try again in the morning perhaps."

I set aside my empty bowl, then stood and stretched. The night sky was full of thick clouds, blocking my view of the stars.

I wondered what the sky would look like in the Southern Plains. Would the same stars shine there? Would they shine as brightly?

Damn Quinn for leaving without me.

A dampness hung in the air as if the sky wanted to rain, but stubbornly refused. I'd bet all my belongings we'd be soaked before the day's end. We cantered ahead, hoping to catch Quinn sooner rather than later.

It was midday when the dampness became more than just the threat of rain. A thick fog descended, coating the road and trees in a soft white cloak. We slowed the horses to a walk and plodded ahead. At first, nothing seemed amiss, but within the hour, the fog had grown so thick I couldn't see Brigantino and his horse ahead…and we weren't that far apart to begin with.

This fog was…odd. One might call it unnatural.

Another minute and I could no longer see Niles.

"Captain," I called ahead to Brigantino.

But there was no answer.

"Brigantino!" I said louder.

No response.

Knowing he was much closer, I called to Niles instead. "Niles, tell Brigantino to stop, please, would you?"

I expected a quip about relaying the message. Instead I was met with eerie silence. I halted Aeros and spun in the saddle, looking in any direction for something—anything—recognizable.

But I was isolated in a disorienting white haze and could make out nothing of my surroundings. Not even the hint of a bush or a tree.

I contemplated dismounting, just to have the ground beneath my feet, but thought better of it, worried I'd lose Aeros, too. The mare snorted a little with my thoughts, sensing the tension in every inch of my body.

"Easy, girl," I said. "We'll figure this out. Just keep plodding ahead. We have to catch up to them eventually, right?"

Unsurprisingly, Aeros didn't answer.

Instead, the forest around me—if there still was a forest

behind the white curtain of fog— began to whisper.

Laughter at first, girlish giggles that had no business sounding in the middle of thousands of acres of woodland.

I turned again in my saddle, searching through the indistinguishable whiteness. "Hello?" I called.

Stupid, Reina. Do you think someone will answer?

All at once, a dozen whispers assaulted my ears. Harsh words pelted me from every angle—words I couldn't make out. The voices taunted, the tone rising and falling, mocking me—mocking the fact that I couldn't understand what was being said. If the words had been in my tongue, I might have had a chance at understanding a couple phrases here or there, but multiple voices all speaking something different in a language I couldn't begin to decipher? I had no chance.

Aeros danced beneath me. Could she hear the whispers, too? Or did she sense my unease? Saints above, were the voices getting louder? I spun, trying to orient myself in the fog, attempting to pinpoint just one voice, anything to keep me from my dizzying spiral.

Just when I thought I might go crazy from the noise, it stopped, a thundering silence filling the void.

Then a single voice, one syllable.

"You…"

The word wavered between a song and a scream, drawn out, successful in sending chills racing down my spine. I gripped the reins tighter, knuckles turning white.

"H-hello?" I said, scanning the fog uselessly.

Another laugh.

"Hiss." The voice whispered almost into my ear. My

hair stood on end.

I whipped back around, searching for the source of the voice.

More laughter.

"Be careful," it sang.

"What? I don't understa—"

With no warning, I was shoved from my saddle, falling head over heels over Aeros's neck, the ground rising to meet me quickly. I put my hands out to brace myself for collision, but they were knocked from beneath me by something I felt without seeing.

I gave a cry of pain when my head and shoulder took the brunt of the impact and rolled forward with momentum to ease the hit on the rest of my body. When I came to a stop, I lay sprawled on the ground, chest heaving. Fear coursed through my veins.

I stared at the unyielding whiteness.

"Sibyl! Are you all right?"

The words floated to my ears as though far, far away.

Who's Sibyl?

"Sibyl, can you hear me?"

A strong hand propped up my head, trying to help me sit and I looked about in a daze. My gaze fell on Aeros first. The dappled mare had taken the opportunity to pull a couple large leaves from the branch above her head. She chewed noisily, then ripped another leaf from its place on the tree.

"Don't let her do that," I said, pointing to the mare. "She'll choke herself with the bit in her mouth."

Niles grabbed Aeros's reins and pulled the half-chewed leaf from her mouth, then wiped his hand on his breeches.

"I'll take that as a 'yes, I'm fine, Captain Brigantino, thank you for asking.'"

I shot Brigantino an annoyed glare, then sat forward on my own, putting a hand to a tender spot on the back of my head.

"Ow," I said, pulling my fingers away to check for blood.

There was none, but a wicked bump had already begun to form.

"What happened? Did the horse spook? How did you fall?" Brigantino asked as. He searched me for additional bumps and bruises.

I pulled my arm from his grasp and stood shakily.

"I didn't *fall*. I was pushed."

Brigantino raised one silver eyebrow.

"By whom?"

"I don't know. Blasted fog made it impossible to see anything six inches from my face!" As I said the words aloud, I realized there was no longer any fog. Not just that the fog had thinned, but there was…none.

Brigantino looked to Niles for a moment—a motion that should have worried me on its own—the two of them exchanging concerned glances.

"The fog that was so thick a few moments ago," I elaborated.

"Sibyl," Brigantino said slowly as he examined my eyes.

Probably checking for a concussion. "What did you see?"

I blinked a few times, attempting to recall what happened through a different kind of fog that had taken over my head.

"Well, I was riding behind Niles. The fog got worse and we slowed to a walk. Then…then I called ahead, but neither of you responded. And then there were these…voices all around, these whispers in the fog. I tried to hear what they were saying, but there were so many of them and they were speaking another language. At least I *think* they were speaking another language. I'm not even sure now. And there was this laughter."

"Laughter?" Niles asked, eyebrows raised in obvious disbelief.

"Yes, right after all the voices stopped. And then the laughter stopped, too. And a voice whispered in my ear to be careful."

"To…be careful." Brigantino clearly thought I'd lost my mind.

"Yes, and then I got shoved out of my saddle. I would have caught myself with my hands, but they were knocked out from beneath me."

"By what?" Niles asked.

"I don't know!" I growled in response.

"Sibyl…" Brigantino stopped, searching for the right words. "There was no fog such as you've described. The morning started out damp for certain, Sibyl, but there was never anything nearly as dense as what you claim to have experienced. When we were separated, it was because you pulled your horse back while Niles and I rode ahead unaware.

By the time I realized you weren't with us and we returned, you were on the ground."

"Are you implying I imagined it? The bruise on my head feels real enough."

"Clearly, you fell from your horse. But the rest of it… Maybe you fell asleep in the saddle? No one got decent sleep last night. I couldn't fault you if you were that tired."

"I didn't fall asleep in the saddle."

Brigantino hesitated before speaking his next words. His scowl deepened.

"A…dark magic?"

It was the only explanation. I'd come to the same conclusion, but that didn't mean I liked it.

A moment of uncomfortable silence dragged on. Did Brigantino really believe me or was he humoring me?

Niles finally spoke, breaking the quiet. "If you're not hurt, we should probably get back to trying to catch up to your beloved king *before* he diverts from the main road."

I stood—faster than I should have—and suppressed a wave of dizziness as I grabbed Aeros's reins from Niles.

"Let's go."

Brigantino hesitated. "Are you sure you're all right, Sibyl? If we need to slow down—"

"We'll never catch up to Quinn if we slow down. Let's go."

I put a foot into a stirrup and threw a leg over the saddle. Ignoring the throbbing at the back of my head, I urged Aeros forward. I didn't wait for Brigantino or Niles to mount and I didn't look back to see if they followed.

The sooner we reached Quinn, the sooner I'd have someone to confide in…someone who could help me make sense of what was going on.

Oh, Quinn. What have you dragged us into by leaving us behind?

CHAPTER SIX

Together Again
Quinn

The horses told me I was being followed long before I sensed it on my own. Their ears flicked backwards repeatedly, straining to hear the sounds behind us. Or maybe they could smell the approach of a familiar equine scent.

The pack horse gave an eardrum-shattering whinny, leaving little question as to who followed.

"One of your friends, is it?"

I pulled up the horses, turned to face the empty road behind me. A few minutes now.

And there he was.

Brigantino rounded the bend. It wasn't difficult to tell who was seated on the enormous draft horse. There were few men with Brigantino's physical presence.

I should have guessed he would come. He would have followed in the name of 'protecting' me even if Reina hadn't sent him. And I was sure Reina had. She wasn't one for sitting around and waiting for answers.

I didn't have a chance to greet Brigantino when two more riders rounded the bend. Both of them sent the blood thrumming in my veins. Of all the stupid ideas…

I said nothing as they approached, instead focusing on relaxing a jaw that had painfully clenched. My expression would reveal nothing, none of the anger I sorely wanted to let loose right now.

Finally, the three riders stood in front of me.

"My king," Brigantino said with a nod of his head.

So, he would take the diplomatic approach. I nodded back to him but let my gaze roam over the other two riders, my mouth resolutely clamped shut.

Niles Ingram. I despised no one on Liron more than Niles Goddamn Ingram. I should take some consolation in the fact that he no longer looked the part of the suave, self-assured soldier he believed himself to be. I should rejoice, at least a little, in his ragged, short hair and his gaunt face, but it was no use. There was no consolation in these things. They'd still brought Ingram, whether I wanted them to or not.

And Reina. I expected uncertainty when I met her eyes, a worry and anxiety that was all too often an integral part of Reina's very nature. Instead, there was anger. So much anger.

That was a surprise.

"I wish to speak with Reina alone."

I could have been wrong, but as she dismounted, I swore I heard Reina say, "Oh, I bet you do, but you won't by the time *I'm* done speaking with *you*."

I dismounted, took a moment to stretch my legs, and waited for her to follow. I guided us behind a thick spray of bushes and trees that would block our argument—for it would *be* an argument—from view.

"Blast it, Reina! You were supposed to stay in Irzan. What were you thinking?" I hissed at her as soon as we were far enough.

"What was *I* thinking? How about what were *you* thinking? Quinn, have you gone daft? Did you forget about the prophecy entirely? The part where we have to travel together, you, me, and…and…*him*?" She swung a pointed finger to where Ingram sat on his horse, somewhere behind the bushes we'd put between us.

I shook my head. "*Why* did you bring that conceited fool?" I asked.

"You know I can hear you, right?" Ingram's voice rose from behind the curtain of greenery.

I ignored him. "I *told* you I'd return soon, and with more information. How else are we to find out where we need to go and what we need to do?" I said.

"You told me? You did no such thing! Or was that in one of the notes you left for your advisors?"

I narrowed my eyes at her.

"No, it was in the note I left for you," I said, forcing the calmness in my voice.

"The note you—"

"—left in your medicine bag. You're always in that blasted bag. I figured it was the best way to make sure you saw it."

Reina's face went pale.

I reached out to steady her with a hand on her arm. "What?"

She swallowed. "I left the medicine bag in Irzan."

"You never saw my note?" I groaned and put a hand to my head, rubbing my eyes, then pulling my hand away again. I'd never be able to tolerate the feeling of fingers on my eyelids. Not ever.

"No, but Quinn. It's worse than that. I left the bag in Irzan. The bag with all my supplies."

She turned, sat on the trunk of a fallen tree, and put her head in her hands.

"But you've got the talisman."

The medicines in her bag were helpful, but not having them wasn't the end of the world. She could heal faster with the talisman than with any amount of her herbs and tonics.

"The talisman hasn't been…working right," she said reluctantly.

We'd remedied the need for me to be close in order for her to access the power of the talisman. At least, theoretically.

Reina needed to be able to protect herself even when I wasn't around—*especially* when I wasn't around—and the talisman, as it turned out, could be fooled.

"We never tested our theory long distance. My hair wasn't enough?" The locks of hair sewn into the lining of her boots was supposed to fool the talisman into believing I was nearby. It worked in our early tests. Now, it seemed, it wasn't enough.

"No, it wasn't quite that. It was…different."

"You've got to give me more to go on, Reina."

She shook her head to clear it. "When I tried to use the talisman when you were away, way back when it was just you and me, traveling the mountains and hiding from

Bruenner, the talisman glowed while you were gone, but I couldn't grow anything. It was almost as if I could *feel* you were far away."

"All right."

When she spoke again, her voice was lower. "This time, when I tried to grow something to eat yesterday, what I grew…died."

"Perhaps you grew it too fast, aged it too quickly?" I asked.

She shook her head. "No, it grew as it always does, and then the fuisberry vine simply blackened, curled, and withered away until it was nothing but ash."

"Have you tried again since? Maybe it was a fluke."

"I didn't tell Brigantino because I didn't want to worry him, but I tried twice more after Niles and Brigantino turned in. Both times, the result was the same. It grew strong and green, then withered before my eyes," she said, scanning my face for my reaction. I was careful to keep a neutral expression.

"Try now."

"But Brigantino and Niles—"

"—can wait."

Reina nodded, then took a breath and closed her eyes, one hand wrapped around the talisman at her neck. Within seconds it was glowing brightly, illuminating her hand and face in an aqua blue light.

A curl of a plant began to sprout at my feet, a little green shoot that could have been the start of a callogh root or the greens of a potato. It flourished into a larger plant, its leaves growing and unfurling before my eyes.

It didn't matter how many times I'd seen Reina work the talisman. The magic never ceased to amaze.

All at once, the plant shriveled and curled into itself, the leaves and stems darkening with disease. It blackened into a charred memory of something green, then dissolved into the air at the first hint of a breeze.

Reina opened her eyes again, glassy eyes filled with fear.

"What will we do?" she whispered.

I grabbed her shoulders. "We'll figure this out."

"Where *were* you going, if you weren't headed to fulfill the prophecy without us?" Reina asked, dark eyes alight with suspicion, her hands soft on the horse's reins.

I let a moment of silence slide by, listening to the satisfying creak of saddle leather with each step forward. The treetops far above our heads swayed with the breeze, dappling Reina's hair and face in sunlight and shadow. Aeros plodded along beside Chiron, the two horses as amiable as if they'd been stabled together all their lives. Brigantino and Ingram followed far enough behind that I held no hesitation in sharing my private thoughts with Reina.

Finally, I said, "I wanted to see the creatures for myself, to see if what we're up against really is the chaos mentioned in the prophecy. I suppose I hoped it might be a convenient misunderstanding."

"And now?"

I took another long breath, thinking through what Reina had detailed since we'd been on the road again, about the unnatural fog and the voices, about someone—or something—shoving her from Aeros's back. And I thought about how I'd do anything to protect her at any cost.

"There's no longer a question where chaos is concerned, is there? Something is stirring trouble. I've seen you ride, Reina. Even if Aeros acts like a silly yearling on occasion, she wouldn't throw you. Not ever. *Something* pushed you from your horse."

"At least you believe me. I'm almost certain Niles and Captain Brigantino still think I fell asleep."

"Ingram maybe, but Brigantino knows better. Even if what he says aloud is something else entirely, trust me, Brigantino knows when something is amiss," I replied. "He said what he did with the hope he might bring you some sense of comfort."

"Comfort!" Reina scoffed. "By doubting me? Implying I can't ride a horse? By insinuating I fell asleep? That's not encouraging."

She had a point.

"He's…not the best at expressing himself sometimes," I said, registering the irony in speaking the words. I wasn't much better at working through emotions myself, tongue-tied more often than not.

"Maybe. So, if you no longer need to see McElson's creatures for yourself, may I make a suggestion?"

I nodded.

"Let's head straight to the Southern Plains and find the

Heart of Death, whatever it is. The three of us—you, me, and Niles are all here. If we start deciphering the prophecy *now*, we stand a better chance at solving the riddle before it becomes deadly."

There wasn't a point in searching for the undead now, not since I'd seen the talisman's magic turn foul with my own eyes. The chaos was already well underway. What good would seeing an undead creature do? What purpose could it serve? Other than to satisfy my own curiosity, of course.

"All right," I agreed. "You make a good point. We'll head to South Trellington and cross there."

"I ran the calculations for the next eclipse," Reina said.

"And?"

"Two months, seven days."

Finally, good news. There was time to travel well into the Southern Plains, time to discover what the Heart of Death was, and how we could stop the Chaos Wielder from turning the world upside down.

"You're sure?"

Reina cocked her head in response, her pressed lips an expression half-insult and half-amusement. "Believe it or not," she began dryly, "the Royal Library contains far more resources than just prophecies about death and chaos. I was able to use at least some of the astronomical and celestial calendars to pin down our date."

I smiled, something I'd tried to do more of in Reina's company, and gave her a nod. "I never doubted you for a moment."

"What about that moment when you left Irzan without

me?" she asked with a smirk. "Did you maybe, just a little, doubt me then?"

I cleared my throat and swallowed.

"I didn't… Let's not talk about that one."

Traveling with company was good for keeping memories at bay. The conversation I tried to avoid was now a welcome distraction instead. Not that any of us were exceptionally talkative on a day-to-day basis, with perhaps the exception of Ingram, whom no one particularly wanted to hear from today or, in my case, any day.

The wind rustled the leaves in the trees, sending plumes of sweet-scented pollen dust floating through the air. At least the forest road was clear and quiet. Blessedly quiet. So different from the chambers with the citizens and their problems, with the advisors and their solutions, with one man after the next seeking help, begging for guidance.

Here, at least momentarily, I could ease the tension from my shoulders and release the breath it seemed I was always holding while on the throne. Here, things were—

"Something's wrong." Reina pulled her reins, signaling Aeros to stop. The mare's hooves dug into the packed dirt as she skidded to a halt, and she threw her head upwards, expressing displeasure at being made to stand.

I held in my sigh.

Reina searched the forest, then turned her face to the sky. I followed her gaze but detected nothing. Brigantino looked to the trees around us, studying them with the intensity of a fellow agent.

"What do you—"

I stopped mid-sentence. I felt it now. The air hummed, practically vibrating. Something approached.

Ayrelings. I'd recognize their trill anywhere. With an abundance of tall, looming pines, Barnham was home to a large nesting ground of ayrelings, but outside of nesting, I'd never heard so many in my life.

I turned my gaze upward, shielding my eyes though I hardly needed to. In seconds, a flock of ayrelings blotted out the sun. They streamed through the air in a giant, shifting murmuration. Without warning, they turned as one, plummeting straight for the ground.

The horses danced beneath us, tossing their heads, unnerved at the birds' unnatural action. The first ayreling crashed, full speed, into the middle of the road, followed by a dozen more. Beside me, Reina gasped, holding her hand to her mouth and flinching at the crunch of bones. Niles cursed loudly. I remained silent, but every muscle in my body coiled and tightened, screaming at the wrongness of what unfurled before my eyes.

I waited for the remainder of the flock to change direction when they saw what happened to their fellows. Instead, they pounded the ground, breaking their necks in an instant death, hundreds at a time in sickening cracks and thuds.

In less than thirty seconds, every bird in the flock lay dead and mangled in a heap on the road in front of us.

"What the bloody hell?" Ingram said, breaking the eerie

stillness left in the birds' wake. He looked to Brigantino, then to me. "What was that?"

I shook my head, words evading me.

Brigantino answered, "No idea."

Reina leaned forward in her saddle, closing her eyes and clenching her teeth in pain. Death always affected her physically, no matter how much she tried to hide it. I hated it, the unfairness of it. Though I wanted nothing more than to jump to her side and hold her through the pain, I kept to my own saddle, letting her fight through it as she needed. She wouldn't appreciate my coddling, not in front of Niles.

The wind rustled the leaves of the trees above, sending them spinning, but down below, on the ground, there wasn't even a solitary flap of a wing in the heap of dead birds before us.

No predator roamed the sky, no impending storm on the horizon. What on Liron had caused a thousand or more birds to turn and plummet to their deaths? It made no sense. The horses hadn't sensed the event beforehand. It wasn't until the birds fell from the sky that they started to dance and shy beneath us. And now? Now there was nothing. No indication at all that anything had been amiss.

Other than the pile of dead birds blocking the road.

"I don't care what caused it," Reina said, her voice low and choked. "I want to get out of here."

I couldn't agree more.

"Into the trees," I said. I didn't want to take time to clear the bodies off the road and the horses wouldn't react well to being asked to crunch the bones of the tiny, winged creatures.

"Off the road, D'Arturio? You think that's wise?" Niles eyed the dead birds.

"If I wanted your opinion, Ingram, I would have asked for it."

I gritted my teeth and urged Chiron between the trees and into the forest beyond.

"What if whatever caused that…atrocity *wants* us to go this way?" Niles hesitated at the edge of the forest.

"Enough, weasel," Brigantino said.

Ingram had a point, but it was one I'd already thought through. We'd circle around the birds and get back to the road, but I'd be damned if I explained my methods to him.

The plan was a good one. I just didn't expect the woods to become a swampland. The ground beneath the horses' hooves grew spongy, the moss blackened. A foul, nauseating odor permeated the air. The horses stepped over dead limbs of trees that had fallen to the ground.

I angled Chiron back to the road after we'd traveled far enough to have passed the birds, but instead of the land becoming more solid again, the ground *liquified*, pulling the horses in past their fetlocks and halfway to their knees.

"Dismount!" I yelled from the lead. My feet hit the muck and the filth rose to my knees.

I didn't want to get lodged in the mud, but our horses were priority. If they got stuck, we'd lose half our supplies or more. Cold mud seeped into my boots with each step. I lifted my feet above the muck and down again, stepping, pulling the reins forward and urging Chiron to keep moving. Nostrils wide and flared, the gelding wasn't happy about the situation. He pulled back, snorting, the whites of his eyes flashing.

I placed a hand to his neck. "Easy, boy," I murmured.

I looked back at the others. None of the horses were as deeply lodged as Chiron, thank the Saints, but they were equally unhappy with the situation.

Aeros gave several deep snorts, tossing her head and chewing on the bit in her mouth. For a moment, I forgot Reina's attachment to the horse, her love of animals, her experience in the saddle. For a moment, all I wanted to do was grab the reins from her hands and keep her safe from a panicking horse.

Which was ridiculous.

Because she had Aeros under control before I even had a chance to get Chiron settled. Our pack horse and Niles's and Brigantino's horses were fetlock deep in the muck and were able to pull free easily. With some finagling, I managed to get both myself and Chiron free of the mud and back on semi-solid ground again.

"Around that way," I instructed, lifting a hand to show which path the others should take.

Filthy and covered in muck, we found the road again, but brought the stench of the swamp with us. The odor lingered, a reminder of the near loss of horses and supplies.

"Are you all right?" Reina pulled Aeros beside me on the road, eyeing me with concern

"Aye. Fine."

"You're scowling again."

Of course I was.

The decaying bog should not have been where it was. In this part of the kingdom, the forest was lush and full, the land covered in large trees and heavy green underbrush. But that underbrush had died.

No, not just died. Putrefied.

In an otherwise healthy section of forest.

"Too much on my mind, Reina. The forest isn't right. First the birds, then the bog," I said, sharing my thoughts with her. "Add in the undead McElson spoke of and it's a recipe for—"

"Chaos," she uttered softly. "It's begun."

I didn't reply.

CHAPTER SEVEN

What's Alive is Dead
Reina

The cool, spring-fed pool near our camp was a welcome sight. After the stench of the bog, I couldn't wait to wash. The muck coated my boots, but the smell was so overpowering that I had resorted to opening and sniffing a bottle of briarmint oil I carried in my saddle bag. The oil was soothing on dry hands, but, more importantly, the aroma was strong—strong enough to overcome the smell of decay that had glued itself to our horses and our legs.

I brushed the dried muck from Aeros's knees, hocks, and fetlocks with a stiff brush from my bag. The crusted stuff came off in waves of dust that burned my lungs and sent me into a coughing fit. Once the dappled mare was clean, I was covered in a layer of fine, very foul-smelling dust.

I'd never before looked forward to an ice-cold bath in my life, but I couldn't wait for this one. I slung a drying cloth over my shoulder and picked my spare set of clothing and a bar of soap from the saddle bag.

Given that my attire needed as much of a washing as I did, I was prepared to bound into the spring fully clothed. Only seeing Quinn standing at the edge of the pool with his boot-clad feet spread wide and his hands on his hips stopped me from jumping headfirst into the water.

"I thought you'd already be in," I said to him, skirting a few rocks in the path to keep from rolling an ankle.

Quinn turned to me, and the pure horror on his face hit me like a wall. I swallowed.

"What is it? What's—"

Then I saw. I gasped, shaking with anger.

The pool was littered with dead bodies. A deer who must have come for a drink after we'd decided on our camp location lay half in the water, a milky film over her eyes, a trickle of blood from her nose, her swollen tongue pushing from a partly-opened mouth. Several dozen fish bobbed sideways across the water's surface, moving with the current of the spring from below.

The bloated bodies of the two adult ducks that had been happily swimming a few hours ago floated on the water's surface, their four ducklings dead and drifting, the little bodies no longer staying close to the protection of their parents.

Quinn watched me closely as I took in the terrible scene.

"What...what could have..." I couldn't finish my thoughts. So much death all at once, all while we were just a short distance away, setting up camp and taking care of horses. How could this have happened right beneath our noses? How could things have gone so wrong so quickly?

I stepped backwards, away from the horror, shaking my head. The spring was just one more awful event, one more sign of death from today.

Quinn continued to study me.

"What?"

"Just waiting."

"Waiting for what?"

He furrowed his brows and squinted his eyes, peering closer at my face, then tilting his head.

"It's not going to affect you," he said.

"What—"

My lips parted. Despite staring death right in front of my eyes, no fire lit my bones, no pain doubled me over. I wasn't necessarily unhappy about this, but the revelation was shocking regardless. What did it mean?

"Why hasn't it affected you?"

I shook my head. "I can't even imagine. Is it…is it maybe because of the chaos thing? The part about life and death being interchangeable? What's dead is alive, what's alive is dead. Are they…not really dead perhaps?" I couldn't even speak the words without an ominous shiver dragging cold fingers across my spine.

Quinn looked back to the dead animals, then to me again. "They *look* dead. Whatever the case, stay away from the water."

No matter how much I needed a clean bath and my clothes needed a washing, I wouldn't dream of touching the water. Swallowing, I turned back and headed to the camp, Quinn following.

I was silent for several moments before asking the question on my mind, "What caused it, do you think? It's a spring-fed pool. Fresh water should be filtering through the rock and soil beneath and into the pond."

"Perhaps a vein of sulfur deep below mixed with the water as it rose to the surface?" he suggested weakly.

I pressed my lips together. Sulfur wasn't poisonous in water unless present in a large concentration…and we'd detected no odor near the pond. No, this was further chaos, chaos wielded by some madman intent on ruining the world.

"No bathing," Quinn announced as we returned to camp. "And be sparing with your drinking water. We'll get none here."

Brigantino looked to Quinn for clarification, pausing in whittling pieces of kindling from the branch in his hands. Even Niles, who sat beneath a tree, the same small book open in his lap again, paused to look up.

"Spring's poisoned," Quinn said simply.

"There's got to be water somewhere else," Niles said. "A stream or something, right? Let's mount up and keep going."

Brigantino looked almost amused at Niles's suggestion. "Water is sparse from here to the crossing," he said. "If we're lucky, there might be a stream not yet dried up for the season, but otherwise, we'll have to conserve. Settle in, weasel. We're not going anywhere this evening."

Niles turned back to his book, ears reddened with the insult, whether from embarrassment or anger, I didn't know. I almost pitied him.

After placing my spare clothes back in the saddle bag, I sat beside him, folded my knees to my chin, and wrapped my arms around my legs, trying to focus on the scent of briarmint over the stench of bog.

"What are you reading?" I asked.

"Am I not allowed to read?" he said, closing the book on his lap and placing a hand over its cover.

"I was just curious," I said quietly.

Niles closed his eyes for a moment and took a breath.

"I'm sorry. I'm still…irritable." He looked away, finding an interesting patch of dirt to study.

I nodded in understanding.

"You see that plant over there?" I asked, unsure why I felt sympathy for him. "The one with the long thin leaves and the tassels on top? That's sweet angel fern. Bite off the tassels and chew them. It will help."

Niles eyed the plant, then looked back to me.

"Why would you help me? After everything. Why?"

I didn't have an answer for him. Not really.

Finally, I said, "You're recovering from the drink, Niles. That doesn't mean you should suffer."

He grunted in reply.

"For what it's worth, it won't always be this bad. It's only been a few weeks. In another two weeks or so, it'll be out of your system completely."

He was silent for a long while.

"The Art of Being."

"What?" I asked.

"The book. It's called The Art of Being. It's a collection of poems."

I nodded, but my expression must have shown my surprise.

"Yes, he can read. And yes, he can think," Niles said of

himself.

"I never thought you couldn't."

That was only partly true. After my last trip with Niles, I'd be lying if I said I thought him to be a deep thinker.

"The world is a funny place," he said. "I swear things that once seemed so clearly black or white are blurred into mottled shades of gray the longer I live."

"Is that from the book?"

He gazed at me a long moment, his expression unreadable.

"No," he answered. "That's just an observation."

I didn't miss Quinn's stare from across the camp, but he knew better now at least. Niles presented no threat, romantically or otherwise.

Nonetheless, I tapped Niles's knee before I stood. "Chew the tassels. As many times as you need. And if you can, pick some for later. They aren't as potent when they're dried, but I'm not sure there will be *any* where we're going, so better dried than nothing."

He nodded and gave a soft, "Thank you."

Clear water ran across the rocky bed, trickling above and around black, tan, and gray stones of varying shapes and sizes. The tiny creek seemed unassuming enough, but after our last encounter with fresh water, I wondered if we'd be denied drinking water again.

"Dare we drink?" Niles asked, surveying the cold, clear creek with apprehension.

We'd packed up early this morning, traveling during the coolest part of the day, though the heat in the air was noticeable now. We were far enough south to feel the warmth of the sun overhead just about all day long. Sweat slid down the center of my back, and my tunic stuck uncomfortably to clammy skin.

Quinn inspected the stream, searching for signs of death or poison. He poked the dirt of the banks with a stick until he found a fat earthworm, then he kneeled and dropped it into the water. Despite my sympathy for the creature, I watched over Quinn's shoulder, waiting. The worm writhed and twisted, sinking to the bottom of the creek's edge, then slowly crawled out from the water and into a tiny crevice between two stones, disappearing from sight.

Satisfied with his results, Quinn led the pack horse to the stream and when the gelding took long gulps, we breathed a collective sigh of relief.

As I filled my water skin, I commented, "You know, I'm sure the water seemed fine when the deer was drinking, too. We don't know what happened to the worm after he went between the rocks."

"Well, it's been a long minute, and Sky is still alive, so I imagine we're in the clear at this point."

"But you'd sacrifice a horse?"

"Not intentionally, but given our options…"

I pursed my lips in disagreement but didn't argue. What choice was there? Sometimes I hated when Quinn made the difficult decisions without consulting me.

As though he needed to consult me.

He'd been an agent of the Order of the Southern Cross for three years, and now ruler and king of Castilles for two months. He didn't need my approval for anything.

I didn't speak for a long time after we returned to the road, thoughts churning in my head. Quinn still made decisions I didn't like. My feelings for him wouldn't change that part of him.

You don't know the things I've done.

Quinn said that to me once, long ago, when he thought I could never love him. Maybe he was right, though. Maybe it was better I *didn't* know.

"I don't like the look of that." Brigantino's words sliced into my thoughts. I turned my focus to where he looked.

"Of what? It's a log," Niles said, squinting at a large fallen tree on the ground beside the road. Judging by its condition, it had fallen many years ago.

"Not the log, inside it."

I saw what he pointed to but couldn't make sense of the dark mass in the hollowed center.

"A hive," Quinn said.

"Doesn't look like there's any activity," I said. "Dead?"

"Mmph," Quinn replied.

"But what killed it? This time of year, this far south, a hive should be rampant with activity," Brigantino said.

Quinn dismounted and I followed suit, unsure I wanted to learn anything more where chaos was concerned. Hives didn't die all at once in the middle of a warm spring. They just...didn't.

Quinn poked around the tree trunk with a stick, ensuring

the hive was inactive before prying the rotted wood open with large, capable hands, and exposing the inside of the hive to sunlight.

Neat, even stacks of golden honeycomb lined the inside, large sections brimming with honey. Hundreds of bees huddled together against one whole piece of comb, silent and inanimate as though they'd made the decision to die all at once.

"Could someone have poisoned the hive?" Niles asked. "Like the water?"

"Not poison," Quinn said, taking in the surrounding area. A chipmunk ran from the cover of the tree trunk into nearby underbrush.

Poison would have killed the chipmunk, too, and any other critters or insects near the log.

"They froze," I said. "In the hive."

It felt ridiculous to say the words aloud when another bead of sweat trickled down my back, but it was true, nonetheless.

"In this weather? Impossible!" Niles exclaimed.

"Right now, anything is possible," Quinn muttered.

"I've seen whole hives die in sudden cold," I pressed. "It doesn't happen often, but when it does, they huddle in a giant mass to keep warm. Then they don't want to move out of that huddle even to eat the honey that would give them energy to continue to vibrate to keep warm. They simply… freeze to death."

"There must be a dozen other ways they could have died," Niles said.

"Like?" Brigantino questioned him while Quinn squatted beside the hive, studying pieces of honeycomb curiously.

"I don't know! You're agents," he said, motioning between Quinn and Brigantino. "You've seen more than I have. Figure it out."

"Reina's right," Quinn said. He stood. "The honey is cold, too."

He bent and took his knife across the front of the honeycomb. Where freed honey should have flowed, the viscous liquid hardly dripped.

CHAPTER EIGHT

Ghosts of the Past
Quinn

"That's why they call it the Order of the Southern Cross?" Reina said, her round, dark eyes wide with disbelief. She scanned the barren landscape, the rope bridge spanning the enormous chasm, and the wide swath of empty air below.

I nodded letting my own gaze fall across the V-shaped suspension bridge. The rope bridge wasn't the kind made with wooden planks for walking across, nor was it the type that had a wide rope base to place one's feet. No, this bridge allowed a single, thick, reinforced rope for footing, two ropes for handholds, and that was it. Certainly, there were support ropes to keep the entire bridge secure, but nothing that would help in trying to cross it.

"Tell me we're not crossing that."

Ingram, white as a sheet, appeared genuinely terrified. He took several steps backwards, putting additional space between him and the edge. A fine sheen of sweat that had nothing to do with the sun overhead shimmered on his forehead. Heights. I wouldn't have guessed it from him. It explained why he'd never gotten close to the edge of the bluff at the Plymann Cliffs those months ago…and why he was so eager to get off of them.

Despite taking some satisfaction in watching him squirm, I replied, "No, we'll be taking one of those."

I pointed downward into the ravine, far east of where we stood. Even at this time of day, there were several South Trellington boats ferrying paying customers between the boundary of Castilles and the Southern Plains.

"But *that's* what you had to cross in your final test?" Reina asked, looking back to the bridge again. It swayed a little toward the middle, from wind or trembling earth, I wasn't sure. It could be either.

I nodded in response to her question, remembering my test all too well. I'd been lucky. No one died during my run. All too often, that wasn't the case. Seasoned agents accepted it when they took opposing roles on the bridge. The hazard pay was coveted, though. Ten times the normal amount. It was enough to make men volunteer to occupy the position for months at a time.

Now the bridge stood eerily empty, never again host to another of the Order's tests. Sometimes I still didn't believe it. The Order was no longer. Was I glad for it?

I caught Brigantino staring at the bridge, too, and wondered if my expression mirrored his. Was he remembering his own test? Or was he thinking of the times he played an opposing force? He was old enough. Had he ever taken on a counter role? Had he seen men fail?

"So you, what, cross that and then you're an agent?" Ingram asked. "Given the Order's reputation, I expected worse."

I didn't take the opportunity to bring up Ingram's obvious fear of heights. Instead, Brigantino plunged right into the terrifying reality of what a test entailed.

"You really think walking a rope bridge is what the Order considers a challenge?" he said, his voice thick with memory.

Ingram had the good sense not to answer.

"There are five opponents you must face before, on, and after the bridge. Five of the Order's best, most-seasoned fighters. Five of the men who trained you, now set out to watch you fail, watch you fall, or both."

Ingram and Reina shared horrified expressions. Shame burning in my soul, I turned from Reina's gaze, not wanting to see the judgment behind her eyes.

"You mean to tell me they let their own men *die?*" Niles asked.

Brigantino shrugged. "The men who died weren't fit to serve the Order."

His words said one thing, the strain in his voice another. I understood all too well. I'd watched men die at the crossing bridge. I'd watched *friends* die.

"That's barbaric!" Reina said. She'd never been good at holding back her thoughts. She whipped her head around to face me again, but I kept my gaze on the ropes, seeing ghosts from a past that existed only in my memory.

"Is this true?" she asked me.

Silently, I gave a curt nod.

"Oh, Quinn…" Her voice was soft, full of sorrow, whether for me or the men who died, I couldn't say.

I didn't want her pity.

"They knew the price and they accepted it," I said harshly, my tone a little too short, my words too clipped. "The Order wasn't made for sitting around, darning socks, and staying safe by the fireside at home. It was meant for men who would do anything to protect the sorceress who would one day save Castilles—men who *did* do anything to protect her—*you*."

I'm not sure why I said it so, why I made it seem like somehow Reina herself was responsible for the deaths of the men she'd never known, of lives she had no control over. The effect was instant.

Reina stepped back as though she'd been hit.

I was a fool.

"Once you're out there," Commander Three said, pointing to the long rope bridge behind him. *"There's no turning back. You're in. Or you're dead."*

Next to me, Kreitz swallowed hard and Ash went pale beneath his solid tan. All the training in the last year had come to this. Crossing a bridge...and living to tell about it. Not that any of us could tell about it. Perhaps the first and most important lesson when it came to the Order was secrecy. Those with a penchant for talking didn't make it past the sixth month of training.

The sun beat against the hard-baked ground, the dirt scorched into a hellish landscape—the kind of land that contained not a single drop of water, yet looked to be home to lake after lake somewhere over the horizon no matter which direction one looked. I ignored the sweat trickling down my temples.

Hundreds of feet below the bridge, a river wound through the ravine—the same river that cut the giant chasm into this land—heedless of what was about to happen on the ground above.

"You," Three said, pointing to Ash. "Go. May the wind guide your feet, the Saints guide your soul, and the Order have your back always. Honor in duty."

"And duty with honor," Ash replied.

Three gave a sharp nod, then stepped away from the mouth of the bridge, allowing Ash to proceed.

The difficulty with the Order's testing process was that they gave no indication of the true nature of a test every step of the way. In this—the final test—perhaps even less so. Was it a test of character to see how far a man would blindly follow?

Ash moved into position at the edge of the bridge, studying the structure and the men waiting on it. I didn't know Ashford's first name, just as he didn't know mine. Much like the Order's commanders going by number instead of name, agents-in-training were instructed to go by last name only.

Ash studied the ropes, the height of the bridge over the plummeting ravine below, and the first agent who waited on the ropes just ten feet from the edge. Arguably, the first agent had both the best and the worst fighting position. As the first to face Ash, he stood before a fresh opponent, one who hadn't yet spent himself fighting others. At the same time, he was closest to the end of the bridge, land, and a safer position should he need to get there. Like all agents playing the opposition role, he was masked.

Was that to make it easier for agents-in-training to strike without worrying who they might be defending themselves from, or was it to make it easier for the masked agents to take out an agent-in-training without feeling responsible for his death?

Ash stepped onto the bridge, throwing caution to the wind, racing head-on into the first masked opponent. Then, instead of plowing into him, Ash used one of the rope handholds at the last minute and swung himself out and around the first masked agent. It happened so quickly, I hadn't expected the move. Neither had the agent. That didn't stop him from trying to keep Ash from gaining his footing back on the ropes.

For one heart-stopping moment, I thought he might not make it back to the bridge again. As his body swung in an arc through the air, over the empty space above the ravine, the masked agent kicked a leg into the space where Ash needed to land at the same time Ash's body came downward. It hit Ash's abdomen as he landed, knocking him to the bottom rope.

My friend rolled with the momentum, easing the kick and safely making it past the point where the first masked agent was allowed to attack. Or so I thought.

But rules didn't apply here. The first agent continued to attack even while the second masked agent advanced on Ash. Within a breath, Ash was fighting both sides, using the ropes and the narrowness of the bridge to his advantage.

Somehow, he managed to make it past the second agent. I'd lost track of how. He was halfway across the bridge, fighting the third agent when things began to go wrong. Ash made the mistake of trying to swing out over the side rope of the bridge again, but the agent had seen his trick twice before.

Instead of landing back on the bottom rope, Ash's feet were knocked out from beneath him in mid-air. The arc of his body as it flew through the air suddenly and violently altered when the third agent's foot connected with his lower half. Almost at the same time, the agent grabbed him and threw him to the base of the ropes.

On his back, Ash was visibly winded, but fought on as he'd been trained to do. He shoved his hands to the side ropes and kicked upward into the agent's midsection, using the man's forward momentum to toss him over Ash's own head and onto the rope floor. The trouble with this move was that now Ash had to get past the agent a second time.

They grappled hand to hand, the minutes dragging on. I held my breath as they teetered precariously over one of the rope handholds and then over the other.

Finally, Ash whirled around, flipping the agent off balance, enough so that the man let go of Ash and held to the ropes instead.

Almost to the end of the bridge, he encountered the fourth agent, but instead of trying to whip out and around him as he'd done before, Ash made a move to plow right into the man—a man half the size of most agents. Instead of fighting

the incoming blow as expected, the masked agent simply...
danced around Ash as lithe and agile as a dancer upon the
stage. There was no other way to describe it. One minute he
was in front of Ash, about to be plowed over and the next he
was behind Ash as Ash skidded off the suspended bridge and
wildly into the air.

Ash didn't have a chance to grab for the ropes. He fell
through empty space and into the ravine. The shock knocked
the breath from my lungs.

What the blazes! What was all this for if good men died?

I looked to Commander Three, ready to speak out, to call
out the atrocity for what it was. I didn't get far.

"Fiermi! What—"

Ignoring me completely, Commander Three turned to
address Kreitz. "You're up."

Already the men on the bridge were changing out,
refreshing with new individuals from both sides, taking their
spots and preparing for what was to come.

Ash and I hadn't been close, but he was as close as one
came to having a friend in the Order, and I couldn't stop
staring at the space he'd occupied just twenty seconds
earlier. If I looked down, his body would be gone, carried
away by the current of the river below. Had he been alive
when he hit the water?

"May the wind guide your feet, the Saints guide your
soul, and the Order have your back always. Honor in duty,"
Commander Three said once again.

"And duty with honor," Kreitz replied, stepping forward.

Honor? What honor? Where was the honor in watching

good men die?

I didn't want to watch Kreitz on the bridge. Hell, I wasn't even sure I wanted to cross the bridge anymore.

Heavy doubt must have shown on my face. Commander Three stood beside me, hands tucked behind his back, watching Kreitz battle for his life and his future with the Order.

"He was never going to make it, you know," he said.

"What?"

"Ashford wasn't cut out for it. That's why he went first. I wanted you to know what failure means, what it really means."

I scoffed and flung out a hand. "'Tis not hard to see. Death! How noble of the Order."

I was too angry to care about insubordination. A man had died for no good reason. I wasn't going to curb my words. Not anymore.

"What do you think would happen if we let men lesser than the smartest, most skilled, most cunning, toughest of men into the Order, D'Arturio? What do you think the Order would become then?"

"You don't have to admit everyone for Saints' sake! Just...let them walk away. Give them a chance to live their lives! Allowing good men to die so you have great men in your Order just means more terrible men walk Liron by comparison in the long run."

Commander Three faced me, leaning in, drilling holes into my eyes with his own unwavering gaze. "Ashford, and every man before him, died exactly as they lived—for the

Order, for the chance to protect the White Sorceress, whoever she is and wherever she might be. He knew the consequence of failure on the bridge, same as you. He stepped up anyway. Will you?"

In the heat of the moment, I had argued with Commander Three right through Kreitz's successful run to the other side. Kreitz had made it through. He was a full-fledged agent.

My relief for him was short-lived.

I turned to face the bridge, my anger racing high at the price demanded, at the loss already sustained today. Did I want to be part of the Order? Was this where I fit?

What choice did I have?

I already told my father the Order was my future. I promised him. I wanted to serve. I wanted to protect. I wanted to do the right thing.

Didn't I?

My heart set an unsteady rhythm in my chest, pounding in time with the thoughts that tumbled through my head. I stared at the bridge.

I'd left Reina behind for the Order.

I'd seen her last over a year ago. Was she still at the cottage farm? Had she taken on the role of Healer? Was she married?

My heart lodged in my throat.

I'd been gone long enough that she could have married and had a babe already. The very thought made me ill.

What kind of life awaited me if I returned?

The question lingered in my mind as I stepped forward to the threshold of the bridge. It lingered when I placed my hands on the rough rope handholds, when my feet found the rope below, when I threw kicks and punches in a whirlwind I couldn't later remember. And when I reached the opposite side of the bridge and the agents waiting there slapped my back in congratulations and welcome, the question remained.

What kind of life?

CHAPTER NINE

Illusion of Safety
Quinn

Two separate towns composed South Trellington, Upper and Lower. Upper South Trellington stood on the plateau overlooking the canyon, a dusty desert town that blended into the baked red dirt surroundings and looked as scruffy as the random scrub brush that grew throughout.

Because it was easier for riffraff to go undetected, Upper South Trellington was a rougher place than Lower South Trellington. There weren't many who found the town a place they wanted to visit for long. As a result, those who had a reason to go into hiding found the town perfect. Naturally, that was where I'd been stationed just shy of two years ago.

We rode through Upper South Trellington with the intention of taking the quickest path to Lower South Trellington, but when it came time to break for lunch, I lost the vote against stopping to eat. Now we sat at a table in one of the pubs I had once often haunted. The establishment was innocuous enough midday, but I wouldn't have dreamed of letting Reina see the place after dark or venture upstairs to the rooms above and those who occupied them. She'd die of shock. Or maybe not. But there was still no reason to linger in the vicinity.

"What do you suppose Tarrowburn meant when he said the veil has thinned, in places shred?" Reina mused, pushing her empty plate forward. "The veil between what?"

"Life and death," I answered. I speared a forkful of bland fish that could have used about a pound of seasoning, missing my mother's cooking with each bite. "What's dead is alive, what's alive is dead."

"Right," she said slowly. "But that's not a physical thing. How can you shred something metaphorical?"

"You can break a heart," I said.

Reina furrowed her brows at me, giving an indiscernible frown. "I hope you're not planning on doing that anytime soon."

I kept my gaze trained on hers as though I might send my thoughts directly to her mind.

"Of course not."

Ingram elicited a groan. "Ugh. I'm going to be sick, and it's not from the questionable inn food."

I ignored him and leaned back in my seat, crossing my arms across my chest. "I think it's more important we focus on the Heart of Death part of the prophecy."

"That's nearly as obscure as a veil. What is it? Where do we find it? What do we do with it?" Reina asked.

"Personally, I'm not particularly interested in finding anything associated with death," Ingram said.

"Lucky for you, you don't get a say," Brigantino told him.

Ingram shut his mouth and turned his head to the bar,

eyeing the pints of ale in the hands of several customers. Up north the drunkards preferred pine ale, but down here it was a dark stout made from dried ugadu beans spiced with chervil, which I found to be nothing less than exceptionally odd. Men here—and even some women—drank it like water. By now, Ingram was probably dying to get his hands on a pint.

"Break it down," I said. I pointed to Reina. "You're the Bringer of Life, I'm the King, Niles is the One Who Failed, and Brigantino...probably shouldn't be here."

"Good luck getting rid of me." Brigantino leaned forward in his seat, challenging me, resting his elbows on the table.

Amused, I nodded my head in concession. "Hence, why you're still with us. Anyway, each of those titles is capitalized in the prophecy, as though using our names. So is the Heart of Death."

I leaned back in my seat, waiting.

"You're saying we're searching for a person," Reina said.

I knew she'd be the first to put the pieces together. I nodded.

"You think the Heart of Death is a person?" Brigantino didn't sound like he believed the possibility.

"Why not? The problem with prophecy is that it's written in a very specific way so even if it sounds like a million different pieces could fit, specific words or phrases often indicate the true meaning behind the words. Paying attention to those kinds of bits is really important when trying to decipher the true meaning." I paused, letting my words sink in. "What I wouldn't give for my father to get a good look at this prophecy."

"Supposing you're right, how do we find this person? We can't just go around asking random people if they know the Heart of Death," Reina said.

"Not random people," Brigantino said. "Very *specific* people."

His eyes were trained on a familiar figure who was currently pouring another round of stouts for several customers at the bar. Eliza was as tough as any man in Upper South Trellington. She had to be to run a pub, even the least rowdy one in the town. She was tall and brawny, her arms and thighs nearly as thick around as my own. Her once dark hair was cropped short and dyed a bright red, probably to intimidate the customers who would think of causing trouble.

Eliza was a wealth of knowledge, one of the Order's top informants at the border. If anyone could coerce her to help, it'd be Brigantino. He had more experience than I when it came to pulling information from a source. It didn't hurt that she'd been eyeing him since we first walked in the door.

A history perhaps? I watched Brigantino's face as he took in Eliza at the bar, his gaze fixed on her. I'd only known Brigantino as an agent—a hyper-focused agent who thought of nothing but the mission he'd been assigned. But who had he been years ago? Back when he'd first joined the Order, when he'd scoured the lands looking for the White Sorceress, Bringer of Life?

Had he given up a chance at his own happiness to see to it that I, the prince baby, was hidden and Reina—wherever she was at that time—was safe? His expression gave nothing away.

Not that I expected it to.

"I'll be back," Brigantino said. He stood, straightened his tunic, and strode to the bar.

He must have ordered one of those horrible stouts because Eliza placed one in front of him with scarcely a glance.

"Come," I said to the others. I stood and left payment for our meal on the table. "Brigantino will do better without us staring over his shoulder."

Eliza provided minimal information to Brigantino. Maybe she was mad he'd left her years ago. Maybe she didn't have much information to share. It was impossible to say.

She had at least confirmed the Heart of Death was rumored to be a person in the Southern Plains, and she recommended seeking out one of the Jyngabé tribes for more information. Despite my time in the south, I hadn't spent much time with the Jyngabé, but Brigantino had, so even though he wasn't *supposed* to be on our journey with us as per the prophecy, I was glad he had come.

As we zigzagged down the cliffside path that led to the ravine floor, the sun blazed at our backs and shoulders. While we weren't pushing to move quickly, the horses breathed hard from the exertion, their sides heaving, nostrils flared wide while they maneuvered down the steep, winding path.

I turned in my saddle to steal a glance at Ingram riding

behind Reina. With his fear of heights, he couldn't appreciate this trail any more than he did the rope bridge we could have crossed on foot, but at least this way he could close his eyes.

Sure enough, Ingram's eyes were shut, his knuckles white around the pommel of his saddle. At least he had the good sense not to hold the reins too tightly, giving his horse its head.

Reina followed my gaze and turned to look behind her.

"It's not far now," she called.

He nodded but didn't open his eyes. It figured she would soothe him. Even after all he'd done to her. Despite the fact that we needed him to fulfill the latest prophecy, I still wanted to kill him for the things he'd done to her. Of course, I'd wanted him dead for past crimes and atrocities committed even before he'd touched her, but when he laid a finger on Reina, he'd taken our quarrel to a personal level. That we were traveling together without my murdering him straight out was a testament to how seriously I took the words of Magnus Tarrowburn.

By the time we made it to the ravine floor, the sun had nearly set, but the temperature in the ravine soared, the walls of the canyon serving to hold the heat like a blast furnace. The increase in heat was opposite to what one would expect, but to get caught on the canyon floor anywhere except Lower South Trellington was a slow death from heat and exhaustion.

Aside from the town of Lower South Trellington, a dusty canyon floor and a churning river were the only landmarks for hundreds of miles in either direction, and in many places on the canyon floor, the river was unreachable unless one was willing to jump in without the need to get back out. The ravine floor narrowed in some places so it was almost filled by the river. The landscape was so different from anything in Castilles that I could imagine what it must look like through Reina's eyes.

I'd spent so much time here that I hardly remembered the first time I'd seen it. Lower South Trellington was a semblance of the ordinary in the middle of the very unordinary. Like many other small villages, the town thrived on goods and services that could be provided only here. Indeed, Lower South Trellington *thrived*.

Here, the ferry service was key to its prospering economy. Nowhere else could one cross into the Southern Plains and still bring along horses and supplies. At least not for hundreds of miles. The Lower South Trellington ferries were enormous, flat barges that could accommodate horses, carriages, even large pens of sheep and goats. It was the perfect market with a never-ending supply of customers doing business back and forth between both lands.

"We'll stay here tonight." I dismounted in front of a whitewashed inn with red, clay roof tiles and a faded wooden sign above the door that read *Ravine Blessings—Lodging, Food, and Stables.*

We could have crossed the river tonight and spent the night in the Southern Plains, but there was no town nearby once in the Plains. As the sun was quickly setting, it made better sense to stable the horses and get a night of proper rest before crossing the river, climbing the steep path off the canyon floor, and embarking into the harsh desert.

Ingram couldn't help himself. "A real bed? One with a mattress?"

How had he ever survived a day in the army, let alone six years? I shot him a look of disgust. He'd done it by lying and cheating to keep from harm's way.

Brigantino glared at him.

As it turned out, the inn had a single room available, so Ingram didn't get a bed to rest his pretty head after all. Reina and I took the bed while Ingram and Brigantino slept on the mostly-even wooden floor. They had a throw rug for cushioning at least.

But Reina felt guilty that Ingram and Brigantino were relegated to the floor and gave up her pillow which meant I had to offer up mine as well, if begrudgingly.

Still, Ingram was deprived of his bed.

Was that satisfaction taking root in my chest? Probably. Perhaps a warm meal that was a hundred times better than the questionable lunch we'd had in Upper South Trellington, a bed, and the promise of sleep without having to stand guard half the night had me feeling more content than I had a right to feel. Still, regardless of the inescapable heat of the ravine floor and despite sharing a room with Ingram, I slept long and hard.

I woke before dawn, and though the innkeeper tried to temp us with breakfast, I insisted on catching the first ferry of the day. Ingram's grumbling about being awake before the birds annoyed me less than usual. Perhaps I should think about getting better sleep on a regular basis. If ever I got the chance to be free of fulfilling one prophecy or another, which, admittedly, seemed less than likely anytime soon, I'd give it a try.

"Let's go, weasel."

Ingram's muttering might not have irritated me, but Brigantino wasn't in the mood to hear his complaints.

"The sun hasn't even risen!" Ingram said as we stepped onto the inn's front porch. "You've gotten us up, denied us food, and want us to travel a hundred miles or more before the *sun* has even come up!"

"Shh, be quiet!" Brigantino said, alarm on his face. He searched the ravine for a grinding sound somewhere in the distance. Alert, I tried to focus on the direction of the noise. Given that noise echoed off the canyon walls, it was difficult to pinpoint where the sound was coming from.

If not for my travel companions, I would have snuck off into the darkness to identify its source, but Brigantino would never allow it. He would protect his king at all costs. In a way, it was maddening since, as a former agent, I was every bit as capable as he. The hair on the back of my neck stood on end, the unidentifiable sound growing ever more persistent. Closer, even.

"*What* is that?" Reina asked, leaning on the porch railing and peering into darkness.

The terrible din grew louder by the minute. A gnashing and crunching like the breaking of bones by the dozens. My gaze darted from one hiding place to the next, trying to pinpoint the location, but the sound was pervasive, eluding capture. Right, then left, then right again, all the while coming directly in front of us.

A pack of wolves with a carcass?

This far south? On the ravine floor? It couldn't be.

And as the sky began to lighten, I could barely make out the shapes lumbering toward us, the horrifying, monstrous things steadily moving forward.

"The undead," I said, my heart plummeting into my stomach.

CHAPTER TEN

What's Dead is Alive
Reina

I didn't react when Quinn identified the threat as the undead. Neither did Niles. As sunlight began to brighten the canyon, we stared at a moving wall made of hundreds of bodies walking, dragging, crawling their way towards us. They shimmered in and out of existence, solid one second, a ghostly image the next.

They were everything I imagined…and worse. My stomach churned at the putrid stench accompanying the mass of undead, the odor more potent than any rotting animal corpse I'd come upon in the woods. I pulled the neck of my tunic upwards to shield my mouth and nose, unable to drag my eyes away from the sight before us. I put one hand to my racing heart, taking in the sightless white eyes—in some cases empty orbital sockets where eyes should have been—and rotting, gray flesh that fell from bones in chunks even as the undead continued to advance. *What's dead is alive.*

I might have stayed in a terror-induced paralysis, but Brigantino and Quinn jumped into action, herding us back to the trail we had traveled yesterday.

"To the canyon cliffs," Brigantino said, shoving his pack

on his back. "Quickly."

"But the horses!" I cried, not wanting to leave Aeros with the undead. Still, I cinched my pack to my own back and ran.

"There's no time to ready them!"

We raced to the path we'd taken last night…only to find it already occupied. Along the path, dozens of undead trudged downward to join their brethren, flashing in and out of being like some deadly, ghostly horde. With each flash, they grew closer, as though moving faster during the times they couldn't be seen.

"Where do we go now?" Niles asked, looking between Quinn and Brigantino.

Quinn's face darkened with a scowl, and he conferred with Brigantino. "Fight or take the western pass?"

The look on Brigantino's face did little to reassure me. As an experienced agent, I expected he would have seen everything, feared little, and that nothing would make him hesitate, but he hesitated now.

"I…I'm not sure they can be fought. Take the western pass and pray to the Saints they haven't made it there, too," he growled.

We hurried along the ravine floor, north of the river. All the while, I wished for a saddle beneath me and four sturdy hooves to carry me away from the monstrosity in Lower South Trellington. Was Aeros safe in the barn where we'd boarded her and the other horses? What about the people of the town?

Lost in my worries, my foot slipped on a boulder. I righted myself and took the opportunity to check behind us for any sign of the undead. The sun had risen and the landscape in the ravine behind us revealed nothing I wouldn't normally expect to see. The river, its rocky rust-colored banks, canyon walls, and the scrub brush growing in every rocky crack and crevice glowed with reflected morning sunlight.

We'd made it far enough that the undead were no longer in sight. It didn't stop me from worrying about the way they flickered in and out of existence. If they moved like that, how long until they caught up?

The memory of milky, sightless eyes and mottled, dead skin sent shivers down my spine. Most of them moved on two legs, but there were undead who were reminiscent of animals, too, mindlessly moving on four legs with muzzles and snouts that reminded me of horses and wolves. Were they already waiting at the western pass, too? The thought alone was enough to make my feet move faster.

It was well over an hour before we reached the base of the pass and Brigantino instructed us to stay behind while he rounded the final bend leading to it. When he returned and beckoned for us to join him, I let out a breath of relief. The pass was clear.

Only when we began our ascent, did I realize why we hadn't traveled to Lower South Trellington this way. It was treacherous, slow, and much steeper than the way we'd traveled yesterday.

"Where else can we cross to the Southern Plains?" I asked. "Since Trellington ferries are out."

There was a moment of quiet before Quinn answered. "You're not going to like it."

"Oh, no. No way, D'Arturio. We're not taking that rope *thing* you call a bridge," Niles said, echoing my own feelings.

Quinn stopped in his tracks and turned to face Niles who was on lower ground behind him. "You want to travel two hundred miles west *on foot*? Because that's the only other way to get across. This ravine? It splits the land for six hundred miles, four to the east, two to the west."

Niles turned white.

"There have to be other places to cross the middle, other canyon floor cities like South Trellington."

Quinn shook his head, turned his back to Niles and resumed the upward climb. "The canyon floor is the widest at South Trellington. That's the only place big enough for a town. After that? Nothing. Any town built would be washed away during flooding."

"Aren't there other bridges? *Real* bridges?" The desperation showed in Niles's voice.

"There's nothing," Brigantino confirmed. "We get to the ropes and we go. Simple as that."

Nothing seemed simple, least of all crossing a giant, gaping chasm in the earth on nothing but a few flimsy ropes. But that was something to worry about later. Right now, I'd just be glad to reach the top of the canyon and get off this wretched path.

Sweat trickled down my back uncomfortably, but we continued higher, alternately walking and climbing depending on the slope of the ground. After a long period of silence, Niles finally spoke.

"Someone please tell me why it seems I'm always

climbing up or down cliffs when I'm with the two of you," he huffed.

Quinn didn't reply and I was too winded from exertion to answer. Not that it mattered since I didn't really think Niles was looking for an answer.

When at last we crested the rim of the canyon and stepped onto the flat open land, we paused to catch our breath. I bent and put my hands to my knees, letting the open air dry the sweat that had coated every inch of my skin. Then we moved forward again, slowly growing closer to the rope suspension bridge somewhere in the distance.

At least we wouldn't be fighting trained agents. I could take hope in that.

Heights didn't bother me, but the thought of a flimsy bridge stretched hundreds of feet across a gaping chasm made me lightheaded, and we hadn't even gotten there yet. Because we'd taken the western pass back to the canyon rim, we now needed to head several miles back east again to get to the bridge. We'd essentially lost an entire day of our journey in just getting and leaving Lower South Trellington without reaching the Southern Plains at all.

About a half mile from the rope bridge, I began to notice some sort of secret exchange between Quinn and Brigantino. Not that they spoke aloud, but there was a conversation taking place with eyes and nods of heads. Infuriating.

I searched the distance where their attention seemed focused. The cracked, red earth was flat, barren with the exception of a sad-looking scrub bush dotting the landscape here and there. Heat rose from the ground in shimmering waves, making the horizon appear a constant reflecting pool, its waters just out of reach.

I saw nothing out of—

I squinted and cocked my head as though it might help to clarify what I thought I saw. The shimmering mirage. The mirage moved more than it had yesterday when I'd remarked on it. It was…

Saints, it was the undead. How could there be so many blasted undead all at once?

"Quinn…"

He only needed one glance at my face to realize I was no longer unaware of our situation.

"Don't stop moving," he ordered.

I hadn't realized I stopped. I hurried onward, wanting to run.

"What is it?" Niles scoured the landscape for what he was missing. "Are you kidding?! What the bloody hell!"

The undead were still a long way off, but so was the bridge. We'd be lucky to make it in time. I moved faster between Quinn and Niles, all the while Niles muttering by my side.

"Goddamned cell would have been preferable. No blasted pension is worth this. No land. No matter how far from Irzan."

"We'll make it to the bridge. Just keep going," Quinn said. "Don't run. I don't want to call attention to us any more than we have to. There's no telling what they'll do with a clear target."

They weren't moving quickly, at least not while in sight,

but every time they flickered out of being, they covered double the amount of ground. I wasn't at all certain we'd make it to the bridge before they did, and my galloping heart was proof.

By the time we reached the rope bridge, I couldn't be sure if my heart was giving a panicked thump due to the ropes in front of me or the undead behind me. They were closer now, close enough to make out the sheer number of them crossing the wide expanse of land.

"Reina, go," Quinn ordered.

"First?" I squeaked.

"Just go!"

Gripping each of the ropes at the sides, I placed one boot onto the bottom rope, took a breath, closed my eyes, and began walking forward. The bridge might hold, but my own legs felt as though they would give out at any moment.

Breathe.

At Brigantino's urging, Quinn was behind me on the bridge. He probably could have crossed it in half a minute by himself, but he was stuck. Waiting on me.

There was wind out here over the canyon, a strong wind that almost seemed annoyed the bridge existed. It wasn't the best moment for me to contemplate how old the bridge was, who'd constructed it, and if it had ever seen repair. Knees weak, I squatted, my hands still gripping the side ropes.

"Reina, are you all right?" Quinn's voice carried despite the whipping wind in my ears.

"Just catching my breath," I replied.

It wasn't a lie. I steeled myself and stood again, inching

toward the lip of the Southern Plains, the sun-worn rope fibers rough beneath my palms. I focused my eyes on the end of the bridge, the land slowly growing closer. Oh, so slowly.

Don't look down. Don't look down.

I didn't look down, but when an inhuman shriek pierced the air and shouts came from behind, I turned and gasped.

Impossibly, the undead were closing in on the mouth of the bridge where Niles and Brigantino still stood, salivating at the possibility of closing in on their prey. They grew wilder by the minute, decaying limbs flailing as they climbed over one another to gain ground. My heart leaped into my throat in terror.

Brigantino shoved Niles onto the ropes of the bridge. Niles stumbled forward, grabbing at the side ropes while Brigantino slashed at the onslaught of undead with his sword in one hand, knife in the other. Pieces of undead flew through the air as Brigantino defended our position. I might have vomited to witness such violence at any other time.

"Go, go!" Quinn yelled from behind me.

Suddenly the height of the bridge over the ravine was no longer a concern. I ran as fast as I dared along the ropes, using my hands as much as my feet to move forward, ignoring the fraying fibers that bit into my fingers. Quinn followed close behind, almost ready to throw me to the opposite end of the bridge if needed, I suspected.

When I dared to risk a look back, Brigantino was backing his way along the bridge, facing the undead and slicing away at the rotting flesh and bones. And yet, it didn't matter how many he cut down. They kept coming, forcing him backwards one step at a time. When he stumble-stepped, my breath caught in my throat, but he righted himself and moved steadily backwards again, towards the safety of the Southern Plains.

Was *any* place safe anymore? I pushed forward, Quinn almost on top of me, Niles several lengths back.

Then the unthinkable happened. The very thing I'd feared the most. One of the undead shimmered out of existence and reappeared between Quinn and Niles, a gaping black mouth hanging open on one side from a half-attached jaw, filmy eyes glistening. It cocked its head in Quinn's direction, then turned to Niles. It swayed once, ever so briefly, then went after Niles with the speed and intensity of a rabid dog.

"Quinn!" I screamed, pointing.

Niles's eyes grew wide with panic. He had no way back, no way forward, and no weapon to fight off the crazed thing that was quickly advancing on him.

For all his hatred of Niles, Quinn turned, drew his sword, and began slashing at the undead intent on reaching Niles. He sliced it clean through its middle, but there was no time to feel relief. The thing fused back together before my eyes.

Something squeezed the air from my lungs.

What are *these things?*

Quinn didn't hesitate. He kept slashing and moving, whirling and slicing, in the narrow space of the bridge. It seemed the undead should have turned to face Quinn, but it continued creeping forward toward Niles, focused on him with an eerie intensity.

Quinn released a growl of frustration, thrusting the

sword downwards, slashing the undead in two, then slicing sideways again so half the body was thrown from the bridge. That moment alone should have been the end of the fight, but the *thing* wouldn't give up. One armed and with no legs, it still dragged itself forward.

Niles backed up against Brigantino, who continued to fight the undead coming from the Castilles side of the bridge. Niles kicked outward, trying to send the remainder of the undead thing off the bridge. Instead, with a speed it shouldn't have possessed, the thing grabbed his leg with one hand and sunk its top teeth through the fabric and into his flesh.

I screamed at the same time Niles howled, but his cry of pain was far louder. Finally, Quinn slashed the remaining arm from the undead's body, sheathed his sword, and pulled its head and torso from Niles's leg. Without a body to control it, the hand that had gripped Niles's leg released and fell.

"Reina, *go!*" Quinn screamed. He slung Niles's arm around his neck, took the brunt of his weight, and awkwardly moved forward.

Brigantino continued across the bridge behind them, fighting one undead after the next. Bodies fell from the bridge again and again—whole bodies, but also torsos, arms, legs, all falling through the air, grotesque mouths opening in surprise as gravity claimed them. Could they be surprised? Did they have minds?

I hesitated a second, then turned and raced to the other side of the bridge. I didn't look back again to see what was coming. I only prayed nothing would appear in front of me.

I almost didn't believe I had reached the end of the bridge when my feet fell on the firm ground of the Southern Plains. Instead of collapsing as I wanted to, I turned to watch Niles and Quinn's progress behind me. I slipped my knife from its place in my boot, quivering at the thought of facing one of the undead up close with the small blade.

I took some of Niles's weight as he and Quinn crossed into the Southern Plains. He leaned on my shoulder, and I nearly buckled as I lowered him to the ground. His leg bled profusely. I tied a makeshift tourniquet from my belt, then turned my gaze back to Brigantino.

"I'll be right back," I told him, though I wasn't sure he heard my words through his pain.

Brigantino wasn't yet halfway across the bridge—a bridge now full of rotting bodies steadily advancing on him. It was only a matter of time before one of them flickered to his other side with free access to the Southern Plains.

"Quinn," I said, breathless. "We've got to help him."

I said 'we,' but I'd never felt so useless.

But Quinn had dropped his pack and was already working on slicing the ropes of the bridge, dragging his serrated dagger across the thick ropes. My lips parted, and I stood rooted in place.

Quinn was going to destroy the bridge.

"Brigantino—" I started.

Quinn looked up for a split-second, then back to the ropes again, drops of sweat falling from his face and hair into the parched ground.

"He's got it," he said.

"The ropes, D'Arturio. Cut the ropes!" Brigantino backed toward us, hacking away at the undead.

"On it," Quinn mumbled, not taking the time to yell back to Brigantino.

I didn't hesitate. As Quinn finished sawing through one of the hand ropes and moved to the thicker foot rope, I threw my own pack to the ground and began slicing into the other hand rope with my own knife. The fibers seemed to fray all too slowly, releasing their tension one by one, surrendering to the blade.

My heart pounded beneath my ribcage, pulse roaring in my ears, and my hands began to redden from the bite of the coarse rope. Halfway through, it seemed like the knife would never slice all the way. Brigantino would die on the bridge. The undead would make it to the Southern Plains. We would *all* die.

I fought against the rising swell of panic, against the animal instinct to turn and run. My focus sharpened on the ropes. I forced myself to breathe, to calm, to do what needed to be done. Like a surgery. This was nothing more than setting a broken bone. I could do this.

Quinn and I sawed through our ropes at the same time. The bridge fell away with a final snap and I looked, panicked, to where Brigantino had been, but he was no longer there.

Instead he was hurling through the air towards us, his body on a collision course with the side of the cliff. He wouldn't make the leap.

Hundreds of bodies, undead bodies, fell in hoards from the bridge as the ropes collapsed and fell to the other side of the canyon. Still they kept coming, falling off the side of the canyon and into the ravine below, their stench carrying on the wind.

Quinn reached out to Brigantino, but he was too far. I turned away as Brigantino hit the cliffside with a sickening thud. Clenching my eyes shut, I pulled my chin to my chest and tried not to hear the sound replaying itself in my ears.

The silence was overwhelming now that the bridge had fallen and the remaining undead were halted by the gaping canyon.

And then I heard something—a grunting and a scraping from just over the canyon wall. I looked to Quinn, but he was no longer standing where he had been.

Instead, he was lying on his belly on the ground, one arm extended downward. I swallowed and risked a look over the edge, then placed a hand to my mouth.

Brigantino had both hands wrapped around the hilt of his dagger—a dagger embedded in a crack in the canyon wall. The veins in his neck strained as he held himself in place, his legs searching for a foothold. His pack was dead weight on his back, adding to his struggle, but there was no way to rid himself of it without letting go of the dagger.

"Can you get just a bit higher?" Quinn called. "Just a little. I can almost reach you."

Brigantino's response was muffled. He'd probably cursed anyway.

"Reina, hold my legs," Quinn instructed.

Returning to where I could no longer see Brigantino, I clamped my hands around Quinn's ankles and arched myself backwards as a counterweight so he wouldn't slip over the edge.

Long moments dragged on, my back burning with the strain of pulling against Quinn's weight. He slid forward to reach farther for Brigantino. I dug my heels into the ground, finding little I could use to brace myself, my boots sliding in the red dirt.

"Hold, Reina!"

I wanted to scream that I was already holding. Instead, I pulled harder, my arms straining with effort.

"Climb, man. A few inches. You're almost there."

Tense moments of silence followed with the scraping against the canyon wall and Niles's groans of pain from somewhere behind me the only sounds heard.

My hands grew slick with sweat, sliding on Quinn's boots—just a hair, but enough to ignite panic.

"Hurry," I called between gritted teeth.

Then a bloodied hand appeared at the top of the cliff, Quinn grabbed Brigantino's arm, and, with a single motion, flung him onto the hard, flat ground beside us. Brigantino collapsed onto his side, wriggled from his pack, then rolled to his back. His enormous chest heaved from exertion, rising and falling with each pant. He closed his eyes against the deep blue sky above and breathed.

I let him rest.

I'd look over his wounds later. For now, I would leave alone the man who just escaped death ten times over. Whatever contusions and abrasions he had could wait.

I stood, shaking, dusting the dirt from my pants, then

bent over to catch my own breath. I turned to where Quinn and I had set Niles down.

Eyes shut tight, lips pressed together in pain, he was pale under the tan he'd gained over the last few days. I didn't like his pallor.

"Let me see," I said to him.

Reluctantly, he pulled his hands off the bloodied mess of a pant leg and leaned back on his elbow. There was a lot of blood, more than I could handle without the talisman. Without my medicine bag.

Fiermi! Why had I left the medicine bag?

I kneeled beside Niles and said, "I need to see the wound. I've got to pull up the fabric. It's going to sting. Will you be okay?"

Niles swallowed and gave a short nod. "Do what you have to do."

"Lie back."

My gaze flicked to Quinn and Brigantino, still on the ground, but sitting up at least. It would be a long time before any of us felt untroubled rest after today, I suspected.

Niles hissed in pain when I lifted the shredded material from the shredded skin and muscle beneath. No bone was exposed, but the wound was…like nothing I'd seen before.

I'd have to try the talisman. I *had* to.

"All right," I said. "Sit still, I'm going to use the talisman."

"What! No. Didn't you say it wasn't working right? Isn't that what you and Quinn were talking about a few days ago? What if you use the talisman and it kills me?"

I looked into his eyes, trying to convey the situation with every ounce of seriousness I possessed. "Niles." I took his hand and squeezed. "There's no choice."

Let him see the truth in my eyes. He'd die here in the desert if I didn't do *something*.

His lower lip trembled once, then he closed his eyes and gave one small nod. I tried to give him a small smile, some reassurance that the talisman *would* work this time, but my own fears had begun to creep in and a thousand 'what ifs' went through my mind.

With resolve, I shoved them away and tapped into the talisman, extending its healing power to Niles's leg. The talisman would work. It would. It had to—

A pained scream snapped me from my vision state, flinging me almost violently back into the moment, and I pressed my hands to the wound that bled profusely again despite the tourniquet.

The talisman was supposed to heal the blood vessels, not tear them further. I pushed at the panic and the guilt in my chest, shoved them away, and held my hands tight to Niles's calf. When the bleeding abated enough that I could relieve the pressure again, I stood.

I would find no help in the talisman. Not this time.

"Stay here," I said.

Niles gave a strained laugh through his nose.

"Wouldn't dream of going anywhere."

I grabbed my pack from the ground and the water skin within. The water wasn't sterile, but it was better than nothing.

And it was better than leaving filth from the undead's claws and teeth in Nile's exposed muscle. At least until I had access to real medicine.

"Have to clean it," I said. "Before we go anywhere, I need to irrigate it."

"Irrigate? Are we farming on my leg now?"

Well, Niles's sense of humor was still intact even if his leg wasn't. I didn't reply. Instead, I poured the water over the wound. Thanks to the tourniquet, the blood no longer welled, and no major arteries appeared to be severed. Still, I couldn't be too careful. It had to be cleaned and dressed before we moved.

Saints, how *could* he move?

Quinn and Brigantino, mostly recovered, joined us, looking on with concern.

"He's not going to be able to travel," Quinn said, voicing my thoughts.

I pressed my lips together.

"Can you carry him? Between the two of you, I mean."

Brigantino held out raw, bloodied hands. "I might be able to help get him a few miles if he can lean on me while we walk, but if it requires my hands, I'm not going to be good for much help."

Not to mention whatever other bruises covered the front half of his body. I hoped he didn't have internal bleeding from the impact. I should have thought of that earlier, but Niles's wound occupied my thoughts, leaving room for little else.

"Leave me," Niles said softly.

"What? No!" I scolded. "Have you forgotten the prophecy says we need you?"

A sliver of guilt sliced through my mind at the callousness of my words. I closed my eyes. I should have said something else, something more along the lines of not leaving *anyone* behind because we were all in this together. But I hadn't.

"I know," Niles said. "The one who failed."

I swallowed.

"That's not what I mean."

"But it's true all the same. Who's to say this wasn't what I was here for to begin with? Let the one who failed get mauled by a monster so the others might survive to save the world."

His words dripped with disgust. Was he really this angry…or just in so much pain that he didn't care anymore?

"Get your head out of your arse, Ingram," Quinn said with a scowl.

"We won't leave you behind," I said softly.

Niles scoffed and let his head fall to the ground as he leaned back again. "We've no horses and you've already said you can't carry me."

Quinn stepped aside and pointed to riders in the distance steadily growing closer. "No, but they can."

CHAPTER ELEVEN

A Jyngabé Welcome
Quinn

The Jyngabé riders of Ndoyo couldn't have shown up at a better time. While they patrolled the area regularly, the Konaho Desert was so large it could have been days before we saw anyone at all.

Niles didn't know how lucky he was.

To be honest, without horses and sufficient supplies, we were just as fortunate.

"Who are they?" Niles asked from the ground, leaning on his elbows to sit up.

"Jyngabé riders. You're one lucky bastard," Brigantino said before I could reply.

Reina shielded her eyes from the sun with a hand, squinting at the approaching group.

"*What* are they?"

I smiled. I'd had the same reaction to seeing the beasts for the first time years ago. The men and women riding them were exactly as one would expect, but the beasts themselves…well, they were unlike any creature from the northern lands.

"Nudes," I answered automatically.

Reina's dark eyes grew large. "Excuse me?"

"Nudromedaries. They call them nudes. Few horses can handle the desert climate for extended periods of time. Nudes are much better suited to the environment. They can travel hundreds of miles without stopping for water, and their large feet keep them from sinking in the sand."

"That's...incredible," she whispered. The riders grew close, Reina's focus never leaving the animals. "But they really could have come up with a better name."

The nudes slowed to a walk and then stopped before us, and I lifted an arm in greeting. The riders didn't look happy when they observed the cut bridge behind us. Or perhaps they'd noticed the thousands of undead gathered at the border of Castilles. I looked back at the strange sight again. It didn't seem likely that they should be able to cross the ravine without the bridge, but I didn't want to take bets on how long it might take them to flicker out and back into existence in the Southern Plains.

Turning back to the Jyngabé, I stated the obvious. "We've a hurt man. He needs medical attention. Can you take us to the shongoman? There's danger and we need to warn him." I beckoned to the undead across the border.

A dark-skinned woman with a scar high along one cheekbone and hair braided to her scalp urged her nude forward a few feet, her gaze never leaving the horizon with its line of broken bodies and bones, tattered clothes, and sightless eyes. People, yes, but there were also animals in the undead, or what I assumed were once animals.

"You have seen these in the north often?" she asked in the

Ndoyo native tongue, nodding her head to the undead, gold cuffs around her arms gleaming in the sun as she shifted.

"As of late? All too frequently," I replied.

She nodded, then focused on Niles with concern. Turning, she beckoned another rider forward, one who appeared to have medical supplies, thank the Saints.

Her gaze then fell on Brigantino, shock and recognition flickering in her eyes. She blinked rapidly and hid behind diplomatic words, looking to me again when she introduced herself.

"I am Ywelo Trymamo. Ndoyo is near a day's journey southeast. We will take you to Yagaman Insweli. Your friend will live."

"What's she saying?" Reina asked.

I nodded to Ywelo, then turned to Reina. "They'll take us to the village."

"What did she say about…them?" She cocked her head toward the undead still swaying, watching us from across the canyon.

"Not much."

"I suspect they aren't all that unfamiliar with them," Brigantino said.

"Well, that's not comforting." Reina turned to help the medic rider bandage Niles.

With Niles tucked away under the medical care of Ndoyo's best yagaman and Brigantino reconnecting with old

Ndoyo friends to see what he could learn about the Heart of Death, Reina and I met with the shongoman in his tent.

Ndoyo was the closest oasis to the border, a fertile bubble in an otherwise vast desert full of shifting white sands. The village offered shade, water, and respite from the sun's wrath. Here the earth was cooled by hundreds of large palms and air that somehow seemed impossibly cooler than the sands just a few feet from its border. As a prized piece of land, it also offered the opportunity for invasion, which is why the Jyngabé riders were as fierce as any agent I'd ever known.

Showing no sign of the fierceness she was capable of, Ywelo escorted us to the shongoman's tent, walking with purpose in her stride, as every Jyngabé warrior always had. We walked the path between various tents and palm trees amidst the open stares of the villagers who paused in their conversations and their actions as we passed.

Reina drew close, watching them in return.

"Quinn," she whispered, leaning close. "The people here. They're…every shade of brown." Her eyes darted from face to face, taking in the rich colors in the fading light of the evening.

I almost smiled at her innocence. How would she know people came in different colors? Until the last few months, she'd been resigned to life in Barnham, and even once she'd left, it had been to travel halfway across the northernmost parts of Castilles.

"Aye," I answered. "One might say Barnham is a bit"—I searched for the word— "starched."

She lifted her eyebrows in amusement. "I never knew.

They're…so beautiful."

She meant it. The awe on her face as she took in the Ndoyo people around us was genuine. A mother shifted a thumb-sucking toddler from one hip to the other so she could continue weaving colorful threads into the blanket on her loom, and a smile appeared on Reina's lips as she watched. It'd been too long since I'd seen Reina smile, truly smile.

She was beautiful. Even covered in dirt. Even bruised and battered, her dark hair half released of its fastening, she was still beautiful. Were we not in a dire situation with another life-or-death prophecy once again threatening us and all of Castilles—hell, all of Liron—I might have taken her aside and kissed her senseless.

For now, it would have to wait.

Again.

"Here," Ywelo said when we reached a small tent in the middle of the village.

I hadn't met Ndoyo's shongoman before. When I ventured through the village two years ago, it was in a flurry of activity after I'd become an agent for the Order, and I was quickly sent on my way once more. The newest agents were allocated their assignments and made to leave immediately, so I hadn't spent more than two days here. Now I wished it had been longer. I wished I'd made connections who might aid us without the need for convincing.

Ywelo reached the open side of the tent and motioned for us to enter. I nodded my thanks, passed her, and entered the space. She didn't join us, but rather turned and went about whatever normal business she had. Warrior business.

Probably preparing for the next day's ride to check perimeters and ensure the village's safety from animals and pillagers.

Maybe from the undead.

Neat and orderly, the shongoman's tent was what I'd expected. Rugs and pillows of every color and texture on the floor for seating, a low, small table for meals covered in a deep vermilion tablecloth, the center poles decorated with colored rope and trinkets. An intricately carved staff leaned against one of the poles, a gemstone at its top surrounded by wood carved into a claw-like embrace. In one corner, on another low table, were an array of small pots and jars that drew Reina's eye.

The shongoman himself was not a large man. Lean and wiry, he was younger than I thought a village leader would be. He stood about even in height with Reina, clad in a long white shirt and loose white pants, his feet set in sturdy sandals. When he smiled in greeting, he revealed teeth that were straight save for two, and dimples in both brown cheeks.

"Welcome!" he said. "Please sit, my weary travelers. Come, come." He beckoned to the pillows laid out on many rugs of varying patterns.

I nodded my head, Reina following suit though she didn't understand his words, and we sat upon the pillows provided.

"I am Shongoman Aleshkatel Bhalehi," he continued in the Ndoyo tongue.

"Do you speak the Northern tongue?" I asked.

"Some," he said, switching languages so Reina could follow our conversation.

"Much thanks," I said. "My companion doesn't speak

your language. I am Quinn D'Arturio and this is Reina di Bianco. We thank you for receiving us so willingly and for having your yagaman tend to our wounded friend."

I hesitated on the last word for Ingram had never been, and never would be, a friend, but it seemed easier than trying to explain who he was and why he traveled with us. Reina glanced at me curiously after my introduction, surely wondering why I hadn't introduced myself as King Eron, ruler of Castilles.

I had my reasons.

"We could do no less. You know the Ndoyo people always offer assistance to the Order."

Had he guessed?

"How did you know I was with the Order?" I asked, narrowing my eyes.

He threw his head back and laughed. "Your kind, you have"—he waved a hand— "a sense about you. It could not be more obvious if you stripped and stood naked in the Konaho sun. You and the other one you came with."

Brigantino.

I nodded. "He's spent time here before. You already knew he was with the Order."

"Agent Brigantino lived with us for a time in the past, yes," he said with a sincere smile that touched his eyes. "But I suspect you are here to discuss more important things than another agent's history of residence."

"Indeed."

The shongoman was welcoming in his words, but his demeanor spoke of thoughts hidden—evident in the shift of his shoulders, the way his dark eyes never moved from mine. This was someone who had trained himself to hide things he didn't want seen, a man who would shrewdly assess his opponent before sharing information.

Which was fine. I could do the same.

"The undead plague the north," I said. "Ywelo implied they were here as well."

His pleasant smile melted from his face. "*Acaffilé.*"

Not dead.

The word was easy enough to understand.

"Those who die in the desert…they have had trouble passing on," he said.

His gaze shifted from mine and stared at a spot on the rug beneath his fingers. There was something in his words, an unwillingness… He knew more than he let on.

"What do you mean *trouble* passing on?" Reina said.

I took a moment to study the shongoman, *really* study him as he thought through his answer.

"The people—and the creatures—they don't leave their *zimbayas*"—he snapped his fingers together repeatedly, searching for the word— "bodies. The soul has left the body, but the energy stays behind. An empty shell roaming the land, fighting for survival while already dead."

"Then you have them here," Reina replied, her shoulders falling in disappointment.

"Not as many as Ywelo says you left behind."

That was comforting at least.

"And why have you come to the Konaho?" he asked. "What do you seek here, in our midst?"

"We believe the center of the chaos that has brought the undead is here, in this land, and we think this land also provides the means to stop him," I said.

There.

A flash of understanding. Brief, but the tell was there all the same. The shongoman's eyes lit with a recognition he quickly smothered.

"Chaos, you say," he said slowly.

I nodded. "Undead, certainly, but more than that. Birds turning downward mid-flight into the ground by the thousands, bees frozen in their hives as though hit by instant frost when the days are warm and the nights mild, and fresh springs turned poison overnight."

"And those are the instances we *know*," Reina added, leaning forward.

"Nothing like that has happened here," he said. "Aside from the *acaffilé*, we have seen nothing to indicate chaos."

Reina stared at him, her expression guarded. "I would think the undead would be enough for anyone to be concerned."

The shongoman raised his hand in acknowledgment and nodded. "Yes, of course. We want to discover why this is happening and how to reverse it so our dead may rest."

"We're in search for the source of the chaos," I said. "It would be good to have Ndoyo help."

I *could* play the King Eron card now. I knew it would get me further than we'd managed to get with the shongoman so far, but I was reluctant to reveal that information too early. I wanted to know what he was hiding, and, more importantly, why he felt he needed to hide it at all.

"We will do whatever we may do to assist you in any way," he said. "Tonight, though, our village is your home. Rest from your journey, heal your friend, and we will visit again tomorrow."

I didn't miss Reina's wince at the mention of healing Ingram. She'd never forgive herself for not being able to use the talisman to fix his injury.

We thanked the shongoman and left, weaving our way back to our assigned tent along the outskirts of the village. I waited until we were far from the shongoman's tent before speaking.

"He's lying," I said.

Reina didn't question how I knew. "About what?" she asked instead.

"The number of undead here, and how close to home it's hit."

She looked on, waiting for me to elaborate.

"He said he wants to reverse it so *our* dead may rest. He means here. At least some of the undead have come from Ndoyo. There's a personal connection."

We neared our tent, Niles and Brigantino already inside, oil lamps burning bright, a surprising murmur of conversation from within.

"Hopefully tomorrow I can get something more from him," I added. "He knows a lot more than he's letting on and I won't let up until I find out what."

CHAPTER TWELVE

Of Family Found
Reina

I still didn't understand why Quinn didn't just tell the shongoman who he was. It seemed like it would make quicker work of opening doors for us and we needed every advantage we could get. Still, I didn't question him.

Now, sitting on an array of giant red and yellow striped pillows with the shongoman in his tent once again, Quinn asked at least one of the questions I wanted to ask first thing yesterday.

"We're looking for a man," he began. "He is known in certain circles as the Heart of Death. A friend in South Trellington recommended seeking him in the Southern Plains. Do you know this man? Or do you know how we might reach him?"

"Yes," the shongoman said slowly, his eyes shifting. He touched a finger to the beautifully carved staff that rested on his lap, its ruby-colored gemstone seeming to wink at me every so often. "I know of whom you speak."

My heart fluttered with hope. This was the first piece of good news since leaving Irzan.

"You do?" I asked, unable to suppress a smile of relief.

"I do. But he's a fickle man and you're not likely to get help from him," he said, stiffening.

I stole a glance at Quinn while the shongoman rose to retrieve a wooden tray from the table nearby, hoping he also noticed the same change in demeanor from our host. He gave a slight nod. It wasn't my imagination, then. He was uncomfortable today.

The shongoman brought the tray and set it on the floor in the midst of where we sat. Taking hold of the pitcher, he poured a pale honey-colored liquid into each of three silver cups, then offered them to us.

Quinn accepted his without hesitation. The healer in me sniffed at the drink first, much to the shongoman's confusion. I couldn't detect anything familiar in the citrusy scent.

Wait, a hint of mint maybe?

"I don't poison my guests. This I promise you." He raised his own glass and drained it in a few quick swallows.

Heat rushed to my ears at the misunderstanding. The last thing I needed to do was alienate our ally.

"I would never think as much," I replied. "I was trying to see if there was anything familiar in the drink. It's habit, I fear. My apologies."

"It's in her nature, Shongoman. She's a healer by trade. I've no doubt she's attempting to determine how she might use your drink, or the ingredients in it, to help her next patient." Quinn's words made quick work of smoothing over the misunderstanding.

Our host nodded with a smile, and I sipped from the cup. The drink was cool despite the heat of the afternoon sun high above us and I couldn't help but wonder how it had been cooled with nothing but desert surrounding us in all directions.

"Is it to your liking?" the shongoman asked in his lilting accent, his eyebrows raised.

"Quite." It was delicious and refreshing in a way I didn't even know I needed. "Thank you," I added, hoping to win him over again.

He nodded. "Good."

"So, the man we're in search of, you said we're not likely to get help from him. Why is that?" Quinn asked, steering the conversation back on course.

"He doesn't take kindly to strangers and he'll lead you in circles before he'll give you any answers you seek."

"What if we offer him something in return for his help?" I said, thinking of my deal with Niles.

"Bribery! He'd be offended by such a notion. Here, in this place, we do not imply our people are so shallow that favors may be bought so easily."

Quinn pressed his lips together, scolding me with his eyes. He probably already knew this about the southern people. He never would have suggested offering something in return. I clamped my mouth shut and vowed to keep it that way. Saints, Brigantino should be here with Quinn. He would have known what *not* to say at least.

On second thought, that would leave me alone with Niles. No, thank you.

"Shongoman, she meant only that we would offer him our highest thanks and praise. And we would tell tales of his greatness throughout the lands for such honor and assistance," Quinn said with a firm nod.

The tightness in Quinn's jaw was the sole indication of the tension in his body, the fear that the shongoman wouldn't lead us to the man who could help.

"And what good would tales of greatness do? No, if you want his help, you'll have to do better than that."

"What would he accept?" Quinn asked.

"You'll have to earn it in the sand."

I didn't know what earning it in the sand entailed, but it didn't sound promising, let alone straightforward. Earning something in the sand sounded an awful lot like earning it in the ring, which even I knew entailed a fight.

Quinn closed his eyes for a second, then opened them again and met the shongoman's gaze evenly. "Very well."

"You accept this offer without knowing what awaits? You don't ask to know more?"

The shongoman examined Quinn, his eyebrows furrowed. He took in this strange man from the north lands who wanted something so badly he was willing to fight for it without asking who he'd be fighting, when, or how.

"The details won't change my mind, so if setting foot in the sand is what gains his trust and convinces him to help us in our quest, then that's what I'll do."

"Oh, but you'll have to do more than just step onto the fighting sands. You have to survive it."

Quinn just nodded. "Very well," he said again.

I wanted to scream in frustration. These negotiations had gotten us nowhere and might well get Quinn killed. The fighting sands? Surviving? Against what? Another horrid desert animal? A skilled killer? A ring fighter who did nothing but exchange blood and punches with his opponents? This was absurd. I bit my lip to keep from voicing my thoughts. I'd already made too many mistakes.

"You must want this very badly to seek him out and fight for his attention," the shongoman said.

"We do, indeed."

"Good, then tonight we eat, and we prepare. Tomorrow, you enter the ring."

"We're in a hurry," Quinn said, surprising me. Thank the Saints we were on the same page for once. "I would prefer to fight tonight if that's not too much to ask."

The shongoman just cackled. "No, there will be no sands tonight. There is much to do before the fighting sands can be used. Tomorrow, at dusk."

Quinn stood and gave a short bow to our host. I followed despite wanting to throttle the man for making us wait even longer.

"In the meantime, if there is anything else you need, any accommodations I can provide, please ask any of the Ndoyo."

His words were spoken out of custom, a politeness issued to guests of the Ndoyo village, but I wasn't about to let the moment pass.

"Actually," I said. "I am in need of fresh salve and bandages for our companion. If you could have some brought to our tent, I would be much obliged."

There. I'd been polite, right? Nothing offensive in my

request.

He nodded, then said, "I've already had the yagaman send what you need. You will find it in your tent when you return."

"Thank you," I said.

"Thank you, again," Quinn said, a hand on my elbow. "For hearing our words."

The shongoman nodded, and, in another moment, we were back in the heat of the sun and sand. I waited to speak until we were outside of the guards' hearing.

"*That's* the plan?" I said. "You're going to fight someone or *something* tomorrow and *hope* it wins you an audience with the man who's known as the Heart of Death? There's got to be a better way, something else."

Quinn shook his head. "No time for another way."

"Isn't there someone else we can speak to? Something else that could be done?"

"We'll do as they say. It would take too long to seek out one of the other tribes. We're at the mercy of the Ndoyo, Reina. We have no horses and few supplies, and we're surrounded by miles of desert. We must play by their rules."

"You make it sound like we're being held prisoner," I said, my mind working uneasily.

Quinn was silent for a moment. "Guest or prisoner," he said. "We're at their mercy either way."

"But you don't even know what you've agreed to!"

Quinn paused and turned to me, his dark eyes fatigued, seeming older beyond his years. "Does it matter, Reina?" he said.

"Of course it does. There are a million reasons we can't afford to lose you, not the least of which is that I love you."

His expression softened. He put an arm around my shoulders, curled me into him, and kissed me.

God, how I missed this. How I missed being held. How I missed being close!

"I know," Quinn said, pulling back. "And I love you, too. I have no intention of losing tomorrow."

I wanted to ask how he could be sure, but I wasn't so certain I wanted to hear the answer. Whatever horrid things had been done during his training for the Order, I didn't need to know the details.

"You're back. That was quick," Brigantino said when we entered our tent. "Too quick."

His eyes darted between the two of us, gleaning whatever information he could from our body language.

"The shongoman won't reveal the man who can help us," I said. I flopped onto a pillow similar to those we'd just been sitting on in the shongoman's tent.

Brigantino scowled and looked to Quinn.

"I enter the sands tomorrow night."

Brigantino nodded. "Can we afford to wait that long?"

Brigantino didn't seem to care that Quinn would fight to win us the opportunity to speak with someone. What was it with them? Why was this acceptable?

"They won't move it up. I already tried."

"Lovely. So, we need to hope our undead friends back in Castilles don't make their way into the Southern Plains before then." Niles said from the bed, where he lay with his injured leg propped on a pillow.

The sight of the blood-soaked bandages around his calf flooded me with guilt. I still couldn't heal him.

I wouldn't risk trying again. Not with my magic out of control.

I could too easily picture the tissue of Niles's calf withering and blackening into itself. Saints, he could lose his whole leg. Or his life. No, I wouldn't risk it.

Even if he did deserve it for what he'd once done to me.

"I need to change those bandages again," I told him, standing once more and ignoring his quip about the undead while the horrors of the day before still played fresh in my mind.

Niles pointed sullenly to a basket near the side of the bed, regarding me beneath heavy-lidded eyes. "That came for you while you were gone. I hope you're not thinking of putting whatever's in there *on* my leg."

The shongoman was true to his word…and fast. I picked up the basket and laid it on the bed, sorting through the contents. It wasn't difficult to see why Niles was wary. The smell of the ointment inside a small clay jar was potent to say the least, but if it contained what I thought it did, it should go a long way in helping with the pain in addition to healing the muscle and tissue. The other bottle held a liquid that wasn't nearly as enjoyable as what Quinn and I had just been served by the shongoman.

"Did they leave any water?" I asked.

"It's in the clay pot over there," he answered.

I tried to listen to Quinn and Brigantino's hushed

conversation while I worked, but they spoke in tones meant to keep me from making out their words. Just as well. They were probably talking in some sort of Order code anyway. I shoved down the hurt I felt at Quinn confiding in Brigantino over me. It didn't matter. It was business, not personal. It wasn't about me.

But still…weren't we a team, the two of us?

The pot Niles pointed to was covered with a dark, wet cloth. I folded the cloth back to reveal a second pot inside the first, and the space between the two pots filled with wet sand. When I pulled the carafe of water from the inside pot, the temperature of the liquid surprised me.

"So that's how they do it." I examined the contraption. Intriguing.

How had they thought up such a technique? How did it work? I'd have to ask someone later if the time presented itself. Not that I had much use for a cooler in Barnham, or even in Irzan, but it was fascinating, nonetheless.

I poured the cold water into a cup for Niles and handed it to him. "Hold this."

"Well, thanks. Do I get to drink it, too?"

"Sure, but save a few sips because you're not going to like the taste of this." I dosed the medicine in the glass dropper provided and handed it to him. "Take this."

He eyed the dropper from over the rim of his cup as he drank, then accepted it with one hand. Sniffing at the dropper, he grimaced, then tried to hand it back.

"I am not taking that."

"Saints, Niles, you're as bad as a six-year-old. It's a good thing you *didn't* get injured in battle. God knows you never would have survived."

My words were enough to shut him up. He grabbed the dropper and swallowed the medicine down without further complaint, then followed it with puckered lips and long swallows of water.

Once he was done with the water, he coughed. "Do you even know what was in that?"

"Not pine ale," I replied.

Actually, I was pretty sure there was some sort of alcohol as the base, but it wasn't going to have the same kick pine ale gave him. I pushed the sliced remnants of his pant leg up to his thigh.

"More water?" he croaked, and I obliged, refilling his cup.

"Now the unpleasant part," I warned him, examining the sight before me.

"That wasn't unpleasant enou—"

He hissed in pain as I unwrapped the bandage that had glued itself to the skin and muscle of his leg. After everything that happened months ago, I should have enjoyed his pain.

Disappointingly, I didn't.

I guess that made me a true Healer after all, for what Healer wishes to see her patient suffer?

"I'm sorry," I said. I softened my approach and tried to peel the bandage with a gentler hand.

"Are you?" he asked. "I wouldn't be if I were you. For all the things I did?" He snorted, laid back on the pillows behind his head, and looked away.

"I'm sorry regardless," I said. "I'm a healer, Niles. I wish suffering on no one."

The skin was a mangled mess, the muscle beneath it shredded to ribbons. How we'd even gotten him off the bridge was a miracle. It would take weeks to heal.

What I could fix in minutes if I had the magic of the talisman at my fingertips would take weeks to heal. Weeks we didn't have. I cursed silently.

I cleaned the wound with water and a fresh cloth from the basket, then slathered it in the potent ointment before wrapping it again. I wanted to stitch it. The layers of skin would mend together cleaner with the wounds sewn shut.

But I wouldn't dare stitch a wound from an animal because of the risk of infection…and it only made sense to treat a wound from the undead in the same manner.

I shivered at the memory.

The way their lifeless eyes stared. The dirt and filth that hung off their bodies and their clothes. The mindless way they moved forward, attacking with bare hands and fingernails, with mouths and teeth. They were human…but not.

Best to treat the wound as though Niles had received it from a wild animal. I couldn't be sure what kind of disease the undead might carry.

"Is that better?" I placed two large pillows beneath his knee again and rolled the pant leg down to cover his muscled thigh and calf.

"To the extent it can be, I suppose." Then he issued a long exhale and let his eyes roll back into his head. "Oh.

Oh, that's good. Whatever's in that nasty-tasting stuff is suuuuuu-perb."

I bit back an amused smile.

"Pain eased a bit?"

"Pain? What pain? I don't have a *body*."

I pressed my lips together and furrowed my brow. A smaller dosage next time, perhaps.

Just then, a man we hadn't seen before peeked through the flap of the tent, announcing his presence with the clearing of his throat. Like everyone else in the settlement, he was dark-skinned, but his black hair was streaked with silver and his square face held wrinkles around kind eyes. He was twice my age, perhaps a decade more than that.

"Excuse me. Forgive the intrusion, but I've been informed there's someone here in your company from Castilles." When no one replied immediately, he went on. "The Kingdom of Castilles, someone with the surname of di Bianco. Is this true?"

"Who asks?" Quinn replied, on guard, shrewd eyes assessing the newcomer despite his unthreatening image.

The man stepped inside the tent, stood tall and folded his hands within one another. He caught sight of me, smiled, sending crinkles to his eyes, and said, "Her father."

CHAPTER THIRTEEN

Smoke and Mirrors
Reina

"I thought never to see you." He held a hand to his mouth, his eyes welling with tears.

I stumbled backwards half a step, my mind a mess of confusion and panic. A strong hand touched my arm—Niles, bedside beside me still. I didn't have the sense of mind to shrug him off.

"My father's dead," I blurted, but even as I said it, I recognized the shape of his eyes, the familiar way he held his hands.

They were mine.

It couldn't be, and yet it was.

He looked wounded at my words, this man who claimed to be my father.

"No, didn't your mother tell you…" His voice failed him.

"Also dead," I confirmed, lifting my chin defiantly.

Her death came as a surprise to him. Now it was his turn to stumble back half a step. He looked as though he might faint. Brigantino pulled a pillow forward for him, guiding him to it.

"Sit, friend, please," Brigantino said.

The man sat—fell, actually—into the pillow, his gaze searching the tent for something or someone who wasn't there.

Quinn looked to me, his gaze falling from my face to where Niles still held a hand to my arm. Belatedly, I pulled my arm from his fingers and straightened my spine.

"Who are you?" I asked. "And why should we believe you?"

He focused his eyes, *my* eyes, on me. "She said I should go, insisted. I didn't want to go."

Brigantino pulled up a second chair and sat opposite the man.

"Easy, friend," he said. "What's your name?"

"Adan," he said. "Adan Iyer."

"Well, Adan, why don't you tell us a little about how you found us here and what's going on?" Brigantino urged.

"I live here. Well, I didn't for a long time, but ever since I left Castilles, this is where I've made my home, here in Ndoyo. And then today, the shongoman said 'di Bianco' and I just knew, only I thought it was her mother for sure. I was wrong." His gaze looked upward at me again. "But, oh, how you look like her."

"Why did you leave her?" The words slipped from my lips. "You left her—us—alone, to fend for ourselves."

If someone had asked me if I was angry about growing up without a father, I never would have said yes. As a child, most days I didn't even think of one. So the words that tumbled from my mouth were every bit as surprising to me as they were to him.

"No," he said, shaking his head vehemently. "No, I didn't leave her. She made me go. She said it was for the best. She didn't think it would go well with me being able to—" Abruptly, he stopped himself from speaking.

"Able to what?" Quinn prompted.

Adan hesitated.

We waited.

"I possess an unusual trait—a gift, if you will. Most would not understand. She didn't…want my gift to hurt the baby, to hurt *you*."

Quinn pressed on. "And how would it have hurt her?"

"I can…see things."

I couldn't hide my gasp. Quinn looked to me, his thoughts mirroring my own. My ability had come from my father.

Adan went on. "I had a vision, you see. When she was still carrying the baby. It was horrible and wonderful all at once. She didn't want to hear the words, didn't want to know the future of our child. There would be greatness in her, more than we ever could have dreamed, but at what price?" Adan's eyes fixed on the far wall of the tent, seeing something none of us could see. "She began to have dreams—nightmares— about me seeing things I shouldn't, knowing an awful truth and telling her, or worse knowing the truth and keeping it from her."

Inside my head, my mind railed against Adan's portrayal of my mother. She wouldn't have been so weak. Not my mother. She was the strongest person I'd ever known. She wouldn't have been afraid of words—not his or anyone else's. She'd once accepted my own visions without a hitch.

"She sent you away?" I asked. "That seems…extreme."

"It was a difficult time," he replied.

I narrowed my eyes at him. "What was her favorite herb?" I asked. "What did my mother drink in her kai almost every day?"

He blinked, wounded by my words.

"What?"

"What is her *name*?" I demanded. He'd hadn't mentioned it, not once.

"Child, what—"

"I am no child, and *you* are not who you claim."

Adan stood sharply, sending Quinn and Brigantino into immediate protector roles, on their feet, legs splayed, ready to go for both weapons and fists. Even Niles in his drugged state sat forward on the bed.

"*Who* are you?" I said, throwing steel into my voice.

Adan looked from person to person, then to the tent's exit, plotting his escape. Making the same observation, Quinn lunged for him.

Instead, he caught only air. A plume of sickly-sweet scented smoke lifted into the air where Adan had been standing, leaving nothing behind in its wake.

Adan had disappeared.

"What was *that*?" Niles asked, his eyes wide with fright.

My own face must have looked much the same, my gaze darting around the tent and the dissipating smoke.

"Nothing I've ever seen before." Brigantino's coarse voice echoed my thoughts.

But I'd seen a lot less in my life than Brigantino had seen

in his, so something that surprised him was something very unwelcome indeed.

"That man—he looked like me. He did. I saw it."

"That man…clearly wasn't," Brigantino said.

"Wasn't what?! A man?" Niles exclaimed.

"Have *you* ever seen a man disappear into thin air?" Quinn asked. "That wasn't a man, Ingram."

"What did he—it—want?" I said.

"I don't know," Quinn answered. "But given the circumstances, it appears he wanted to get close to you. I can guess why."

He looked at my tunic, beneath which the talisman lay, its hum a low buzz against my skin. My breath caught.

"He was after the talisman?" I asked.

"I think it's a good bet," Quinn answered.

"I'll talk to the shongoman, see if I can find out more about this Adan Iyer. Perhaps he knows something," Brigantino said. "Until we leave Ndoyo, we're setting watch. We won't be caught off guard."

"What need is there to catch us unaware when whoever—whatever—this was can disappear in a puff of smoke?" I said.

Quinn took my hand in his and pulled me close in an embrace.

"Brigantino's right. We can only do so much. Here? Here and now? *This* is what we can do."

When Brigantino returned to the tent, I didn't expect to hear much in the way of news. Perhaps that's why I was shocked to learn that Adan Iyer was a bachelor who lived in a tent just a few hundred feet from our own.

"What?!" It didn't seem possible.

Brigantino held up a hand. "I haven't even told you the worst of it yet."

"Well, get on with it then!" Niles exclaimed.

Shocked at his outburst, I turned to face him, eyebrows raised. Clearly the pain-relieving medicine was working well for him.

I leaned closer. Judging by the size of his pupils, it was possible he had forgotten he even had a leg injury. I shook my head and sighed. *Definitely* a smaller dose next time.

"I spoke with Adan Iyer myself. Whoever we met wasn't Iyer."

"Why give his name?" I asked.

"I think the better question is 'Why take his face?'"

I blinked.

"Adan Iyer looks *exactly* as we saw. Only he wasn't who we spoke with. Three different witnesses place him caring for the nudes at the exact time he appeared here in the tent."

"Are you sure? He could be lying," Quinn said.

Brigantino gave him a look as if to ask if Quinn was questioning a job he'd been doing for over thirty-five years.

Quinn shook his head. "You're right."

"Then what did we see if it wasn't Adan Iyer? And why use Adan Iyer's appearance to confront us?" I asked.

"I can't say who—or what—we actually saw, but after

talking with Iyer, it's clear why he was used." Brigantino paused before meeting my eyes. "He really is your father."

I stepped back.

I'd learned of—and lost—a father in a matter of minutes only a short time ago.

And now I'd just learned of him again. I heard the words, but my mind was slow in understanding.

"You're saying…"

"The reason why Iyer was chosen is because he *is* your father. The real Iyer, that is."

Had the air become thinner?

"I think I should sit." I fell into the seat the Iyer lookalike had taken a short while earlier.

Quinn handed me a cup of cool water and I gulped even though I knew it would be better to take small sips. The liquid hit my stomach in a rush and my stomach gurgled in response.

I handed the cup back to Quinn.

"I want to talk to him."

"Are you sure?" Quinn asked, grabbing my hand.

I nodded.

"I need to."

"Do you want me to come?" he asked, squeezing my hand tenderly.

I squeezed back in return but shook my head. "No, I… need to do this alone."

I stood, took a breath, and moved forward before my mind could make an excuse not to go.

"Left, fourth tent on the right," Brigantino said.

In a matter of another half a minute, I made it to the fourth tent on the right. I stood, staring at the fabric that separated me from the man who *was* my father, the one who *had* left me and my mother behind. The palms overhead rustled with a breeze and the shouts of children playing nearby carried on the air. It all seemed so…normal. And yet, nothing was normal at all. I raised a hand to knock, then hesitated. I stared at the fabric.

Exactly how did one announce one's presence at the door of a tent?

I was saved the trouble when the flap swung open and I met Adan Iyer's surprised face on the other side.

"Esmé?" he said, wide-eyed.

He dropped the basket he'd been holding, figs and some sort of legume I'd never seen before spilling to the floor onto the rug and into the sand.

"Reina," I said softly, bending to help him pick the food from the ground. "Esmé's daughter."

I fought the urge to pick a fight with him, reminding myself once more that the man I'd met an hour earlier wasn't the same person. Adan paused, his hand halfway to a fig, and met my eyes, searching them. He sat back on his heels, figs and legumes forgotten, and swallowed.

"You're…"

I nodded.

"Well, of course you are. You look so much like her."

And like him, but maybe he didn't notice that part. He said nothing more, but began gathering the figs into the basket again. I waited for him to speak, to show some emotion at learning he had a daughter.

Maybe he doesn't know.

Brigantino said Iyer was my father, but what if Iyer didn't know? If he thought…if he believed I was Esmé's daughter with another man…

"You're my father," I blurted as I handed him the last fig.

He stood slowly, the basket on his hip.

"Come, please," he said, beckoning with a free hand. "Share isufuzi with me. We'll talk."

I didn't know what isufuzi was, but I followed him back inside the tent and to large wine-colored sitting pillows. He put the basket down on a low table, then reached into a deep ceramic bowl much like the one that contained Niles's medicine. Instead of medicine, though, he pulled out a carafe and poured two cups of pale blue liquid.

I accepted one when he handed it to me, tasted it, then drank the fruity liquor down, the fluid burning all the way down my throat and into my stomach.

Perhaps even I needed a little liquid courage at times. Besides, Adan did the same, so maybe I was just keeping custom.

"You're sure?" he said.

I didn't think before I spoke. "Have you looked in a mirror lately?"

To my surprise, he laughed, a husky sound accompanied by a genuine smile. I smiled in return, whether I intended to or not. He rested his chin upon a hand, his elbow on his knee and looked at me, examining me from head to toe.

"I didn't know," he said. "We parted before…well,

before she could have known."

Adan reached to the table to pour himself another drink. I declined with a shake of my head when he offered it to me. I needed my head clear and my muscles already felt deliciously warm from the effects of just one cup of whatever the blue stuff was.

"I don't know," he continued. "Maybe she *did* know. Maybe that's why she made me leave."

"Why *did* you leave?"

"I stood out in Castilles, especially so far north. Esmé didn't think it was safe for me, but she wasn't ready to leave her home. I don't know if she ever would have left. Mercia was where her heart belonged, and even my love couldn't fight against that."

"She raised me in Barnham."

"Well…hmph," he said, the noise indiscernible. "I guess she left after all. I'm…well, I'm not going to lie. That stings a bit."

He drained the liquid from his glass again.

"Why?" I asked.

"We…well, your mother and I were together for a few months. I traveled a lot back in those days—trade mostly— but when my boots hit Mercian soil and my eyes caught sight of her tending the gardens in front of one of the grandest homes in Mercia, I knew my traveling days were over. Esmé? She didn't know like I did. Took three tries before I finally got her to agree to even walk with me. I didn't realize the grand home I'd seen her in front of was *hers*, or her parents' in any case. Had I known, I might not have worked up the courage to ask her out at all."

He chuckled at the memory.

"By the time she allowed me to court her properly, I'd already fallen hard. I planned to ask her to come home with me, to Tihanya here in the Plains. Saints, I love that city. I love the pulse of it, its vibrance, the money a trader can make… And I thought of her future as a healer. Her skill was unmatched. She would have been an asset in a city like Tihanya.

"I should have talked to her, given her a choice, should have considered staying where she wanted to be. But I didn't. I made grand plans for our future in my head, but never discussed them with her, never asked her what *she* wanted. I was an idiot."

A dark sorrow crossed his eyes, his expression pained with the memory of loss. We'd all lost.

"What happened?" I asked softly.

"She fell apart when I asked her to come with me. Now that I think on it with the wisdom of an old man"—at that, he winked— "I pushed too hard. I didn't listen to what she tried to tell me. We had an argument. I'm not proud to admit much of the groveling was on my end. My pride was too large. I thought if she loved me, she could see how I wanted to care for her, how I wanted to give her a city that could offer the finest of everything life has to offer."

"Then why didn't you just stay in Mercia?"

He looked downward, examined something at the bottom of the cup.

"I offered. After all the arguing to get her to come with

me to Tihanya, I finally offered to stay in Castilles with her."

"And she said no."

"She didn't think it was safe. Echhh. But what *is* safe?"

"If Mercia is like Barnham, the people aren't used to seeing anyone who looks like you," I said. "I imagine it caused some…distress when you weren't just passing through."

Ignorant people were stubborn. Always would be. They looked at a man like Adan with suspicion and disdain. His skin, his hair, his speech, his clothing—nothing about him was familiar to them. As a trader? Sure, they would accept any number of differences if it meant they could get their hands on the kinds of goods they couldn't otherwise buy, but as a villager? To accept someone like Adan in their midst, to smile, tip a hat, or shake a hand with him? Could they do that?

"I wasn't worried about what they thought. Not even when the threats became physical. If I'd given Esmé more time before pushing to move south, maybe…*maybe* I could have convinced her, but she panicked. She was certain the Mercians would kill me, and that was it. Just like that, she ended it."

"She…ended it?"

"Not in so many words. She told me she needed space, asked me to return to the Plains and said she would send for me when she found someplace safe for both of us. I never should have listened. I should have insisted on staying with her to find someplace we could settle together, but I was desperate, I guess. Afraid of losing her if I pushed too hard."

I regarded the sadness on his face, the pain in his eyes. On instinct, I reached out and squeezed his hand.

"She never sent for me." He paused a long moment before continuing, "I waited forever. I'll *wait* forever. Why do you think I'm still in Ndoyo instead of Tihanya? It's closest to the crossing. She'd have to come here first."

Saints. He doesn't know.

My breath hitched for a moment. I forgot that the man—or thing—I informed of my mother's death a few hours ago wasn't Adan. The man in front of me knew nothing. He sat, eyes shining and hopeful that my mother might someday return to him…and she'd been dead for nearly four years now, murdered at the hands of a madman.

"How is she?" he asked. I tried to think of a way to break the news to him. "Is she…happy?"

My gaze fell to the pillow beneath me, and I let out a choked, "She's…fine."

CHAPTER FOURTEEN

A Warrior's Promise
Quinn

"I don't know why I lied." Reina paced the floor while I kneeled on a pillow, preparing my mind for the battle ahead.

I took a deep breath in and held it.

Here. Here and now.

Slowly, I exhaled.

Our day with the Ndoyo people, waiting for the challenge, passed without event, thank the Saints. While Ingram slept on in oblivion and Brigantino gathered whatever information might be useful on the sands tonight, Reina spilled the details of the conversation with her father the night before.

"You wanted to spare his feelings," I said.

Reina had always been that way. She couldn't tolerate being the bearer of bad news, the deliverer of pain. She was terrible at inflicting pain, even when we were kids and I wrestled her to the ground. She could have gotten up easily with a squarely placed knee to my groin, but she hadn't. Even then.

She would have made a terrible agent.

I fought a smile. I didn't want her to think I was making light of the lie she'd told and how it weighed on her conscience.

"You should have seen him, Quinn," she said, one hand on a hip, the other by her mouth as she bit a cuticle.

"He was—no, he still *is*—smitten with her. That should make me feel better, knowing my parents loved each other and that I was somehow a product of that time, however short it was, but it doesn't. I lied to him. I finally got to meet the father I didn't even know was still alive…and I began our relationship with a *lie*."

She groaned and sank to her knees on a pillow, letting her chin fall to her chest. One would think she was regretting a murder with her theatrics. She was so…pure. So good.

Too good for me. Always had been.

Push it aside. Don't think on it.

I closed my eyes and breathed in.

Here and now.

Exhale.

The tent, and everything in it, fell away, secondary to my mind, my preparations.

"You're meditating," Reina said, breaking the quiet.

I nodded in reply, focusing on my breaths just the same, partitioning my mind. One part for Reina. One part to still my thoughts. One part to gather my wits. One part to wall away the regrets. And one part to accept whatever I'd soon add to those regrets.

Acceptance. It was part of my training years ago.

Not that it was a part of the training I'd excelled in.

Reina took a hesitant breath.

"What is it?" I asked, my eyes still closed.

"I was just wondering. What do you…think of when you meditate?"

"I try not to think of anything. That's the point."

"When I meditate, I recite an oath to help me channel my energy and prepare to heal. Is that…what you do?"

"Something like that."

If she knew the bloody images I saw every time I had to close my eyes.

Ingram groaned from the bed, catching Reina's attention and saving me from an explanation. Would I have an excuse the next time she asked me to share a piece of myself I detested?

The sands were exactly as Brigantino described—small. It seemed ridiculous to me that in the vastness of the desert, there was a tiny area marked for the challenge. A fighting ring more or less. The boundaries were marked by thin, unadorned wooden poles that looked as though they might snap in a stiff breeze. Not that there was much of a breeze in the Konaho. With the exception of infrequent sandstorms, the wind hardly moved at all.

Two openings marked the entranceway where each fighter would appear at the beginning of the match. I had yet to be informed of anything beyond that.

An intimate affair, this fight. What did that say about the shongoman? What did it say about the Ndoyo people and the Jyngabé warriors?

Their fights were not for spectacle. They fought with a purpose, for a goal…which would be harder than fighting for an audience.

I shook out my hands and bent my head side to side, loosening the muscles in my neck that seemed tense no matter what I tried.

"I don't like this," Reina said.

I wasn't excited about it either.

"It'll be fine," I said, if only to calm her nerves.

"All this preparation the shongoman spoke of, and I see nothing here. What preparation did they need for *this?*" She gestured to the circle of sand, no more than twenty-five paces across.

Without any embellishments, the basic ring proved that the kind of preparation they needed was also the kind there was no physical evidence of, which was a hundred times scarier than if I'd faced a pen full of raging beasties with fangs and claws. Animals were predictable at least—far more so than humans.

"The Jyngabé were close-mouthed about the sands," Brigantino said. "I couldn't get a word from any of them, not even the ones I've known for some time. When I stayed in Ndoyo, there was no ring, at least not to my knowledge."

"The Ndoyo don't seem the most forthcoming people," Reina mumbled.

"Secretive, perhaps, but they are good people. Do not doubt that," Brigantino reaffirmed.

"Ah, good, you have found the sands," a voice said from behind.

The shongoman arrived, leaning on the staff he didn't seem to need in order to walk, the same staff I'd noticed in his tent each time we'd visited. A quirk? Or a weapon?

He was followed by two dozen Jyngabé warriors who came either to watch or to participate against part of what I would be fighting today.

"I am ready," I said with a steady nod.

Here and now. Center. Focus.

The shongoman regarded me for a long moment. He leaned on the staff, the blood-red gem at its center flashing with the sun's rays. For a moment, it was almost as if the staff itself were trying to convey a warning.

What absurdity.

"Are you?" the shongoman asked. "We shall soon see. Please, choose your entrance."

He gestured to the ring in front of us. He still hadn't told me what I was to expect. Perhaps the test was to see how long I could go without asking.

The answer was forever. I'd had enough of *those* tests in the Order to last a lifetime.

Always expect that which cannot be anticipated. Always.

So, I didn't need to ask. I was already prepared for whatever the shongoman had chosen for me.

I approached the entrance on the right, but not before Reina grabbed my hand and gave it a tight squeeze. I locked my gaze on hers and squeezed her hand in return. If the concern in her stance wasn't enough, her worried eyes and downturned mouth said it all. I gave her a small nod of encouragement.

To my surprise, the shongoman placed himself at the other entrance.

Unexpected.

"The rules are simple. We fight until death…or until one of us can take no more, at which time the loser places his left hand in the air like this." He raised his left hand high in the air.

I nodded slowly, indicating I understood even though my mind was reeling. I had seen small men fight and fight well. I'd seen them take down men twice their size in the blink of an eye. I'd seen time and again men my own size underestimate them…and get beat.

But the shongoman wasn't just a small man. He was lean—wiry in a way that looked as though he might break if hugged too tightly. I a full head taller and outweighed him by sixty pounds or more.

Regardless, I acknowledged the rules for the end of the fight.

"Additional rules?" I asked.

Straight white teeth gleamed. A smile spread across his dark, desert-weathered face. His eyes danced in amusement, crinkles appearing in each outside corner.

Odd that he seemed to have no nerves at all. Had he done this often? Or was he *that* confident in whatever fighting ability he had?

Assess. Assess. Find the weakness. What are you missing?

"No rules," he said.

"No rules," I repeated, my own words sounding more like a question than a statement.

I nodded again to indicate I accepted the terms of the fight.

Come on. Come on. Give me something.

There.

The shongoman's glance to his staff. Brief, but there.

Of course, he would use the staff. In the right hands, it was a lethal weapon. It wasn't much of an assumption to assume the staff was in the right hands.

There was no time to think. The assault began. Even expecting the staff, even knowing I couldn't guess what the trial would bring, I couldn't have predicted what was waiting for me.

The blindness struck first.

I had no reason to anticipate it, having not been physically touched. But I had fought blindfolded before, so even with the advantage of surprise, the blindness didn't faze me the way it might another opponent.

Magic. Shongoman Aleshkatel Bhalehi possessed magic.

Swinging to my left, I blocked a blow meant for my side. The staff hit my arm and slid off as I followed through with my turn. A rush of air blew past—the shongoman following through with his own motion to alleviate the rebound.

"Something's wrong," Reina said to Brigantino somewhere off to my left. "Something's not right."

I didn't have a chance to soothe her fears.

The shongoman came at me again, but this time I was ready for him. I tracked his movement as he crept almost silently to my right, then behind me. I kept my back to him, letting him believe I didn't know he was there. I needed the element of surprise this time.

As he came at me from behind, swinging his staff through the air at my shoulder, I turned and grabbed, swinging it—and the man holding it—around and to the ground in front of me.

There was a surprised murmur among the Jyngabé. A thud and a rough cough from the shongoman assured me I'd done well regardless of not having my vision.

But then I lost my hearing.

The silence that filled my head was so dizzyingly absolute that I almost passed out from the impact alone.

How the hell was I to fight blind *and* deaf?

I took a solid hit to the abdomen first—most likely with the blunt end of the shongoman's staff. The air expelled from my lungs as though I'd been squeezed, then a burning pain began just below my sternum, radiating outward like I'd been struck with fire itself.

Stumbling backwards, I fought to keep my balance, reorienting myself with a hand to one of the wooden poles.

Magic was magic.

I couldn't beat it with strength alone. I had to get rid of that staff.

Staying against the sides of the ring meant the shongoman could only attack me from the front or side. At least, that's what *I* would want me to believe if I were in his position, but with that staff, he could come at just about any angle without leaving the ring.

And that's what he would do.

It took him longer than I expected to creep around to my

side and attempt to blast me in the back of the head with his staff and the only indication that he had was the sudden shift of air from behind. I reacted with reflexes honed by years of training.

I pulled the staff from the shongoman's grasp and flung it backwards, far from the ring. I expected some sort of relief from the blindness and deafness, an escape from this prison he'd thrown me into.

To my dismay, the magic remained. For a brief moment, I struggled against the panic welling in my middle. Would I be blind and deaf forever? Could I live that life? Could I help the people of Castilles in such a state? Could Reina still love me?

Ridiculous questions. All of them.

Because none of it mattered when the air grew thick and the blackness became so much deeper than just the dark behind my eyes. My lungs burned in their attempts to get air, but the air wouldn't budge. It wouldn't slide into my throat, or down into the lungs beyond, no matter how much I wished it.

If I raised my left hand in surrender now, we would never find the Heart of Death. The shongoman would send us away to face whatever undead horrors the Plains dealt us. If I succumbed to the death he handed me in this battle, Reina and Brigantino still had a chance. Would Aleshkatel honor his word? Or would my death mean a loss anyway?

I stumbled to my knees, throwing a hand to the ground to steady myself and gasped at the air like a fish out of water.

It was hard to think without air.

Fiermi, I wish I'd sent Reina away.

CHAPTER FIFTEEN

Death Found
Reina

I didn't think.

Hesitating half a second, I didn't think about the consequences of my actions if the talisman still refused to work for me.

The fact was that Quinn was dead if I didn't act anyway. Too stubborn, too proud, he would never raise his hand in surrender. He'd figure his death meant success for Brigantino and me. Stupid man.

Stupid, stupid man.

I ripped the talisman from its place beneath my tunic and held it firm in my hand, saying a prayer to the Saints that it would work.

When I tapped into the power of the talisman, its energy rushed through me in torrents almost beyond control. The aqua hue that accompanied my vision was expected.

The pulsing, dark red-black ribbons that wove themselves through and around Quinn's body, choking him in ever tightening knots were not expected at all. And they didn't come from me. Quinn fell to the ground, fighting against a force he couldn't see. He rolled to his back, hands clutching his chest, ripping at his tunic where the ribbons were concentrated.

The talisman's power collided with the dark ribbons and dueled for control in an angry confrontation, but my own power was nothing like the life the talisman had brought forth before. This, whatever it was, was all-consuming and took every ounce of strength to wield control. I struggled to stay in command of the talisman. The two forces slammed together in a violent collision of black sparks— as though trying to consume one another—in a vision only I could see through the aqua haze.

The redness pulsed again, pushing back against the talisman, against me. I fought the pressure in my chest and threw another burst of life energy at it with all the strength I could muster. If it were possible for energy to hiss, the dark ribbons did as they curled away from the life-giving tendrils.

Quinn's chest rose unexpectedly. He filled his lungs with air the talisman's power provided, but his fingers clutched claw-like at the ground, grasping at the sand.

I pushed harder. The turquoise tendrils began to swirl around him, forming a protective cocoon, pushing the deep red claws of death away.

All at once, the red-black ribbons disappeared as though they had never existed at all. They didn't dissipate or drift away or fade into obscurity. They simply no longer *were*.

I raced to Quinn's side to help him sit upright, placing one hand on his back, the other on his shoulder. The fact that he let me assist spoke volumes of his condition. Brigantino aided him on his other side. Quinn blinked as he took in his surroundings as though seeing through new eyes.

"You were blinded," I realized out loud. That was what had gone wrong during the fight. That was why he hadn't seen the blow that came at his abdomen.

He swallowed with difficulty, then spoke, his voice hoarse. "Deafened, too."

Quinn put fingers to his ear, rubbing back and forth, trying to coerce the hearing back into it, opening and closing his mouth repeatedly.

"You used the talisman," he said, his voice low. "Even with the magic…"

"There didn't seem to be a choice."

The shongoman stood not far from where he'd been when Quinn first fell. Someone had retrieved his staff for him, and he held it reverently, observing Quinn, his eyes blazing with intensity.

Or…was he eyeing me?

"We could have saved this trouble entirely if you'd told me you'd brought the Bringer of Life," he said to Quinn, amusement lighting his eyes.

"I brought the Bringer of Life," Quinn croaked. He rubbed his neck and then his jaw, twisting and turning his head at various angles.

"This, I see."

He extended his hand to Quinn to help lift him off the ground and Quinn took it, but the shongoman didn't release his hand once Quinn was standing.

"My name is Aleshkatel Bhalehi and I am the Heart of Death," he said, with a bow of his head. "Call me Alesh."

"We could have saved this trouble if you'd told us you were the Heart of Death," I said, narrowing my eyes at him. "A fickle man indeed."

To my surprise, Alesh smiled.

"Indeed."

Quinn inspected the staff Alesh handed him. On the surface, it was nothing spectacular. The carved wood at its top was a cage of gnarled fingers that mostly obscured the blood red ruby cabochon beneath.

We left the ring—and Alesh's people—behind and walked the perimeter of the village camp, as much to release nervous energy from the fight as to keep prying ears from hearing our conversation. While Brigantino walked with us, he maintained his distance, acting once again as Quinn's personal guard. I wondered if Alesh suspected Quinn's true identity.

"How long have you wielded the staff?" I asked, eager to learn more about someone who possessed a gift like mine.

Only it wasn't a gift like mine. Not at all.

His was a power far deadlier.

"It was passed to me by the last shongoman," Alesh said. "As per tradition."

"How long have you been shongoman?"

"Too long, I fear. The last shongoman succumbed to an unfortunate fate much earlier than he ever should have."

That caught Quinn's attention.

"What happened?" he asked.

"He sacrificed himself to save his son. As a result, the staff was passed to me."

"The stone in this, does it shock you if you touch it?" Quinn asked.

"I've never touched it." Alesh tapped the wooden cage at the top.

I coughed. "I wish I could say the same of my own token. Would you like to hold it?"

His eyes lit. "May I? I would like to examine it."

I hesitated a moment. I didn't like to hand the talisman to anyone, but if Alesh was the Heart of Death, we wouldn't succeed in reining in chaos without him. The sooner I gained his trust, the better.

I slipped the talisman from my neck, ignoring the jolts at my fingertips, and handed it to him. He nearly dropped it when it made contact with his skin.

"That's…painful!"

I nodded.

"I am glad I do not have this burden to bear." He handed the talisman back. I placed it around my neck and back beneath my tunic, letting it settle into a happy hum on my skin.

"I would think the burden of death would be enough for anyone," Quinn said before I could respond with a sarcastic word of thanks.

"I do not kill living beings," Alesh said, seeming almost offended at Quinn's insinuation.

"What *do* you do?" I asked. "With this power, I mean.

What does the being the Heart of Death mean for you?"

"What does being the Bringer of Life mean for you?" he countered.

"Well…with the talisman, I can bring forth life. I can create life where there was none before. I can nurture life that already exists, speeding it up or slowing it down if need be. Any way that life can be manipulated is in my realm of power, I think."

"You think?"

"I've only been in possession of the talisman for a few months," I admitted, giving a lopsided smile.

"Ah, I see."

"And there was no one to teach me how to use it."

Alesh looked perplexed.

"It was hidden, unused for a thousand years," I explained.

His eyes widened. "Child, how is that possible?"

I almost smiled at the pet name that brought Laurelle Bonverno to mind. Quinn's mouth twitched in amusement, too.

I wondered if Elle had already restored the kingdom in the week and a half since we'd been gone. With her ability to make men quake with a look alone, surely she had made progress. Even with undead roaming the kingdom.

"The last wearer of the talisman hid it based on a prophecy. She meant to keep it safe for the duration of that time," I said.

He shook his head in disbelief. "It seems impossible that such a thing could be lost for so long and then found again. It is lucky that you found it, yes?"

"Luck, perhaps, but there was more to it than that," Quinn said with a shake of his head. "Too much for one tale."

Too much by far for right now. I wouldn't even know where to start if I *thought* about telling Alesh how I came to be the White Sorceress, or, as he called me, the Bringer of Life.

"What *do* you do as the Heart of Death if not use the power to kill?" I asked.

"Ah, to know the answer to that is to explain what death is. It is more than what you know, more than what your eyes can see," Alesh said tapping his own temple. "Define death."

I paused a moment, thinking.

"Death is a permanent end to life," I responded with the medical answer. "When there's no longer tissue growth in the body, or breath in the lungs, or thought in the mind. With death, the body is still, no longer a sentient being with self-awareness. In death, the body becomes no different than a rock or a piece of metal."

Alesh made an amused sound.

"That's death this way"—he held outspread hands far apart from each other, arms wide— "but death can also be seen this way." He drew his hands together so they were a few finger-widths from touching. "Death can be small, slow. One piece of the body may go before others. Your eyes can stop seeing, but you are still alive, even if your eyes are not."

"Until the Heart of Death steals your hearing…and then the air from your lungs," Quinn muttered, handing the staff back to Alesh.

Alesh grinned and accepted the staff. He gave it a lazy

twirl, then leaned on it.

"This is true."

"You mean you…can make certain parts of the body die without killing a person?" I asked. This did not sound like a good power to have, unless one was in battle. Then it was an exceptionally helpful skill to have command over. Incapacitate the enemy without killing them entirely.

"I can."

"Then I'm relieved not to be your enemy," I said.

Alesh outright laughed. "But it has uses for friends, too. In instances of pain or injury, I can deaden the pain so it is no longer felt. Your mind no longer feels the pain even if the injury persists."

My gaze met Quinn's. He nodded. Alesh's gift could be useful on Niles's injury. If he could deaden the pain, Niles could heal much more comfortably. And we wouldn't have to leave him behind wherever this journey took us next.

"That's fascinating," I said, genuinely amazed that the power of death was not the terrible burden I thought it should be. "Alesh…how did you know about the Bringer of Life? When I came to Quinn's aid, you knew who—and what—I was."

"Ah, that. The Ndoyo have long heard stories about the bearers of the three balance stones."

"Balance stones?"

"Life, death, chaos," he elaborated.

"The three talismans," Quinn said.

"And three who wield them," Aleshkatel said. "The Bringer of Life, the Heart of Death, and the Chaos Wielder.

These stories have been passed down from older to younger for many, many years. As long as all three are used with purpose, all things remain balanced and in…in…" He struggled to find the word.

"Harmony?" I said.

"Yes, that is it. Harmony. Together. The world is balanced when the three stones are used as they should be."

"And what happens when they're not?" Quinn asked.

"Great unrest."

Great unrest was an understatement, given what we'd left behind in Castilles.

We lapsed into quiet for a moment before Alesh blurted, "Tell me why you have sought the Heart of Death. What use am I to you?"

"I should think that's obvious," I replied.

"We need your help," Quinn said. "And you know more than you let on."

A smile tugged at the corner of Alesh's lips.

"I know much…but not enough to be of any real help."

"You're named in a prophecy," I told him. "A prophecy issued by Magnus Tarrowburn, who also foresaw my finding the talisman."

He issued a skeptical glare. "Do you have this prophecy? May I see?"

I pulled the handwritten copy from the pocket of my tunic and handed it to him. He stared at the words on the page, deep in concentration. Or so I thought.

"Can you…read to me?" he asked after a moment. "Translate? I do not read your language well. Speak well, yes, but do not read."

"Of course," I said gently, accepting it back from him.

I read the prophecy in its entirety, with Quinn translating the few pieces Alesh didn't understand.

We neared the nudromedary pen, evident by smell alone if not by the constant grunting of one annoyed animal. I had never heard such a sound in all my life. If horses made such noise, I might ship Aeros off to live with someone else.

My heart sank at the thought of the mare in the stable in Lower South Trellington. Saints, I hoped she was safe. Surely the undead wouldn't be interested in stables, would they? Had they ransacked the town? Or had they just been in search of us?

When we reached the pen, I extended a hand toward one of the nearest animals. How odd, these creatures. With cloven hooves the size of saucers and a sinuous neck that looked better suited to a mythical fairytale creature, it was a mystery how such an animal had come to exist. Bushy eyebrows fell across long, dark lashes on one of the large-eyed, droopy-lipped animals who came nearer to inspect my hand. I scratched her jaw lightly, marveling at the difference between her fur and Aeros's. Sparse and light, it was nothing like Aeros's sleek hide.

"You are the three, then?" Alesh asked. He turned to address Brigantino behind us. "You are the One who Failed?"

Brigantino almost choked on his own laughter.

"I am not," he said, his eyes still shining, mouth still twitching with humor. "That particular weasel is under watch by the yagaman in the tent you've provided for us."

"Weasel? I do not understand what is this, weasel."

"He refers to our companion in a less than gracious way," I explained, glaring at Brigantino. "He was attacked by the undead, what you call the"—I searched my memory for what he had called them— "*acaffilé*. He is recovering but could use your help, if you would be so kind as to aid him with the pain."

"I will look at him," he said with a nod. Then his gaze switched back and forth between Brigantino and Quinn. "And which is the king?"

"I am," Quinn said. "Captain Brigantino is head of the Royal Guard, and a fellow brother in the former Order as you already know."

"Why did you not tell me you were king in the beginning?"

"I sought your help, not your judgment."

"Judgment?"

"I didn't want to come to you as a king, a diplomat representing my country and begging for the help of your country and your men. I come to you as a man, as a fellow Lironian, looking to help all of our people, both north and south. This threat extends to us all."

Alesh nodded thoughtfully at the same time one of the nudromedaries let out a giant belch that was almost enough to knock me backwards. I'd take horse-breath a thousand times over nudromedary breath. Saints above!

I coughed and stepped backwards away from the pen.

"Don't mind them," he said. "Always something to say at the most awkward of times, but the milk is good, and they travel well."

It hadn't occurred to me the animals would be good for milk, but with that breath, what did their milk taste like? I was wary.

"Anyway," Alesh continued. "I will help. The eclipse, it is not long now?"

I nodded. "In two months from today, Andra will have already set when Stellon lines up with the sun in its entirety. Full eclipse."

"Two months until the veil is broken forever and chaos reigns," Alesh said, tapping a finger on his staff.

"Unless we stop it from happening," I said.

"And the broken veil is just our guess as to what will happen if we don't stop the chaos from wreaking havoc," Quinn added.

"There's not much room for interpretation there," Brigantino added. "And we've seen what happens already where the veil has thinned."

"*Acaffilé,*" Alesh murmured. "*Acaffilé.*"

Alesh was positive we needed the advice of an old friend from another village a hundred miles to the southwest, which meant…

…another journey.

I should have been grateful that Alesh knew of someone who might be able to guide us further on our quest, but the only emotion I could dredge up was utter exhaustion. I was near certain I'd already traveled more of Liron's miles than any bird, and *they* had wings. When this was all over—if indeed it was ever over, I planned never to go farther than my own two feet could travel ever again.

"Are you sure you can help him?" I asked. Alesh inspected the wound on Niles's leg. Though his brow remained creased in pain, Niles was deep in a medicine-induced sleep, or I wouldn't dare speak so openly. I'd waited until Brigantino and Quinn left to take care of supplies for the upcoming journey before bringing my concerns about the talisman to Alesh.

Alesh placed his fingers on the healthy skin of Niles's thigh, then moved downward to his calf, as though feeling for something only he could detect.

"Yes, I can help him."

"What I mean to say is you haven't noticed anything… strange with your abilities since…well, in these last few weeks?"

He turned to observe me, dark eyes watching closely, reading my face. I resisted the urge to bite my lip, trying not to show the nerves I felt when thinking about the torn veil and the lapse in my own abilities.

Sure, I'd saved Quinn on the sands. The talisman worked, but what choice had I been given? Without my intervention, Quinn would have died. If my abilities had killed him instead of healed him, it might have been a small mercy given how he suffered.

"What has gone wrong with your gift?" Alesh asked pointedly.

I debated how much information to reveal. Now that he

knew who we were, Alesh seemed warm, welcoming, and ready to assist, but why had he forced Quinn into the ring to begin with? Why not just help us from the start? His change in demeanor made me wary. I swallowed, then told him the truth, mostly because I couldn't think of a conceivable lie fast enough.

"There's been several instances when I've gone to grow something, to nurture a plant to life for food on our journey, and instead of growing, it blackened and died."

Alesh breathed in sharply.

"Your talisman, it gives control of life, yes?"

I nodded.

"You maybe used too much life, too quickly? Aged the plant too fast?"

I shook my head. "No. I did that once before when… well, I've done that before—aged someone, I mean. It's not the same. This was different. This was the plant dying before it had even matured. It just…withered away to nothing."

Alesh blinked and turned his attention back to Niles, laying one palm on his thigh above where the undead had shredded the tissue and one palm at his ankle below where most of the damage had been done.

"How many times has this happened?" he asked me, closing his eyes.

Was he going to work on Niles even when I just told him how my own ability had waned?

"Three or four times. It's why I haven't attempted to heal Niles. I tried when it first happened, at the crossing. I tried, but I made it worse, so I…stopped," I told him. "I could have. Any other time, I could have healed this entirely. The wound would be gone, and Niles would be fine."

"I believe you," he said.

"But I won't risk my ability going wrong and blackening Niles's leg the way I did those plants. I can't risk his life."

"You did the right thing," Alesh reassured me.

I shifted my weight.

"And still you'll use your ability?" I asked.

Alesh smiled, opened his eyes again, but kept his hands in place.

"My ability lies in death. If it is reversed—especially at this moment—we would find ourselves in a desirable situation, would we not?"

I opened my mouth to reply, then closed it again. What argument did I have against Aleshkatel's logic? If his magic worked correctly, Niles would no longer be in pain. If his magic somehow reversed as mine had done, Niles's leg would be healed.

Alesh closed his eyes once more and I remained quiet, working at the cuticles of my nails. I waited for some sign that his magic worked, that Niles's pain had lessened.

Then the crease between Niles's brow smoothed. Alesh had altered his ability to feel pain from the wound. I wouldn't have believed such a thing was possible had I not seen it with my own eyes. Alesh removed his hands from Niles's body, stood, and turned to face me. I breathed a sigh of relief.

"He travels with us tomorrow? This, the One who Failed?"

I nodded, hating the term, regretting that I had been just

as quick to label Niles in much the same manner.

"He must," I said. "If you can keep him comfortable and we keep his leg clean and wrapped, the travel should pose no problem for him."

Still, I looked to Alesh to confirm my hopes. He seemed satisfied with my answer, and so I took some measure of relief from his response.

"One thing." Alesh reached into the pocket of the long, dark tunic he wore today and fumbled for something. "Here," he said, fist outstretched.

I extended my hand and he dropped two rough, round, yellow tablets into my hand. I didn't have to ask the question on my lips.

He tapped his head.

"When he wakes, he will wish for death, but"—he squinted his eyes and pursed his lips "only for one hour. Give him these or it will be longer."

He turned to leave, but I grabbed his arm.

"How *much* longer?" I asked. "What if he refuses to take them?"

He smiled. "You are a healer. You will get them into him."

"How *much* longer, Alesh?"

"Without the pills? Three days. Worst pain of his life."

With that, Alesh left the tent. I slipped the pills into my own pocket, then flopped onto one of the cushions on the floor and threw my head into my hands, rubbing at my temples.

Broody Niles was difficult enough to deal with when he

was in a *good* mood. I cursed the undead once more, and the chaos that kept me from using the talisman to heal Niles completely.

A moan from the bed broke me from my self-pity. *Get on with it, Reina.* I had been with patients through pain. I could be with Niles.

Even Niles. I breathed out slowly.

"Here, take these." I helped him sit forward.

"No," he mumbled before letting loose a howl of pain. "No more. No more concoctions, no more foul medicine. Let me die!"

He pushed my hand, and the pills, away. I fought against the urge to roll my eyes. Thank the Saints above that Niles never suffered like this in the army, though maybe he would have been less dramatic about it if he had.

"Don't be infantile, Niles! Your health could get much better or much worse *right now*. Which will it be?"

He turned his head away, eyes shut tight in pain, convinced he was upon death's door.

"Just leave me," he said.

I pursed my lips. Steeling my resolve, I grabbed his chin with one hand, jammed the pills to the back of his throat, then pinched his nose.

Despite the fighting, coughing, and gagging, he swallowed.

He spit yellow goo to the floor as soon as I let go, but there was no sign of the actual pills, only tinted saliva.

"You're the devil's minion," Niles croaked before his eyes rolled back into his head and he howled in pain again.

I smiled.

"You're welcome."

CHAPTER SIXTEEN

Departure
Reina

There was no way to convince anyone I needed time alone, not even to seek a vision, so instead I waited until they all slept, which took far longer than anticipated. It was over an hour before Brigantino succumbed to sleep and I'd resorted to pinching my arms to keep my eyes open.

What thoughts kept a man like Brigantino awake at night? What horrible memories played in his mind after so many years in the Order, being sent to work undercover beneath Bruenner? I shivered and moved closer to the warmth of Quinn's solid body.

Quinn slept on the cushions beside me, his breathing deep and rhythmic. I studied his face by the glow of the lanterns we left burning in case Niles needed anything during the night. After Niles stopped howling in agony and flinging words far worse than *minion* at me, the pain passed just as Alesh said it would, and he thanked me—warily, if not properly.

Now, Niles lay on the bed sleeping soundly, Brigantino slept sprawled on a low, cushioned sofa despite the fact that it was far too small for him, and Quinn and I lay side by side on the floor cushions again.

In his sleep, Quinn returned to the boy I once knew. His brow was smooth, no longer drawn down over his eyes. His jaw was relaxed, his mouth for once not scowling. I resisted the urge to kiss his lips and wake him. Not here, not stirring emotions neither of us could act on.

Like this, asleep, relaxed, Quinn looked…like so many other young men I had known.

My thoughts darkened as they turned to the Order. Had the Order of the Southern Cross stolen his youth, crushed his innocence while beating his body? I'd seen the scars on Quinn's back. Though I'd offered to heal the skin once I'd gained control of the talisman months ago, he resisted, insisting the scars were reminders.

Reminders of what?

What did he need reminding of?

I glanced to Brigantino, another scowler. What had he been like once upon a time? A boy like the Quinn I remembered from before he'd gone away?

So many questions that would never be answered.

My, my, staying up late turned me melancholy.

Get to work.

I closed my eyes, slowed my breath, and focused until a honeyed sweetness flooded my senses and I *saw.*

A small village, but one with a more permanent presence than the desert-dwelling community of Ndoyo. I was drawn down a packed dirt street and through the doors of an ancient-looking storefront with a rainbow-hued glass door. The odor inside was an overwhelming mix of powders, remedies, oils, and dried plants hung from the rafters in bundles ready for sale.

An apothecary.

The shop was empty except for us and a single young woman behind the counter—the shopkeeper, I assumed, though she appeared far too young to be in charge of a store, let alone one selling remedies. I was unable to tell who was in our group—we were shadowy figures—but it looked as though there were more people in our company than Quinn, Niles, Alesh, and I. Brigantino, probably. And…someone else maybe?

An argument ensued when the woman grew agitated with Alesh. Whatever he asked about, the dark-haired girl behind the counter didn't want to give. She pointed to the door, her face drawn in a scowl. Muffled words were exchanged, not pleasant ones by the look of it.

Alesh—I thought it was Alesh—argued with her, and before she could tell us to leave again, an old woman in long robes with wild, white hair emerged from a curtained doorway leading somewhere to the back of the shop. I could see her clearly, vividly, as though I were standing in front of her now, and when she met my gaze with eyes that seemed too black to be human, I was almost convinced she saw me, too—the real me, not the phantom version from my vision. She smiled and nodded. I sucked in a startled breath. Did she know me?

Then she turned her attention to Alesh and pulled a folded leather pouch from beneath the counter, untying the worn fabric fastenings holding it closed and flipping it open to reveal the weathered parchment within. Without warning, bottles on the shelves began to burst, their contents exploding across the walls and splattering onto the floor. I jumped in surprise, but the girl behind the counter looked as though it hadn't been unexpected in the least. In fact, she looked annoyed.

Alesh tried to offer payment to the old woman, but she wouldn't accept. She shoved the parchment into Alesh's hands and pointed at the door—a door that flew open on its own, slamming against the wall. I may not have been able to hear the slam, but it made me jump anyway.

The scene faded and I returned to my own time and my own body. Alesh hadn't shared with us where we needed to go or why we were headed there other than wanting to visit with an old friend. The old woman in my vision, the one who seemed to see right through my vision and into *me*...could that be his old friend?

Alesh didn't seem surprised when we informed him the Chaos Wielder had taken Adan Iyer's form right beneath our noses, here in Ndoyo. Adan, however, seemed plenty shocked.

"Why should he know me?!" His eyes grew wide and he put one hand to his cheek to reassure himself that his face still belonged to him. His other hand remained holding the reins of one of the nudromedaries we'd be taking with us shortly. Just over the horizon, the sun flared brightly, turning miles of white sands into an endless reflecting pool of light. Just looking out into the desert forced me to squint.

To my father's question, I could only shake my head with no explanation. I couldn't begin to understand how the Chaos Wielder's powers worked and what knowledge he was capable of gleaning.

"And how could he know that you were my daughter when I, myself, did not?"

"We aren't sure," Brigantino said with a tired sigh. He pointed between Adan and Alesh. "But we wanted to make you both aware of the kind of danger that exists. This man is capable of changing the weather, raising the dead, and taking another person's form. Be alert at all times."

"I want to travel with you," Adan said, dropping the nudromedary's reins. "I can be of help. I've traveled the deserts and the roads extensively. I know all the trade routes. I can get you where you need to go quickly."

Alesh took hold of Adan's arm. "I know, my friend, but I need you here."

"Alesh, I just learned I have a daughter. Please don't take her away from me. Give me the chance to travel with you. Give me the chance to get to know her." Adan didn't hide the desperate tone in his voice.

A heaviness settled in my chest at my father's words, and I felt guilty once again that I'd lied to him about my mother. *You should tell him.*

Alesh continued, "I need you here. No one here understands the extent of the danger we face. You have seen the world outside. You know what weighs on us all if we fail.

You must lead the Ndoyo and oversee the Jyngabé."

Adan reeled in shock, his eyes wide. "No, Alesh, I am not Jyngabé! I cannot! I have done nothing to deserve—"

Alesh gripped his friend's hands. "You can. You must. We cannot have you with us. The Chaos Wielder already took your form once. He knows you. We cannot risk that he should take your form again. This way, we know you are here. If we see *you*, we will know it is *not* you."

Though hurt, Adan nodded. "What's to say he cannot take the form of any of you?"

"There's no telling what he might be able to do, but we hope our companions know each other well enough so as to know if one of them does not seem true," Alesh said.

"And what if he should take the form of one of you?" He motioned between Alesh and Ywelo, who stood with dark, sculpted arms crossed over her chest and keen eyes observing everything.

Alesh nodded. "He might try, but Ywelo and I are aware of the risk. We will remain vigilant."

Adan nodded slowly, then turned to face me, with a thousand things to say and no time to say any of them. I wondered if he felt lost, too. Didn't that feeling go away as one aged? Didn't one become *better* with expressing feelings?

Tell him.

But I couldn't. Not now. Not when I was about to leave him to head off into whatever unknown the future held for us. Not when things would get much worse before getting better.

"Daughter," Adan said, his voice breaking on the word. "Please be safe. I wasn't there for you as I should have been. I wasn't there to protect you, to watch you grow, to help you along the way. For that, I'm sorry."

Tears welled in my eyes. I cursed them as they streaked my face, and Adan embraced me in a hug. The awkwardness between two strangers was no more. I let myself melt into the arms and chest of the man who shared my blood, the man who loved my mother as I did.

I would tell him.

When I returned.

"I-I want to talk more." I pulled back and wiped my eyes. "When we return, I want to get to know you, the way we should have been able to from the start."

He gripped my shoulder gently and nodded.

"Be safe. Travel with the trade winds."

My face must have shown my confusion.

"An expression. One of luck. Travel with the trade winds. It means 'go in the right direction,' figuratively speaking."

"Oh," I answered. "We'll try."

Hopefully, we'd go in the right direction literally, as well.

Brigantino, Ywelo, and Niles had already mounted their nudromedaries when I turned to step upward onto my animal. I stole a glance at Niles's leg, but it was well-hidden beneath a new set of pants gifted to him by Aleshkatel. Without our horses, we had left most of our supplies in Lower South Trellington. We'd retained only what was in our packs. Staring at Niles's leg, remembering our hasty departure from the border of Castilles, I shivered despite the oppressive heat.

Quinn stood beside me, waiting to help me mount. The animals were nothing like horses at all. In fact, because they were so much taller than horses, they had to be made to lie down to receive a rider. I pushed upward, then centered myself in the saddle and gripped the handle in front of me, grateful for its presence. Otherwise, I'd surely be on the ground, even with so many years of riding horses behind me.

After I settled in the saddle, Quinn took to his own mount and the animals rose when Ywelo issued quick, harsh-sounding commands to them. As my nudromedary lurched forward, her hind legs rising beneath her, I leaned back to balance myself. Then I sat forward again, my back straight, as she stood tall.

In all, we had five people and eight animals in our group that would make the trek to—well, to wherever we were going. All I knew was that it was southwest and would take two days to reach if we didn't want to push the animals too hard.

As we left the oasis of Ndoyo behind, I squinted against the glare of miles and miles of shimmering, gold-white sand. I didn't look back at Adan, at the cool and welcoming village we left behind. An illusion of safety, all of it. Until we found a way to null the Chaos Wielder's power, there would be no safety anywhere on Liron.

CHAPTER SEVENTEEN

Visions Unveiled
Reina

The town and the shop were laid out exactly as I'd *seen*, not that I expected differently. We left the nudromedaries in the care of a stable, or what passed as a stable here in desert lands and traveled the dusty street by foot. If there was a positive to be found, it was in the hardness of the packed dirt beneath our boots, which didn't shift beneath our feet like sand.

We'd crossed the sandy dunes to reach the red dirt plains covered in various scrub and wiry-looking trees that seemed more dead than alive. Though Ywelo swore the same trees were covered in enormous yellow blooms when the rains came once a year, I had difficulty picturing the landscape as anything but dusty, barren, and dry.

The door to the shop, its glass panels a prismatic array of colors, was familiar to my eyes, but my breath hitched anyway when Alesh reached to swing the door inward. Whatever was in that parchment Alesh sought, it was here. And so were the girl and the old woman.

The apothecary smelled as I expected, medicinal wafts of unfamiliar herbs, various jars filled with pungent oils varying in hue from pale yellow to a deep amber, and the tang of something—maybe the girl's lunch—on the air.

The young girl from my vision, dark-haired and petite, stooped in front of the counter sorting something in the cases below. When she saw our party, she stood upright and spoke in an unfamiliar language.

Alesh, thankfully, switched the conversation to the northern tongue so the rest of us could understand. The shopkeeper followed effortlessly.

"Hello and good day," she said. "You are here for something special, hmm?"

"We are, indeed," Alesh answered. "My dear friend and longtime healer has been keeping something safe for me for many years. I hope this is still the case. If so, you have exactly what I require."

"Oh, we always have that which is searched for," she said, giving a cryptic smile. "If intentions are true, that is."

"Our intentions could not be truer," Quinn muttered beside me, but the shopkeeper paid no attention to him.

"And what is it you seek, shongoman, hmm?"

I wondered how she knew Aleshkatel was a shongoman. His clothing? His mannerisms? What distinguished him from Ywelo as a Jyngabé?

"We seek the Map to Balance," Alesh said.

The girl's welcoming demeanor disappeared in the space of half a breath, the smile falling from her face so quickly I wondered if I'd imagined it there.

"Out," she said, pointing to the door. "We have no such thing."

Well. At least this was all going according to my sight. It was good to know at least something still worked as it should.

"Ah, but you do," Alesh replied. "And we come prepared to pay for it."

"Ní. We have no map."

"What is your price?"

I furrowed my brow at Alesh's offer of money. If the map was his and kept here only for safe keeping, why should he have to pay for it?

"The map does not exist!" The girl was angry, a flush growing in her cheeks.

"You have no map, or the map does not exist?" Alesh asked. "Which is it? For it cannot be both."

The old woman with the wild hair appeared in the doorway to the back room at that moment, pushing aside a floral curtain that separated the two areas. Her sight on Alesh, she entered, her hobbling gate telling of old injuries or arthritic bones.

Her gaze flicked to me, and there it was—that knowing smile. She knew. Somehow, she knew I'd seen this all before. She was ancient, this woman. Ancient, but not feeble. Her dark, weathered face was a map in itself marked by dozens of lines—proof of years lived, and days seen. Black eyes darker than any I'd ever seen bored into my soul when she smiled.

She turned her attention to Alesh and reached beneath the counter to pull out the folded parchment. I didn't jump this time when she untied it and bottles began to burst behind us, the door flinging open as though an angry ghost had turned the knob and flung it against the wall.

Alesh tried to push payment into her hand, but she refused to accept his money, instead pointing to the door.

"Out! Out!" the girl cried at us. The dried herbs hanging on the rafters began to swirl in the chaos. She was already picking up a broom beside the doorframe.

The old woman watched us go, her eyes burning a hole in my back. Alesh folded the map again as we moved forward, eager to stop the gusting wind and broken glass that seemed to follow us.

"What the bloody hell was *that*?" asked Niles once we were on the street. I glanced at his bandaged leg. Not even a hint of a limp. Aleshkatel's fix, the unexpectedly useful power of death, was remarkable.

"A map," Alesh answered, storing the now folded and retied parchment in a deep inside pocket within his tunic.

Niles narrowed his eyes as though trying to decide if Alesh was toying with him. The lack of amusement on Alesh's face indicated he was not.

"Yes, I can see that," Niles replied dryly. I meant the whole poltergeist in the shop bit."

Alesh's brow furrowed. "What is this word—poltergeist?"

"A ghost," I answered. "An angry one."

Alesh laughed. "Ah, no, not a ghost. The Winds of Chaos."

"So, why the Winds of Chaos?" Brigantino asked, hoping to get a more direct answer than the one Alesh gave to Niles.

"The Map to Balance will tell us where to find the Chaos

Wielder. Do you think he wants that?"

Brigantino shook his head. "Can't imagine so."

"But it also opens the channel between us, so if we can see his location, he, too, can see ours."

"That's mad! *Why* would you think this is a good idea?" I said.

It would have been good to know this information beforehand. Perhaps we'd never have come for the map at all. There had to be another way to locate the Chaos Wielder, and I said as much to Alesh.

Quinn was quick to stand beside me.

"There are other ways of gaining information," he said. "Ways that don't include letting the Chaos Wielder know we're coming."

"Not to mention exactly where we're coming *from*," Brigantino added.

"We have until the eclipse," Alesh said. "Did you have a faster way to obtain this information?"

Quinn set his mouth into a hard line, unhappy with the truth behind Alesh's words. "Next time," he said. "Tell us the consequences *before* you pull something like that."

"He is always like this," Ywelo said, smirking and raising an eyebrow, her eyes flicking to Brigantino, then moving downward.

"But we know where to go now, do we not?" Alesh said. "Kufataba."

"Kufu-what?" Niles said.

He turned and pointed south. "Kufataba, the mountain."

The land he pointed to seemed unassuming, no mountain

in sight. How far away this time? I thought about the last time I'd taken a mountain pass, about the snow that coated the land and the attack that claimed the life of a horse and rider from our party. The memory elicited a shiver.

This mountain was different. No snow. No ice. No frozen rivers below. At least, I hoped.

"Will nudes make the pass?" Quinn asked Brigantino.

Brigantino shook his head. "You can't go *over* Kufataba."

I groaned. Not caves again. I'd had my share of those, too.

"Caves?" Quinn asked, echoing my thoughts.

Ywelo and Alesh both shook their heads.

"Tunnels," Alesh said. "I have never been, but you"—he pointed to Brigantino— "You have?"

Brigantino gave the slightest of nods.

"Twice."

Was it me or had he paled beneath his weathered tan?

"Do you want to talk?"

Ywelo turned to face me, her expression unreadable. She sat on a dusty blue and wheat-colored mat beneath the shade of a wide palm, methodically checking the nudromedary harnesses for wear, reinforcing the braiding where needed. Instead of answering, she patted the mat next to her, encouraging me to sit, so I kneeled beside her.

"It is hard to talk about difficult things," she said. "But women always find a way, do we not?" One fine eyebrow arched as she regarded me with amused eyes, then turned her attention back to the harness.

"We do," I agreed.

We sat in silence for long moments, Ywelo pulling the rope through strong, capable fingers before she spoke again. "He left years ago. I did not think to see him again."

She could mean only one person.

Captain Brigantino.

There *were* feelings there after all. I thought I'd caught a few shared glances during our travels, but Brigantino and Ywelo were about as willing to show emotion as a box full of rusted nails, so it was difficult to imagine there was any real substance to my observations.

"Imagine my surprise when your group appeared that day, the bridge cut to shreds behind you, hundreds of *acaffilé* standing in the Northlands. And there he was."

"A bit of a shock, I would think."

I leaned back to grab a water skin resting against the base of the palm and drank, letting the unappealing, warm water slide down my throat. At least it was wet. And clean. And free from poison.

"Have you spoken to him, yet?"

She shook her head, her face drawing to a scowl while pretending to focus on a second harness in front of her.

"Why should I?"

I hid a smile behind a hand.

"Because relationships tend to go smoother when both parties share their feelings."

"Feelings!" She spat the word as though it left a bitter

taste on her palate.

"You're both stubborn." I realized the irony since Quinn and I were very much the same in some regards.

"Jyngabé do not grovel. I am a warrior," she said, her head snapping upward as she flung the harness and its mess of cords into her lap.

I ducked to avoid a flailing rope, but as it pulled across the desert floor, I was met with a face full of sand.

"Sorry!" Ywelo cried immediately, leaping to my aid.

I blinked away sand grains in my eyes and waved a hand.

"It's all right," I said. "Refrain from discussing feelings with a Jyngabé while checking equipment. Duly noted." I offered her a smile to reaffirm my teasing words.

She gave a tentative smile in return, then sat back again, and put a hand over mine.

"I am truly sorry," she said. "I would rather fight a hundred sand snakes than talk to *him* about things past."

"Hmm," I replied.

Ywelo grew silent again and I let the conversation drop. I studied the swaying leaves of the palm above me.

"What?" she said finally.

"I didn't say anything."

"Your sound. You have thoughts to share."

"What sound? I didn't make a sound."

She leveled a glare at me, and I was forced to laugh.

"All right, all right! I just think things might be smoothed over if you two spoke privately We'll be moving again as soon as the sun drops enough to let us travel. Now is the perfect time."

"Why is now the perfect time?" she asked, already assessing my motives.

"Because I need your help."

She set the harness in her lap aside and met my gaze squarely. Wow, Jyngabé turned serious fast when a friend asked for help. Good to know. Now I just had to hope she would agree with what I needed to do.

"I need to go back to the apothecary."

She shook her head, confusion in her eyes. "Why?"

"They have medicines I can use to help with Niles's leg. I would have asked them when we were there, but, well… it didn't seem like the right time with everything exploding around us and all."

This was true. It just wasn't the sole reason I wanted to go back. Ywelo eyed me, her stare as intimidating as my own mother's once was. I resisted the urge to wilt under her gaze.

"Why, really?"

My shoulders dropped and I gave a sigh. "I need to speak with the old woman there. I…had a vision of her, and I…I think she saw me. I think she knew who I was. I have to find out."

Ywelo blinked at me. I'd never revealed my visions to anyone, not willingly. Aside from Quinn, no one amongst us knew what I was capable of, how I could glimpse pieces of the future. Sharing that knowledge had always seemed too risky, too isolating, and…too downright dangerous to share.

I couldn't say why I told Ywelo the truth. Maybe I was tired of hiding who I was. Maybe I'd finally begun to believe my visions were a part of me that everyone should accept. Maybe I knew I wouldn't have her help unless I was honest.

Or maybe, just maybe, I wanted a friend.

"You have…"

I lifted my chin and met her eye. "Visions," I said with a nod. "Not always, but when I try, I can often see what the future will bring."

My pulse hammered in my ears. I held my breath, waiting for the disbelief, the disapproval, the revulsion.

It never came.

Instead, Ywelo said, "So, when will you go to the shop?"

I let out an enormous breath, free from the weight of my secret. Unexpected tears of gratitude pricked my eyes. I blinked them away furiously.

"Now, if I can. If you distract Brigantino, I can slip back while Quinn is resting, get what I need, talk to the old woman, and return before we're ready to head to Kufataba."

"And you think it is safe enough for you to go alone?"

I pressed my lips in a hard line. I wasn't convinced it was safe, but was anything safe? Theoretically, Ywelo could accompany me now that she knew why I needed to return, but would Brigantino let the two of us go without also wanting to accompany us?

"It will have to be," I said.

To my surprise, she didn't argue or insist it too dangerous. She didn't demand to come with me for my protection or try to convince me I should tell Brigantino so he could offer protection.

She simply nodded and said, "Go."

"And you…"

She fixed her gaze to the tent, where Brigantino sat in the shade, keeping sullen watch over Niles, though there was nowhere for Niles to go even if he still wished to leave our company. Alesh spoke quietly with Niles, though what *they* might converse about, I couldn't begin to guess. It didn't matter. If Ywelo could distract Brigantino, I had my opportunity.

"I suddenly feel the need to have a long, overdue conversation with a boar," she said, standing.

I smiled. "Good luck."

She gave a reluctant laugh. "*He* should hope for good luck. I've held my tongue too long. There is much to say, I fear."

If our travel-weary crew had set up camp farther from town, I might not have ventured back to the apothecary on my own. I might have instead asked for Ywelo to accompany me, but we were just on the edge of the town, the camp in sight for a good portion of my trip back to the shop.

Since Quinn tended to spend half the night on watch in our camps and we were at last in one place for more than a few passing minutes, he dozed in the makeshift tent beneath a small copse of wide palm trees with large fronds that offered at least some shady relief from the sun.

If there was one lesson I had learned since coming to the Konaho, it was that travel when the sun was at its highest was *not* recommended. If we couldn't find shade, we made our own, waiting out the harshest of the sun's rays. Since I didn't have far to travel back through the town, I wasn't worried about the sun high overhead.

It took me less than fifteen minutes to get through the dusty desert town on foot. Given that the town was smaller than Barnham with only one small shopping outlet, it wasn't difficult to find the apothecary again.

I stopped outside the shop, hesitating at the door with its colorful glass panes, then closed my eyes, took a fortifying breath, then swung the door inward, gritting my teeth all the while. As I closed the door behind me again, the colored glass panes projected bursts of gold and cherry and emerald shapes onto the wall, the movement almost dizzying.

The shop was almost clean from the map's earlier destruction, but the dark-haired girl still dragged a broom across the floor in the back corner, small bits of broken glass tinkling with every stroke.

She turned when she heard the door open and a face that was ready to welcome a customer turned angry in half a second.

"No. Out!"

"Please," I said. "I'd like to purchase a few items. I'm a healer."

I wished I could say I was a Healer with a capital H, but I'd lost that distinction when I'd claimed the title of the White Sorceress and left my village behind.

The girl narrowed her eyes at me, no doubt trying to determine if I was worth her time or if I was here to destroy the other half of her shop's inventory. Slowly, she leaned the broom against a wall and made her way to the front counter.

I stepped further into the store and met her at the desk. She was older than I'd thought, maybe my age, a year or two older than that even. With her short hair, smooth, dark skin, and round face, I'd thought her closer to fourteen or fifteen this morning.

"What do you need?" she asked.

I gave her a list of the few essentials I was hoping to find. Some of the items went by names other than what I knew, but between the two of us we managed to figure out what I could use. My hope was to make sure Niles's wound would heal quickly. Alesh may have numbed the pain, but if the muscle and skin didn't heal, the wound remained open to infection.

The shop had no honey salve, but the girl sold me a thick oil with a stringent odor that she promised would keep a wound free of infection. I wondered if it killed germs by the potency of its scent alone. My eyes watered long after she stoppered the little, green bottle.

I paid for my purchases with coin from Irzan's reserve. Since the girl had no change, I told her to keep the remainder and consider it my thanks for her help in finding the right remedies.

Then I worked up my nerve to ask the question I'd really returned to ask.

"The woman I saw with you this morning. Is she here?"

The girl grew wary, her gaze flicking back and forth across my face as though assessing if she'd been tricked into a conversation she didn't want to have.

"Why do you want her?"

"I just want to talk to her. I think…she might be able to help me."

"And what will *you* do for *her*?"

"I—"

I hadn't thought that far, what I must look like to her—a demanding foreigner who was part of the reason her shop had been destroyed, now returned looking for more, more, more. I'd just hoped she might be able to shed light on why she'd looked at me the way she did, how she *knew* the same things I knew.

"You come here, spoil my shop, upset my grandmother, leave me to clean your mess, and then expect me to disturb my grandmother again for your own selfish reasons? Everyone wants her words. Everyone seeks her sight. Always. She gets no rest. So, tell me. Tell me why you are worth her time!"

I blinked. Had she said—

"I…have the sight," I said, the words tumbling from my mouth before I thought about what I was saying.

Why I should blurt such words to someone I'd never met in a place so far from home I couldn't begin to guess. It had taken all my willpower and a whole barrel of trust to confess my ability to Ywelo a short time earlier. Sheer shock at the old woman's ability must have loosened my lips.

The girl narrowed her eyes, not seeming to believe my words.

I tried to explain further. "It's true, I—"

The floral curtain to the back room separated at that

moment, and the old woman hobbled to the counter beside her granddaughter. I felt small beneath the weight of her gaze, her black eyes assessing everything about me. It seemed she could see right to the core of my being.

"You."

Her voice was stronger than I expected of a woman of her age. It was a sure voice, unwavering and certain. One word was all she spoke, but in that word? In that word, was everything that needed to be said.

"Ugo…" The girl's worried eyes spoke of her concern for the woman, and of her love.

The girl put a hand to the woman's arm, and the woman covered the girl's hand with her own and patted it.

Settle down, girl, that pat said. *I know what I'm doing.*

"You saw me," I said quietly. "Before this morning, I mean."

She nodded slowly, her eyes once again seeming to peer into the depths of my soul.

"Did you know?" I asked, my heart racing. "Did you know I saw you, too?"

"Yes," she said with a slow nod.

Adrenaline rushed through my veins and I swallowed, trembling, before I spoke my next words. I gripped the edge of the counter as much to keep myself standing as to have something to do with my hands.

"Will we…will we succeed? In our task, I mean."

I could have sought the answers on my own, but I was a coward. I couldn't handle seeing our failure, seeing all things lost and our entire world doomed. I didn't want the weight of having to decipher my own visions, and…maybe I didn't want to find out if my sight had been corrupted in the same way the talisman no longer worked properly. What kinds of things might I *see* then? What kinds of *false* futures?

The woman looked down a moment as if thinking. She smacked her lips together a few times, then her eyes rolled back in her head, and she swayed on her feet.

I might have worried, but her granddaughter gripped her arm and didn't seem surprised to see the woman fall into such a state. Instead, she supported her and waited for the fit to pass, but I didn't miss the look she gave me, the one that said, *This is your fault.*

When the old woman came to, she was racked by fatigue and allowed the girl to lead her to a small metal stool shoved against the dingy back wall. She sat and slumped into the wall, catching her breath before attempting to speak.

The girl murmured something to her in their language, something not meant for my ears, and I was left feeling guilty for intruding upon this family with my demands at the cost of an old woman's hardship. What right had I?

"Stay with her," the girl said. "I'll be back."

When the girl disappeared through the curtain again, the old woman took my hand. I gave her fingers a light squeeze.

"I'm sorry," I said quietly. "I shouldn't have asked that of you."

"Success, maybe. The cost will be high," she replied. "He will not make it."

I gripped the wall of the doorway to keep myself from swaying. The room spun wildly around me. *He will not make it.*

"Who?" I croaked.

The girl returned with a small cup of water and held it to the woman's lips. The woman took it from her with an annoyed look that said she was still capable of holding a cup with her own hands.

"You go now. She is tired, needs rest. She has done too much. Again."

I wanted to plant my feet on the floor and tell her I wasn't going anywhere until I knew *who* wasn't going to make it. I wanted to dig my heels into the floor until I was told more, but the old woman's strength was fading, heavy eyelids closing on her, though she struggled to keep them open. Was this my future someday?

Do I have *a future?*

Reluctantly, I nodded and packed the items I'd purchased into the pocket of my tunic.

"Thank you," I said to the girl. She helped her grandmother stand again, and the look she gave me didn't believe I could be grateful. Perhaps she didn't hear words of gratitude often. "Truly," I said. "It means more than you know."

Not the herbs and the remedies. Those were helpful, useful, and I was glad I had them. But the knowledge that there was another woman with the sight? *That* was something I would never forget. It was a knowledge I would hold close to my heart for the rest of my life, no matter how long or short. There were others like me.

CHAPTER EIGHTEEN

Another Face
Reina

Eager to use the new remedies on Niles, I hurried to return to camp, but the tent was still out of sight when a little voice came from behind.

"Mama says you're a healer. Are you a healer?"

Alarmed, I spun to see a little girl standing in the road behind me, large dark eyes taking in everything about me from my head to my toes as though trying to memorize me. She was perhaps five or six, and I recalled seeing her earlier that morning in the town. Why had she followed me? What was she doing without her family?

I pushed my suspicions aside. If the child needed help, my first duty was to help, not jump out of my skin just because she'd approached me. I looked up and down the empty street. Who else *would* she ask for help? In the heat of the day, everyone was deep inside their homes or shops.

"Yes, I am a healer. Are you lost, sweetheart? Do you need help?"

I stepped closer and kneeled to get nearer to the little girl, taking in the black curls that had escaped from a beaded clip, curls that framed her flawless bronze skin. She clutched a well-loved cloth doll in one brown fist.

"Are you here to stop the chaos?" she asked.

I sucked in a breath and my heart fluttered softly at the mention of chaos. I met her golden-brown eyes. "Where is your family?" I asked, no longer sure this was an innocent request for help anymore.

"The chaos," she repeated, her bottom lip quivering. "Are you here to stop it?"

"Is there chaos here, little one? Do you need our help?"

I squinted at her, trying to push away the nagging sensation at the base of my scalp, the one that encouraged me to run away as fast as my feet could carry me. This was a *child* and she needed help. Now was not the time to let fear and paranoia creep in.

I reached out a hand and clasped one of her much smaller hands in it, giving a squeeze. The ice-cold fingers in my grasp shocked me. No one should be so cold with the sun blazing overhead. Was she ill? Maybe she needed a healer after all.

"Are you all right?" I asked, peering at her with concern.

She looked at me and gave a toothy grin, displaying several spaces where she'd lost baby teeth and had yet to grow permanent teeth in their place.

"There's chaos," she said again, repeating her earlier sentiment.

Why did a child so young even know the word *chaos*? This was wrong.

She smiled wider.

"You know," she said, her voice deepening into a child's impersonation of an adult's voice.

I turned my head, searching for anyone within earshot, anyone who might also be witnessing the child's odd behavior. Still, there was no one. Only the town and the desert.

"Why do you want to stop the chaos?" she asked, twirling a length of hair around her finger. "Chaos can be *good*, you know."

I jumped up and stepped back.

This was no child. If I lunged for her at that very moment, she would disappear in a puff of purple smoke…just as the first Adan Iyer had done, the one who'd never been Adan at all. I froze, unsure how to respond, how to deal with the child-who-was-not-a-child.

"Ah, you figured it out," she said, following her statement with a high-pitched giggle.

"Figured what out?" I said slowly, taking another step back.

I didn't need to be close enough for Chaos Wielder to grab for the talisman, if that's what he was here for. If I ran now, could I make it back to the camp?

"That I'm not who I seem."

I narrowed my eyes. "Why are you here? What do you want?"

"What do *I* want?" The girl grinned wider and the toothy grin that seemed charming moments ago turned menacing instead. "I think the question you should be asking is what do I *have*."

"Why should I care what you have?"

"Because what *I* have is stronger than what *you* have."

She stared at my tunic almost as if she could see the talisman beneath the fabric. "And," she continued. "Because what I have works."

He knew. The Chaos Wielder somehow knew the talisman's power had gone astray.

"I ask again. What do you want?" I said through gritted teeth.

"I want to have fun."

As if to emphasize the words, the little girl did a turn on her toes, spinning around with her arms extended.

This was madness.

"Why did you come to me posing as my father?"

"I just wanted to see."

"To see what?"

"If you wanted him. If you needed him in your life."

Hot panic shot through my middle, but I refused to let it show.

"What have you done to him?"

She smiled again, then made her eyes round with feigned innocence. "I've done nothing."

I breathed out, forcing a calm I didn't feel onto my features.

"I swear to you, if you harm one hair on his head, I will come for you—"

"And what? You'll come for me and what? You were coming for me anyway. As long as chaos rules, you can do nothing."

My blood boiled at the words, the truth behind them.

"Then what is all this for?!" I yelled, losing control at the little-girl-who-was-not-a-little-girl.

"Fun!"

And then she disappeared in a puff of violet smoke, just as before. Purple coils of dust rose into the air, then dissipated with the wind until I was left staring at the empty air.

Mad. The Chaos Wielder was mad.

Saints save us all.

"I should have known from the beginning," I said once I recounted the tale to the group long after the sun relinquished its grip on the desert and the stars shone clear overhead.

I'd told them about the Chaos Wielder immediately, of course, but eager to be on our way and far away from the town, I hadn't gone into detail.

Alesh stirred the bubbling contents of a metal pot over the small, crackling fire. For as brutally hot as the sun could be during the day, I welcomed the fire's warmth now that darkness had fallen. I shivered.

"Why would a southern child speak the northern tongue so well? Why would she speak it at all? That should have been my first clue."

"You couldn't have known," Brigantino said.

"*You* would have," I replied.

Ywelo raised an eyebrow, but Brigantino just shrugged his shoulders.

"Yes, but you weren't trained to detect such things," Quinn said, a warm hand on my back.

"I should have gone with you," Ywelo said, reprimanding herself. "I should have insisted."

I tilted my head, dropping my shoulders and shooting her a look. "You had an important task," I told her.

"Distracting me," Brigantino said pointedly, looking unamused.

"I do not understand why the Chaos Wielder keeps contacting you," Alesh said. "It does not make sense. He is not gaining any information."

"And he's not issuing demands, either," Brigantino added.

"He's just…taunting," Ywelo added.

"Fun. That's what the little girl said."

One of the nudromedaries grunted as though in disbelief at my words. I glanced into the darkness where they lay in the sandy dirt, some dozing, some lazily chewing cud.

"Off his rocker," Niles mumbled, shifting the book on his lap. I hadn't been sure Niles was even paying attention.

Ywelo issued him a questioning look, her dark brows drawn.

"Crazy," he elaborated, looking up from the book's pages.

"I don't get it," I said. "The interactions. It's like dealing with a child."

Quinn's eyes lit. He held up a finger. "What if we *are* dealing with a child? Or at least someone who has a childlike mentality."

"Do you think…" Brigantino trailed off, his eyes growing distant. He rubbed one hand on his bearded chin. It was a moment before he continued. "I suppose that makes sense."

"You're saying you think the Chaos Wielder is a child?" I said in disbelief. It's not that I didn't trust Quinn. Saints knew his instincts were correct time and again, and they'd often saved our lives, but a child causing destruction on this scale seemed impossible.

"I'm saying it's feasible. Think about the first interaction we had with him. He pretended to be your father. Why? What purpose does that serve?"

"He wanted to gain her trust," Ywelo suggested.

Quinn shook his head. "No, at that time Reina didn't even know Adan Iyer *was* her father. That means the Chaos Wielder knew before she did."

"But why taunt me with the charade of finding family?"

"Because to a child, what's more important than family? What better way to toy with your enemy than to introduce family they didn't know they had?" Quinn turned to face me. "He was measuring you for a response."

I snorted in disgust. "Well, I hope I measured up."

"You're not going to like this, Reina, but since the Chaos Wielder is keeping tabs on you, I think it's important you're not alone."

He was right. I didn't like it.

"And how's that going to change anything?" I asked. "He appeared as Adan in front of all of you anyway. Do you think it will make a difference?"

"Maybe we should make a plan for the next time he appears," Alesh suggested. "Questions we can ask, something… If we must put up with his presence, we can try to make some good of it, yes?"

Brigantino nodded thoughtfully. "We should come up with a script, each of us. That way we'll have a list of questions to ask to lead him into giving something away. We're heading into this fight blind, which is not a position I enjoy being in. The more we can uncover before we reach him, the better."

"You don't think he's going to cooperate, do you?" I asked.

"Not a chance," Quinn said. "But if we ask *enough* questions, perhaps we'll learn at least a few of the answers."

"All right," I said. "Where do we start?"

CHAPTER NINETEEN

Sea Legs
Reina

Kufataba was farther away than it looked, not just by land, but also by sea. As we boarded the vessel that would take us across the Retryant Sea to the base of Kufataba, I stepped onto the gently bobbing ship with its great, pointed bow and giant, white sails.

"Spectacular," I breathed, and, oh, it was.

The sea here smelled different from the ocean back home. I'd grown up with a tangy brine hanging on the air in Barnham, but here the water smelled lighter somehow. The sea breeze seemed fresh by comparison. Or perhaps so many days in the desert had changed my sense of smell.

Regardless, I closed my eyes, inhaled deeply, and let the gentle wind caress my face and ruffle loose strands of my hair. With the sun shining behind closed eyelids and the breeze on my skin, I could almost, *almost* relax my shoulders.

"I hate boats," Ywelo mumbled, trailing behind me.

"I'll take a boat to a bridge any day," Niles said, following.

The journey would take half a day, just as Brigantino said, so I found a spot at the smooth, wooden rail and watched while the crew finished loading their boxes and crates, tallied the fare we owed for tagging along, then cast off into the clear blue waters. The way they worked together so effortlessly— almost wordlessly—with ropes and oars and sails was nothing short of remarkable.

They did this every day and so to them operating a ship might seem mundane, but to me, this routine, this ritual, was nothing short of a miracle. Within moments, the wind caught the sails and we sliced through the calm water with no effort at all. It was amazing and exhilarating and had I known such a sensation existed, I might have found myself a sailing vessel much sooner.

The water below us was a hue that almost matched the talisman, a sparkling aqua that changed from one moment to the next as it reflected the cloudless sky above. The water twinkled with the sun's rays and, were it not for our immense task, I might have closed my eyes and enjoyed the moment.

"Good day to sail." Quinn leaned on the railing beside me.

In response, I lay my head against his shoulder.

"Y'er quiet."

"Am I?"

He nodded and kissed the top of my head in response. I let my gaze travel to the hazy land in the distance, and the mountain we would soon be exploring in order to get to the Elorin Empire, where the Map to Balance had shown the Chaos Wielder to reside. At least, it was where he currently resided. There was no telling where he might decide to move in the time between when we'd opened the map and when we would set foot in on Elorin lands.

"How long 'til the eclipse?" I asked.

"Seven weeks, two days."

I bit my lip. I'd hoped my calculations were wrong. They weren't.

Seven weeks seemed like so much time…until I thought about traveling half a continent on foot. We'd exchanged the nudromedaries for coin and supplies at the port town in part because the ship's captain refused to take them and in part because we hoped to purchase new animals once we crossed the Retryant Sea.

Regardless, Brigantino had already said there'd be no taking animals with us through Kufataba, which meant we'd be walking. A lot.

"Will we make it in time?" I glanced up at him, searching his eyes for some sign of the hope I didn't feel.

"We will."

I gave a half-laugh, and his eyebrows raised.

"Is it funny?"

"You're always so certain. How? Do they teach that in the Order?"

He gave me a dubious glance. "They teach a lot of things in the Order. Second-guessing isn't one of them. If you plan to get yourself in a life-or-death situation, you'd best be sure you know what you want the outcome to be and how you're going to make it happen. If not, you're as good as dead."

"That is *not* an optimistic outlook," I replied.

He shrugged.

"But the Order isn't exactly optimistic, is it?"

"You're right. In many ways, it wasn't. But the Order is

in the past now. For me, and for all."

"We haven't discussed that," I said. "How you feel about it, I mean."

Quinn gave a strangled laugh. "No, we haven't. Nor will we."

"I think it would help, you know. You're not alone anymore. You're not a"—I bit my lip, hesitating to say the word— "ghost, anymore."

Quinn turned to face me, somber eyes on a solemn face. He rested his hands on my shoulders as if words alone weren't enough to convey his feelings.

"Reina, it doesn't matter what was done in the past," he said. "Right or wrong, the past is done. What matters now is the future. We cannot lose focus."

"Fine, but at some point, you're going to have to come to terms with your past."

A *hmph* from him was all the response I got. Typical.

I reached on tiptoe and kissed him anyway.

At the sound of Ywelo retching over the side of the railing into the glassy surface of the water below, I peeked over Quinn's shoulder. I'd never been on a ship before and seasickness concerned me, but since we'd pulled out of port, I felt nothing but appreciation for the sea and the wind.

I still wished for my medicine bag. Ywelo could have used both the gingerene powder and the briarmint candies. Then again, if I'd predicted seasickness during this trip, I could have added to my list of items purchased at the apothecary. Maybe I should stop being terrified of what I might *see* and allow the visions to come. And yet...

The old woman's words rang in my ears, striking fear in my heart.

He will not make it.

Brigantino rubbed Ywelo's back softly, displaying a tenderness I'd never seen in him. Interesting…the first sign I'd seen from him that there might still be feelings in return.

I nudged Quinn's arm and gestured with my head.

"Guess there's a reason she hates boats," he said, missing the point completely.

"That's *not* what I was pointing out," I said quietly.

"I know very well what you were getting at. Give them a moment to themselves, aye?"

"Ah…I could be wrong, but I don't think vomiting the contents of one's stomach over the side of a boat has ever led to anything romantic."

"I've seen more of that in taverns than you can imagine," he replied.

Alesh took a place at the railing on the other side of Quinn. They settled into a conversation, so I took time to walk the ship's wide deck, admiring the well-worn, but well-maintained wooden surface. A strong breeze sent my gaze skyward again and I inhaled deeply. No trace of death or decay, of dingy streets, or sunbaked bodies.

"Enjoy it while it lasts."

To my right, Niles sat perched on the deck, leaning against a large crate, the book of poetry open on his lap once again.

"I don't suppose it can last, can it?"

He shrugged. "Given that chaos seems to follow us

everywhere, and that the Chaos Wielder is rather hellbent on getting your talisman, I'd say we're probably in for another hiccup soon. I wouldn't be surprised if he whipped up a storm."

Alarmed, I looked again to the cloudless sky.

"Thank you, by the way."

Words of gratitude? From Niles?

"For what?"

I slid down the side of the crate to sit beside him.

"For the tip about the sweet angel fern."

I'd forgotten.

"It's helped," he said. "A lot. I think I'm past the worst of it now. I owe you."

I waved a hand at him even though part of me wanted to remind him he owed me for a lot more than helping him overcome the hardest part of his addiction. I was almost too tired to think on how different our situation was just a few months ago, what he'd done to me—to the Resistance, and how much I hated him.

Anger was funny like that, though. It fizzled after a while. I never seemed to be able to remain angry for long. Even when it was warranted.

"What great ponderings are you reading now?" I asked, pointing to the book. Easier to change the subject than talk about his addiction.

"Musings about addiction," he answered.

So much for changing the subject.

"Light reading," I commented.

"What does a man become, if not the very demons he

consumes, when he allows the spirits to own him?" he read. "What actions does he take, what falsehoods does he make, when he gives himself over to the de'il himself?"

I swallowed and bit my bottom lip.

"I did a lot of stupid things, Moreina. And I'm sorry for them."

"The past is past," I said, echoing my earlier conversation with Quinn. "I don't want to think about it."

"Not just to you," he continued against my plea. "I did stupid things—horrible things—to others. Things I don't think I can ever find forgiveness for. I spent years drowning my past in tankards of pine ale…then concealing it from everyone around me. Innocent people died. Because of me. And nothing I ever do will change that. And the times I was sober, did I behave any better? No! I turned you in to Bruenner."

I wanted to throw my hands over my ears, to drown him out with humming or singing, to mute the words coming from his mouth. It was easier to think of Niles as a monster who did evil things purposely than a man who'd made one very big mistake that led to a few dozen more.

"What do you want from me, Niles?" I asked. "I can't offer you the forgiveness you seek. Not for the…things you've done. You want to change? Now's your chance."

"I don't ask forgiveness. I mean, I *am* sorry for things I've done—the things I *did* to you. I could have ruined everything for everyone. I could have been the reason you were killed. I'm sorry. I'm sorry for who I was and for what I did. But I'm also sorry for what I didn't do. I'm sorry I didn't believe in you. I'm sorry I let my fear of the future control my head. If you can forgive me those things, that's all I can ask." He held up a hand and continued, "And before you answer, allow me to say that it's all right if you don't forgive me. I don't know if *I* could in your position. I'll make peace someday either way. I vow it."

I closed my eyes and issued a long sigh.

"You're very persistent," I said.

He gave something that could have been a laugh.

"When you've nothing to lose, you find persistence is a much easier stance to take."

I let a long moment of silence pass before speaking again. Softly, I said, "I will forgive you, Niles. Maybe not today, maybe not yet, but I will."

He breathed a sigh of what I assumed was relief and leaned his head back against the crate with a thump.

"Just…show me," I said. "Show me you've changed. That's what I ask in return."

He nodded solemnly, finally giving me the peace I wanted. Thank the Saints.

Halfway across the open sea, still three hours from shore, a storm turned our world upside down. Swirling clouds appeared as if by magic from the midst of the bright, clear sky, and the glassy water whipped into a frenzied chop, tossing the ship first one way, then the other.

The storm was anything but natural and I couldn't help

but think of Niles's words a few hours before. I stalked to where he stood on the deck, a cold, heavy rain battering our faces and clothing.

"Did you do it again?" I accused. "Did you work with the enemy?"

Raindrops fell from his lashes, and blue eyes darkened by the clouds widened with surprise. "You think I'd arrange a storm in the middle of the sea?!"

"You said as much earlier, Niles! You said you wouldn't be surprised. Are you working with the Chaos Wielder? Did you plan this?" The accusations flew from my lips. All his words, all his apologies from earlier dissolved into meaningless drivel in my mind.

He'd done it before. He'd nearly gotten us all killed during a mountain crossing less than a year earlier. Why would I think he could change just because he had a moment of repentance?

"Are you out of your mind?" he cried. "After everything I said before? You know—" He paused, taking a deep breath, gripping one of the railings tight enough to turn his knuckles white. The boat rose on another wave and I gripped the railing as well. "Never mind."

"What?" I demanded.

"It…serves me right. After everything, why *shouldn't* I expect to be blamed for something like this?"

I stared hard at him. Water streamed down his face, dripping from his nose and chin, but his gaze never wavered from mine. My shouting had caught Quinn and Brigantino's attention and both looked as though they needed only my approval to toss Niles into the churning sea below.

Instead, I shook my head, cold drops falling from my hair onto my soaked shoulders with the movement.

"Leave him be," I said. Trying to get my mind off of Niles's strange prediction—and hoping it *was* a coincidence—I asked, "What can we do to help the crew?"

"Nothing," Quinn replied. "Stay out of their way. Take hold of something solid and hope the crew is experienced enough to ride out the storm…or we'll all be swimming the rest of the way."

CHAPTER TWENTY

Another Ocean
Quinn

They said the storm was coming. I didn't see how they could know, but since they were experienced seamen and I was not…well, I believed them.

The sea was a creature I hadn't expected—calm and yielding one moment, angry and unforgiving the next. I knew from Barnham's coast that she could be both of these things, but I didn't realize how quickly her temper could change out on the open ocean.

Another towering wave exploded over the bow as the ship plunged into it, sending pieces of the sea raining down from above, drenching us all in salted icy droplets. Most of the sails had been pulled, but those stern-side still flew, their white folds billowed out like the tents Reina and I used to make from bedsheets as children.

The thought shook me. I hadn't thought of Reina in months. I thought…I might be free of whatever hold she had on me. After I'd committed to the Order, I tried to let her fade from my memories entirely.

Strange that now, in the midst of a sky-splitting storm, she would come to mind, and not just that she would come to mind, but that I would choose some of the fondest memories we'd once made.

Did she think of me?

The ship shuddered. I gritted my teeth and held to the ropes as we topped another wave and fell into the trough below, sending my insides for a ride again. The motion didn't bother me. The memories did.

"Are y'all right?" the quartermaster yelled from his position across the ship.

On a normal day, you could whisper, and the sound would carry far and wide. In this storm, I could hardly hear him and he was six feet away and shouting.

I nodded, not that he could see me.

Was I all right? Since graduating from the Order, since giving up any hope of returning to a life in Barnham, was anything right at all?

The ship cracked against the bottom of another trough, sending the bones in my body clacking together. It was fine. My body had taken worse. The Order had made sure it could. But could the ship *withstand such a beating again and again?*

And in the midst of it all, it was the internal beating that did me in, the sudden memory of the way Reina smelled, a mix of soap and herbs and oils—a floral scent that infused into her thick hair, into the palms of her hands, and into my very brain.

How? How could I smell such a thing here and now, in the middle of the ocean, battling to stand upright on a ship that couldn't seem to decide which way was up?

We crested another wave, and I tucked my head into my arm, clutching the ropes, my feet sliding out from beneath me again. I'd received word the Order had need of an agent in Barnham right before I set foot on the ship. Barnham, of all places.

Did I want the job? *they'd asked.*

And did I?

Blazes, no. I wanted to get as far from Barnham as possible. It was why I hadn't returned home since I left for training, other than to tell my father to withdraw my offer to be paired with Reina for her Choosing.

It wasn't like I was being given a choice with regards to my post, though. The Order hadn't actually *asked if I wanted the job. Not really.*

And yet, I'd stepped on the ship anyway, even knowing they were awaiting my response. I'd gone where they couldn't reach me for a month, where I could be free for just four weeks—free of orders, of commands, of pretending to be someone I wasn't, of watching and waiting, of being the good son, the good agent, everything I was asked to be.

One month of blessed freedom before the next job.

Another wave crested the port side of the ship, slapping me in the face and stealing my breath away.

Good. A slap in the face. I needed it.

I'd follow my orders and go to Barnham. It was where I was headed anyway, no matter how many times I denied it to myself.

It was time.

Hours later, when the wind began to slow its howl, the

waves exhausted their anger, and the sky lightened to reveal the most vibrant sunset I'd ever seen, I collapsed on the deck. I sprawled out on the sodden wood, the ship tossing side to side in the chop, and I stared upwards at a sky turning hues of gold and scarlet.

The crew laughed.

"Greenhorn! You still with us?"

"Made it through yer first squall, eh?"

"Did ya faint, big guy?"

"No vomit. That's a plus."

One of the mates offered me a hand off the deck. I took it and pulled myself to my feet. It would be days before the waves would calm, but maybe years before my heart could.

I grasped the smooth, worn railing of the ship, staring at the setting sun and the violet and indigo clouds clustered above it.

I had survived the Order's training, the sea's violence, and at least a dozen attempts on my life in the last year.

Would the assignment in Barnham be it? Would it be the job that finally killed me?

"I'm going home," I said, mind made.

The laughter around me went on and on, but I heard only Reina's voice in my ears, saw only Reina's face in my mind. I'd hidden my feelings from her for so long. I could do it again. I could bury the feelings deep inside. I could hide them deep within, where even I couldn't think to find them.

She doesn't want you, you ass.

I hoped she was married. It might be easier that way. If I returned and she was married and settled and happy, well, then I could focus on the next mission, on whatever the Order wanted me for in Barnham.

At least my parents were there. At least I'd have a decent place to sleep each night and hot meals I didn't have to lay out coin for. The Order paid well, but living on the road meant spending a good portion of my earnings each and every month. In Barnham, I'd be surrounded by familiar faces, people I'd known almost since I was born. My life could never return to what I'd once known, it was true, but maybe...maybe I could learn to breathe in Barnham. At least, for a little while.

I was going home.

CHAPTER TWENTY-ONE

The Vow
Reina

As the boat rocked violently downward again, my feet slid.

"Find a place and hold tight, Reina. Stay with Ingram," Quinn said with a nod. He and Brigantino turned their backs to me.

"Where are you going?" I asked.

"To get Alesh and Ywelo. We stay together. Saints only know how much easier this gets for the Chaos Wielder if we're separated."

The ship rocked again as though tempted by his words. I gripped a nearby rope and held on as we were tossed sideways. If my heart hadn't already been racing and my stomach in my throat, I might have worried about getting sick, but right now I was too terrified to care.

"Are you enjoying the ride?"

I turned to face a man behind me, confused for a moment in thinking it was Niles who had spoken. I couldn't fathom why Niles might tease at a time like this, especially when I'd just accused him of working with the Chaos Wielder to arrange the storm.

Through the rain and the sea spray, a shipmate stood atop

the rail of the main deck, precariously balanced like the most experienced of dancers, leaning one way and then the other as the ship moved through the water.

When I didn't answer his question, he smiled and asked again.

"I said, are you enjoying the ride?"

I shivered and gripped the rope tighter with both hands to keep from sliding across the deck.

"Not particularly," I told him, shaking the water from my eyes to no avail. I wiped my face with a wet hand.

"That's not…one of the ship's mates," Niles said, his voice low in my ear. "Something's wrong."

The man was a shipmate. I'd seen him loading barrels and crates when we boarded, but Niles…was correct. Something about the man wasn't quite right for even an experienced seaman shouldn't have been standing on a railing in the midst of a violent, unnatural storm.

"I'm offended you don't like my gift!" he said. "Storms are great fun."

With that he hopped from his feet to his hands, holding the wet rail, balancing his legs in the air overhead, despite the driving rain and rocking ship. I gasped, my heart leaping into my throat.

"Who are you?" Niles asked, narrowing his eyes at the shipmate-turned-acrobat. I didn't need to ask the question. Only one person would *gift* us with a storm and refer to it as great fun. Still, I had to give Niles credit. At least he had remembered to ask questions of the Chaos Wielder. Still holding a rope to keep himself steady, Niles took a step forward, shielding me as if to protect me.

The man flipped through the air, landing on his feet once more, this time on the deck of the ship instead of the rail. I gave a small sigh of relief even knowing it was the Chaos Wielder and that he could disappear in a puff of purple smoke at any time if he wanted to.

"Who *am* I? What a ridiculous question! I've already spoken to *her* a few times now. I bet she knows."

I swallowed. Niles looked to me for clarification, and I nodded. I stepped out from behind him, the pouring rain making it difficult to see much of anything beyond the sheer gray wall of wet. Where were Quinn and the others?

I narrowed my eyes at the man. "You're the Chaos Wielder."

He smiled, revealing a mouthful of crooked teeth, and clapped like a child. "Yes! I *knew* you knew!"

"I ask again. What do you want?" I said.

"I told you last time. I want to have fun!"

"And what's your idea of fun?" I asked. The ship tipped forward again, and I held to the rope to balance myself.

"I should think that's obvious!"

"Chaos," Niles said with a shake of his head.

"Of course!"

"And what will you do when the whole world is chaos?" I asked.

He laughed, throwing his head back, the dark, wet hair on his head flinging backwards with the motion. Delight shone on his rounded, half-bearded cheeks in a childlike way.

"Dance in it," he replied, grinning.

"Won't you be lonely?" I asked.

"Never! I'll have *you*."

I stumbled half a step backwards before I pulled myself together enough to reply.

"Me? Does the fact that I'm trying to *stop* the world from succumbing to chaos not bother you?"

"It does, but you won't succeed, so I'm not worried."

He followed his sentence with a perfect cartwheel on the rolling ship, unconcerned with the rocking below us. A man this size should not be able to do such things. I narrowed my eyes as though doing so might help me see who was beneath the sailor's exterior.

"Do you think I'd make a very good companion?" I asked. "Seeing as I'm trying to stop you and all."

He grinned again. "Once you and the *other* arrive, we'll have all we need here. We're the same, you and me. You don't see it yet, but we are."

"What do you want from me?" I asked, becoming exasperated with half-answers and roundabout logic. "If you know we're to meet soon anyway, why all this?" I beckoned to the surging storm around us. Lightning flashed dangerously close to the ship and I blinked against the brightness.

The shipmate took a rope in one hand, held it tight, and twirled around it before answering, "Because this part is fun." He stopped and stood upright as though a thought had just occurred to him. "Of course, if you don't think it's fun, we could make a deal and I could end *all* of this right now."

I wiped futilely at the rain streaming down my face, contemplating his words. Quinn would scold me for even thinking on it. Quinn would tell me to cover my ears, close my mouth, and walk away.

But Quinn wasn't here.

"What kind of deal?" I asked.

"What are you thinking?" Niles hissed in my ear. "D'Arturio will kill you."

Placing a hand to his chest, I pushed him back, ignoring his words.

The man had stopped his playful antics and looked to be pondering an offer. I gripped the rope harder when the ship swung backwards and tilted dangerously on a wave, but still the sailor didn't budge from where his feet were planted on the wooden planks of the ship's deck. I had no doubt he was an apparition who would dissolve in purple smoke before succumbing to the sea in any way.

"Offer me the necklace."

My hand flew to where the talisman was tucked beneath my drenched tunic, my pulse thrumming in my veins.

"I-I can't," I said finally.

He closed his eyes as though bored and shrugged. Before I could make a counteroffer, the atmosphere hummed, the hair on my arms stood on end, and a strange charge permeated the air.

"Wait—" I cried all too late.

White hot lightning split the sky, crashing into the ship's tallest mast, ripping it in two amidst a shower of sparks and flame. The wood splintered, and part of the mast came crashing to the deck just as Brigantino and Ywelo crossed below the sails.

Eyes wide, I screamed in warning, but I couldn't stop the falling mast or warn my friends fast enough. With a warrior's instinct, Ywelo hurled her body across Brigantino, pushing him from the path of the falling wood. The two tumbled to the deck of the ship at the same time it rose on the very next wave to meet them. With the driving rain, the fire on the tattered sails hanging above burned out quickly, but the damage was done.

Not to the ship.

I couldn't have cared less about the ship. I let go of the rope to go to Brigantino's side, but Niles grabbed my arm. Ywelo was already there, still with him. He'd been spared the worst of it, but even from here, I could see that a large, splintered piece of wood from the mast had been driven through his shoulder like a spear. A dark stain spread across his tunic. Any lower and it would have hit his heart.

I turned on the Chaos Wielder, racing to the railing beside him.

"Is *that* how you negotiate?" I growled.

"No," he said with a malicious grin. "It's how I get my way. When next we meet, offer me the necklace."

"I—"

"Ah-ah." He held up a finger. "I would think very carefully about your next words…about how many people are on this ship, and just how many of them you care for. I would *hate* to see you lose them *all* in a terrible storm."

I paused, my mind racing for some way out of promising something I couldn't give. Niles was good with manipulating words. He was a master. What would he say?

"Don't do it," Niles said in a hoarse whisper. "Don't. He won't let us live anyway."

"I'm *waiting*."

The Chaos Wielder seemed angry now, impatient with my stalling, his hands on his hips, legs splayed wide.

"Yes," I said, closing my eyes in pain. "I will offer you my necklace."

With a snap of his fingers, the rain began to fall *upwards,* and the clouds dissipated, curling in on themselves until nothing was left but azure sky and a blazing white sun high above. The water below still churned, slapping at the sides of the ship, reluctant to calm so quickly, but like a dog to its master the wind died instantly at his command. After hours of the rain and thunder, the sudden absence of sound was near deafening.

The Chaos Wielder-turned-sailor stepped forward. I refused to back away. Not this time. I wouldn't give him the satisfaction. Then he placed a hand to my chest, directly over my heart, and the skin beneath my tunic burned as though I'd been branded. I *jumped* backwards, checking myself for flames, and putting a hand where he'd marked me. The wet fabric of my tunic remained untouched, but the skin beneath burned with a mark I dared not examine right now.

Horrified, my head snapped upward, my gaze meeting his. The Chaos Wielder grinned, climbed on the rail again, and did one final twirl.

"Excellent," he said.

And then he stepped over the railing and into the water below.

I stood rooted to the deck in confusion. Where was the purple smoke? Where was the disappearing act? I looked to Niles, but he held no answers.

Oh.

Oh, no. *Please, don't let it be true.*

The Chaos Wielder had inhabited the sailor's body—his true body. He hadn't just taken the man's likeness. He'd *killed* him! That's why there was no disappearing act.

"No!"

I raced back to the railing, but there was no sign of the possessed shipmate in the water below. The merciless water had swallowed him. Why…why hadn't the Chaos Wielder disappeared in clouds of purple smoke as before? *Why* possess and kill the sailor?

But I knew the answer.

It was a warning. To me.

"Moreina," Niles said. "What did you do?"

I swallowed the lump in my throat.

"I…saved us all from the same fate as that sailor."

The ship still thrashed wildly in the water, but without the rain pouring from the sky above, it was easier to walk without sliding across the deck. Unfortunately, that meant Quinn was headed straight for me.

I grabbed Niles's arm, my nails digging into his skin.

"Not one word," I warned him through gritted teeth. "You tell him *nothing*."

Niles put his hands up defensively, fingers splayed in the air, and I let go.

"I wouldn't *dream* of it."

The ship bucked and I lost my balance, sliding into Quinn as he arrived at my side. I braced my hands against his chest, and he wrapped solid arms around my waist. It would have been a comforting embrace if not for the glower on his face and the unseen brand burning my chest.

"The Chaos Wielder took the life of that shipmate," I said, my voice unsteady. "Is Brigantino all right?"

Quinn turned back to look where Brigantino lay, Ywelo hovering and Alesh already working his magic to ease the pain.

"He will be." He turned back to me.

"Quinn," I said, trying to change the subject so as not to have to answer questions about what just occurred. I'd examine the brand later, alone, behind a locked door. "I think…I think the Chaos Wielder *is* a child."

CHAPTER TWENTY-TWO

The Mountain's Secrets
Quinn

As Alesh worked on Brigantino's wound and Reina offered guidance, I found myself lingering nearby and inspecting their progress nearly as often as Ywelo did. It wasn't that I felt I could be useful, but Brigantino had become a trusted companion and, besides Reina, he was perhaps the closest thing I had to a friend.

I had to remind myself Brigantino had been through worse. Thirty-five years in the Order? He *had* to have gone through worse. He would be all right.

He would.

The crew had brought the damaged ship into the port of Aberly at the base of Kufataba as we'd agreed upon, and we'd gotten a room at the closest inn so Brigantino could be cared for before moving on. With fatigue plaguing us after the seafaring journey, a night off was well warranted, eclipse be damned. Everyone needed a break.

I studied the grain of the wood in the floors and the walls, the coarse fabric sheets on the bed that were now stained with Brigantino's blood, and the lone painting of a ship sailing on what now seemed a deceivingly peaceful Retryant Sea.

The room might have been pleasant shelter for any worldly traveler to stay. For now, it was a depressing makeshift hospital with few physicians and even fewer supplies.

The healing process was taking longer than it should, not that I'd been present when Alesh had deadened Niles's pain in Ndoyo. I didn't know what the process entailed, but Brigantino's wound should have been better in the half-hour Reina and Alesh spent with their heads bent over him. And yet, it seemed nothing had changed.

Ywelo urged us to get a local healer, but between Alesh and Reina, Brigantino was already in the best of hands. At least, I thought so…until they began working on him in earnest. The howls of pain ripping from Brigantino's throat were almost inhuman. He'd been through the same training I had, the same kinds of torture, the same kinds of pain. This should have been nothing for him.

Ingram's face paled and he put a hand to the wall when Brigantino let out another bellow.

"If you're going to pass out, sit down first," I barked at Ingram.

He had the good sense to listen, though he didn't pass out. Pity.

"You are doing no good!" Ywelo said, hovering over Reina and Alesh. "Something is wrong."

I left Ingram by the wall and joined Reina at Brigantino's side again. His bare chest heaved with the effort of his labored breathing. Bright blood pooled at the wound in his shoulder again, and Ywelo wiped it with a cloth, leaving ruddy, crimson streaks across his skin.

"What's going on?" I asked.

Alesh regarded me, dark eyes filled with concern. He shook his head.

"It is not working as it should. The magic does not want to do as I ask."

Fiermi.

"You said you had more control because you had experience with your gift. You had training," I said.

He worried his hands, then threw his head into them.

"I *have* the experience. The magic is broken," he said, his accent more pronounced in his panic.

On the bed, Brigantino gasped for breath, body rigid, back arched. Ywelo pressed a cloth to his shoulder to slow the bleeding. She clamped her hands to his body as though she could seal the wound through sheer will alone.

"Shh," Reina said. She picked up one of Brigantino's hands. "Still now."

I wouldn't have pulled the splintered wood from his body if I'd known they couldn't staunch the blood flow.

"Do *something*," I growled. "He's going to bleed out if you don't."

"That's the problem! I'm making it worse. Where I tell it to stop, the blood flows freely, and in greater amounts. Where I tell it to deaden, he feels greater pain," Alesh said.

I swallowed and closed my eyes. I'd seen too many agents die in the last three years. Too many. Brigantino couldn't. Not from something as simple as a puncture to the shoulder. Not after all he'd already been through.

"Alesh," Reina said softly, taking a hesitant breath before

continuing. "What if…what if we tried working together? If the power of death isn't working for you, you're increasing the life, increasing the blood flow to the area, which is why it's bleeding worse."

"How can you know this?" he asked.

She gave him the look, the one I knew so well, the one that more or less screamed *Are you really questioning me on this?*

Instead, she just said, "Trust me."

"She was a healer even before she wore the talisman," I said aloud even though I wondered if they were gambling with Brigantino's life.

Alesh nodded. "We do this."

But Ywelo intervened, holding up one dark hand, slick and red with Brigantino's blood. She kept the other on the wound.

"No," she said, eyes flashing. "No more."

"But I think—"

"No!"

A heavy silence filled the room.

"The bleeding has slowed," she said finally.

She lifted the cloth to reposition it, showing that the blood had stopped gushing. Brigantino's breathing was less labored, and he seemed to be in less pain than moments ago.

If Reina was right, Alesh made things worse by trying to work his magic and that's why the blood refused to clot and Brigantino was in such pain. But he'd already lost so much blood. Trying again could kill him.

I nodded once slowly, agreeing with Ywelo.

"Leave him be," I said, praying it was the right decision.

"He's lost a lot of blood," Reina warned.

I tried to fight against irrational anger, my hand curling to a fist at my side. She meant well. She wanted the best for him.

But I wasn't willing to risk a man's life by playing with talismans. Not another agent.

"Leave him be," I repeated slowly.

"But I—" Reina began.

I interrupted. "I'll watch over him," I said. "Go to the tavern and get something for dinner."

"I will stay," Ywelo challenged fiercely.

I closed my eyes for a moment, then nodded.

"Yes, fine. The rest of you, go."

I tried to ignore the hurt on Reina's face, the pain of my dismissal. I'd discharged her just as I would have any member of the court, any of my citizens, or any of the castle's servants.

I put a hand to my forehead and rubbed as she, Ingram, and Alesh filed out the door.

Dammit all. I'd need a hell of an apology later.

Brigantino's color had barely improved, and his breathing was still shallow, but Ywelo was right. The bleeding had stopped. I hoped it had stopped on the inside, too, and that there was no deadly pooling of blood somewhere deep within, hidden from view.

Ywelo didn't leave his side except to wash her hands in the basin of water on the side table. Once she dried her hands, she returned to her bedside watch. The warrior was fierce even in love.

"He would have died without you," I said to her. "If you hadn't been there to push him from the mast when it fell, I mean."

Reluctant to meet my eyes, Ywelo kept her gaze trained on Brigantino's face, his hand wrapped in hers, and answered me with a shrug.

Ywelo was younger than Brigantino, perhaps by a decade, but she was easily twice my age. It wasn't Eliza whom Brigantino had left behind after all. It was Ywelo.

It fit. Both Ywelo and Brigantino were hard-headed warriors who would rather die than admit their feelings out loud, who would rather love and live without than abandon their duties—Brigantino as an agent, Ywelo as a Jyngabé rider.

Brigantino moaned and stirred, opening his eyes for the first time since Alesh had tried to relieve him of the bleeding and pain.

His eyes found Ywelo first and he closed them again, squeezing her hand with his own and wincing in pain. When he next opened his eyes a few minutes later, he took in the room before his gaze landed on me. He nodded.

I poured him a glass of water from the pitcher on the sideboard and offered it once he sat up a few inches. He took the glass with his uninjured arm and sipped, coughing as the liquid soothed vocal cords parched from his earlier screams of pain.

When he handed the glass back to me, he gave what could have been a small chuckle.

"The king serving his captain. That's rich," he croaked.

"Brother serving brother," I corrected him. "Nothing more."

One agent would always care for another, even if there was no longer an Order of the Southern Cross. Captain Brigantino would always be Agent Brigantino first, just as I would always be Agent D'Arturio to him…or at least, I hoped I would.

I didn't wait to spring my next words on him. It was better he knew.

"We're leaving you here." I met Ywelo's surprised eyes. "You, too," I added. "He can't be alone."

"No." Brigantino fought to sit up further. "Absolutely not. I go where my king goes. I serve and protect. That's my job. Don't take that from me." Leaning too hard on his injured shoulder, he winced again

"And what a protector you'll be," I mused. "Injured and half your blood gone."

He fixed me with a glare that might have once been intimidating.

"I will tend to him," Ywelo said, her voice thick with emotion. She turned to Brigantino. "*You,*" she said. "This mission is complete so far as you are concerned. Your only command now is to heal."

"You're not my king," Brigantino mumbled.

"But I am. Your only command now is to heal." I parroted

Ywelo's words.

"There are things you don't know about Kufataba," Brigantino replied. "Important things."

"Whatever it is, I'm sure we'll handle it. I had the same training you did, Captain. Need I remind you?"

"It's not…about the training."

I sighed and put a hand to my temple, rubbing at the pain that had taken permanent residence there.

"Let's hear it."

"Beneath the mountain lies magic," he began. "Deep magic. Magic far more than I ever could have believed to exist. Beneath that mountain, there's a forest of unimaginable beauty, but also unimaginable challenges."

"There's a…forest beneath the mountain?" I said, drawing my face into a scowl Reina would have scolded me for.

"It sounds impossible, I know."

It did sound impossible, but I'd seen so many impossible things over the last several months. How could I discount one more?

"All right," I said, taking a breath and partitioning my mind again. Worries in one section, locked away. A plan for action in another section. *Focus on the plan.* "How do we manage to make it past the unimaginable challenges without succumbing to death, which is surely what you imply waits for us?"

"Not just death," Brigantino said, grabbing my sleeve and trying to convey the gravity of his words. "There are three challenges you must pass to get through the forest beneath the mountain."

Naturally. Why could nothing ever be a simple path? Why was there always something more? At what point would life stop handing out prophecies about death and chaos and give up on sending us on perilous errands one after the next?

"Let's have it."

Brigantino winced again, shifting in the bed.

"You make him talk too much." Ywelo fussed with the bedsheets, pulling them up over the various scars across the skin of his chest. "He is tired. He needs to rest."

Brigantino shook his head.

"I'm fine, you overprotective nanny."

"You need a nanny," she responded sharply. "Fifty-six years old and you will die before fifty-seven!"

He ignored her and continued speaking, but I kept a close eye on how his face paled when thinking about the horrors beneath Kufataba.

"I wish I could tell you what challenges await, but their nature changes with every crossing. The mountain makes demands that are nearly impossible to fulfill, and once you enter, there is no leaving without the sacrifices asked. Turning back is not an option."

I considered his words carefully. Turning back wasn't an option for us anyway. If we'd had the time, I would have taken a much longer route and avoided Kufataba entirely. But we didn't have that luxury.

"I'm serious, D'Arturio. I didn't plan on telling you since I assumed I'd be going with you and that I could *be* at least one of the sacrifices if need be."

Ywelo snapped her head up. "You stubborn goat. We get a second chance and you throw it away?"

Her accent grew deeper with her anger. If I had any doubts there was something between them before, Ywelo's words rather confirmed my suspicions.

Brigantino switched to the Jyngabé tongue and spoke too quickly for me to understand, but I caught the gist of his words. *Too important. Life or death. More than my happiness. No future without. Love doesn't change. Love doesn't cower.*

"Should I give you time alone?" I asked, feeling very much an outsider thrown into the midst of a personal conversation.

I'd heard everything as my time spent ghosting as an agent, but hearing personal conversations while staring the speakers in the eye? That was another story. I'd rather let them have time to carry out whatever needed to be said between them.

"No," Brigantino croaked even though Ywelo's eyes said otherwise. "Since we won't be going with you, we'll have plenty to discuss later. I suspect I'll do most of the listening. In the meantime, it's more important you know what you're up against."

I nodded, surmising he was very much right, given the look on Ywelo's face.

"The challenges will force you to reevaluate how badly you need passage and what truly matters to you. They take measure of your priorities and will make you question the very core of your being."

Brigantino had always been a serious man, but I'd never heard him speak this way. A thousand questions flew through my mind. I locked them behind partitions. This wasn't the time.

"Tell me," I said. "Tell me what happened beneath Kufataba. Even if the challenges change, at least I have a measure of what I might expect to sacrifice."

"Our mission was simple. At least it seemed that way. We were to break the magic beneath the mountain, find a way to make the path more accessible. This was…going on thirty years ago. I'd been with the Order long enough to feel confident in myself and the other agents assigned. I was almost ten years in at that point and there were several seasoned agents in the group. I was confident." Brigantino paused, his eyes searching the room, but seeing something long ago and far away. "I was daft."

The minutes dragged on, and Brigantino collected his thoughts. I knew what it was like, the remembering. Brigantino battled the demons inside his head, the ones he'd kept in the dark for so many years. More years than I could even imagine. Right now, he wished he couldn't remember at all. Right now, he maybe even wished *he* was one of the ones who hadn't made it from Kufataba's depths.

"The forest closes behind you," he said. "It seems unthreatening enough. It's a beautiful place, enchanted. And maybe that's what makes it terrifying. It doesn't seem like something so serene should be so deadly. The trees, the birds—it's a false sense of security meant to lower your defenses."

"I can handle that part. Don't let defenses fall."

He shook his head. "It's not that easy. We went in *knowing* it wasn't going to be easy, knowing we would face awful things, knowing we should keep our guard up. And we still failed."

I nodded.

"The first challenge tested our resolve."

"In what way?"

"I can't say exactly. One minute we were taking a pleasant trail through the woods and the next minute, the trail split into half a dozen directions and each of us wanted to follow a different path, *insisting* the path we chose was the only one that wouldn't lead to certain death. A decision we would have let the most senior agent make without a second thought any other time instead became a cause for childlike squabble. Something happened up here"—he raised his hand to his head, tapping it, wincing with the motion— "to make us forget."

"Forget what?"

"What mattered. It was like nothing in the world was important except for taking the path we each wanted to follow. It took over your mind like nothing I've known."

I wanted to ask him if he remembered mind-control testing for the Order, if he recalled the things they did to try to break us, the men who left that test less whole than they'd started it, the men who had to be held up when they left the room. I shut my mind against the memories that threatened to be seen again, but flashes of bloodshot eyes and nervous laughter, toes of boots dragged across the ground—they took root in my brain, reluctant to be banished again.

Maybe Brigantino hadn't taken that test. Maybe the mind-control testing had been added later. I suppressed the mild nausea that threatened with the memories.

"We lost two men that way."

"To the wrong…path," I clarified.

He nodded. "One we never saw again. He left and kept walking. For all I know, he could still be wandering the forest beneath the mountain. The other…walked off a cliff."

"A cliff…in the mountain?"

"Enchanted," he said. "Beneath the mountain is another world."

I blew out a frustrated breath and leaned my elbows on my knees, running my hands through my hair. What were we up against? Mountains beneath mountains? Forests below Liron's surface? Madness.

"All right," I said, pushing my uncertainties aside. "First challenge takes over your mind. Got it. Second challenge."

"You're my king, so I will go on, but know the first challenge is not like you think it will be. You're still a pup yet, D'Arturio. You're smart, strong, and capable, but don't be overconfident. Don't make that mistake."

"My confidence, my friend, seems to be more and more of an act these days."

He didn't respond. Instead he forged ahead.

"The second test challenges mental fortitude, requiring a sacrifice of sorts."

"Like…an animal?" I swallowed. "Or a person?"

Brigantino shook his head. "No, not a physical sacrifice.

It has to be something from within."

I tried to suppress my confusion. Nothing about Kufataba made sense.

Brigantino continued. "Each person in the party must sacrifice a memory. It could be something you cherished. It might be something you feared, but it has to be potent, a memory that evokes the most emotion inside."

Supposing we even had a way to make this happen, I didn't see this as a problem for Alesh, Reina, or myself, but Ingram…he would be difficult.

"What for?" I asked. "And what happens if they don't?"

"Those who give the sacrifice move on, those who don't…lose themselves."

"You're going to need to be less cryptic here, Brigantino. I know you don't want to discuss the matter, but I need information before I throw us all into the fire."

He tapped his fingers to his head. "They *lose* themselves. All of themselves. You either offer a single potent memory or you lose *every* memory, good and bad."

"And you know this because…"

"We lost another man on the second challenge. Seemed easy enough, right? But some people aren't made to relive the past. It's harder than it seems."

"Everything is," Ywelo muttered and I echoed her sentiments.

"The third challenge?"

"Strength. Endurance. It's a physical test. For us? It was ropes. Climbing. I don't know what it might be for you. I've heard rumors of boulders, of walls, of raging animals weighing thousands of pounds, but I…can't confirm any of that."

I wanted to discount it. It was preposterous. All of it. And yet, Brigantino was the very last person to tell tall tales. If he spoke, he spoke truth.

Which meant we were in for a world of hurt.

CHAPTER TWENTY-THREE

Broken Magic
Reina

Quinn kicking us from the room made at least one task easier. I now had a moment to examine the brand that still burned beneath my tunic.

"Privy," I said to Niles and Alesh before locking myself in the tiny room with yellowed walls and peeling paint. Thankfully, they didn't object, nor offer to escort me.

I peeled the tunic over my head and examined the reddened skin over my heart. I let out an involuntary gasp, and my lip trembled. I peered closer into the dingy mirror, then down at the skin itself.

The image of an eye, lid half-lowered as though bored, had been burned onto my skin. The bastard child had branded me. I gritted my teeth and pumped water to splash on the skin. The aloe I'd gotten from the apothecary would help with the burn, but the scar it would leave behind would still be unmistakable. How would I hide such a mark from Quinn?

I cleaned the spot with cool water, swallowing against the pain. I *could* use the salve I'd gotten for Niles on my own skin, but Quinn would smell it from a mile away and I'd never be able to use it discreetly.

I closed my eyes and breathed. No, I would deal with the pain. I'd put aloe on before bed to keep it from scarring badly, but the pain would have to be ignored.

There was one other task I could complete while in the privacy of the privy, and it wasn't using the pot. No, I needed a vision of my own. I'd been terrified to see what kind success or failure we'd have on our journey. It's why I'd asked the old woman to look instead.

A pathetic laugh escaped my lips. I didn't even know her name. I hadn't thought to ask. Once upon a time, my mother would have chastised me for such a lack of manners. Now? It hardly mattered.

As my fingertips grazed the mark once more, the talisman lit and I gave into the honeyed sensation on my tongue, falling into the vision that awaited me.

The Map to Balance would be opened again…once more unleashing the Winds of Chaos. Grassy plains rolled in the ferocity of the wind, surrounding me as I faced off against a beautiful young girl. The Chaos Wielder, I was sure, in yet another mask. Clear cerulean skies didn't seem right for such a vision. Somehow, it would have made more sense to be surrounded by skies that threatened lighting and rain, but it was not the case.

There was another figure with me, but I couldn't tell who it might be. Quinn, I hoped. For if I was to face the Chaos Wielder with no one else by my side, Quinn would be enough.

We spoke, the Chaos Wielder and I, but like most of my

visions, the words were muted, and I had no way of knowing what was said.

Unsurprisingly, I angered her, and she lashed out, blasting us with wind that knocked me from my feet. And then I reached into my tunic…

I couldn't give her the talisman.

And yet I watched my hand grip the amulet and pull it from my neck. I had promised the Chaos Wielder I would offer the necklace when next we met…

Saints, no.

I withdrew from the vision in a rush, my head spinning so heavily that I had to grip the sides of the basin to keep from falling. I didn't want to see it, didn't want to *believe* it. Oh God, I was going to doom us all. I would give over the talisman.

I gripped the sides of the basin until my knuckles turned white, until the tears no longer fell from my eyes, until the pain from the mark felt as though it had always been there, burned into my skin.

A soft knock at the door startled me.

"Moreina? Are you all right?"

Niles.

"Fine," I said too quickly. "One moment."

I wiped my tears, splashed water on my face, and threw the tunic back on again, cinching my belt at my waist once more.

Chin up, I met my own determined eyes in the mirror.

"I will *not* hand the talisman over. Come death or worse, I swear it," I said to the mirror.

There *had* to be another way.

"Will you walk with me, Reina?"

I considered Quinn's words, then nodded and allowed him to hold open the door to the room as well as the door to the inn. We ventured into the sun again, leaving the inn behind.

Aberly was lovely—a place I could imagine spending months, if not years, on end. The breeze from the sea blew in just enough to offset the heat of the sun, and beautiful large trees with willowy fronds bent toward the ocean as though perhaps wishing they were made for water, too.

We stepped from the inn to the road and followed it until we reached the pink, sandy beach littered with shells of varying shapes and sizes. One of the sailors told me they were made by tiny creatures and I wished there was time to look for one that wasn't just a hollowed shell.

Maybe I'd return someday and search for the shell-producing creatures…if we ever managed to defeat the Chaos Wielder and return to any semblance of normal life. Stepping onto the supple sand, I kicked off my boots, relishing the sensation both gritty and soft between my toes. Low in the sky, the sun lent a blush to the already rosy sand.

"I owe you an apology. I'm sorry. Will you forgive me?" Quinn's voice was strained. He wasn't used to having to apologize.

I bent to pick up a frail pink shell with scalloped edges

and a small hole at one end. I twirled it in my fingers a moment, then slipped it into my tunic pocket. It might make a nice necklace or bracelet if I ever had time to do something with it. The eye branded on my chest burned when my tunic brushed it with the movement, but with Quinn present I didn't give in to a hiss of pain.

"There's nothing to forgive," I said, but even I could hear the strain in my words. An unconvincing performance.

Quinn touched my hand, his fingers brushing against my little finger, seeking reassurance that I wouldn't push him away.

I wouldn't.

If only he would stop pushing *me* away. It seemed every time he had the chance to share a piece of himself, he dug in his heels and locked his past away tighter. If he wanted to isolate himself from me, he was doing a stellar job.

"I mean it, Reina. I've made a lot of mistakes on this journey. You're right, you know. There are parts of my past I need to confront, parts that"—he took a breath— "are painful for me to think about. I'm not proud of them."

"We've all done things we aren't proud of, Quinn. All of us. At some point or another. But we can't do this"—I motioned between us— "unless we're both one hundred percent committed. You can't keep pushing me out because you're afraid I'm going to leave when I learn something you didn't want me to know."

"You're right," he said. "No more secrets."

I eyed him. "You mean that?"

"I do."

"Agreed. No more secrets."

Liar, my conscience hissed, but I didn't dare tell him. I couldn't bring myself to say the words, to admit what I'd promised the Chaos Wielder in order to save Brigantino's life, to save all our lives. I couldn't tell him how I'd been marked.

I would. Eventually. Just…not yet.

I placed my hand in his and squeezed, relishing his strength as he squeezed back.

"I still can't believe Ywelo and Brigantino," I said, happy to change the subject. "Did you have any idea?"

Quinn scratched the back of his neck, squinted his eyes, and scrunched his mouth sideways.

"Maybe?" he answered. "I didn't know before we got to the Plains, but once I saw him with Ywelo, I suspected there was something there. He's not an easy man to read."

I laughed out loud.

"Yes, I know all about men who aren't easy to read."

He narrowed his eyes again. "Is that a jab?"

I held my fingers an inch apart. "Only a little one."

CHAPTER TWENTY-FOUR

Welcome to Kufataba
Reina

Above us, Kufataba emerged larger than life, with a looming, nearly vertical cliff that drew shivers down my spine when we entered its ominous shadow. We were a sullen group, if ever I saw one, but the enormity of the situation was nothing less than overwhelming, so I didn't exactly expect merry songs, laughter, and skipping.

Still.

It would have been better for morale had we not left Ywelo and a wounded Brigantino in Aberly, but even I wouldn't dare move Brigantino in his condition. Stable, yes, but too much movement and he'd start bleeding again. If we had time, we *might* have waited a week for him to heal enough to move on again. But traveling on foot as we were, there was no time.

Aberly hadn't housed any nudromedaries, and horses were so rare that those who owned them weren't apt to give them up easily. It seemed the people of Aberly relied more on large, extremely hairy, and unwieldy animals that were better for pulling carts than for carrying people. A cart wouldn't do for where we traveled, so, yet again, we traveled on foot.

I tilted my head, gazing at Kufataba and the unassuming clear sky behind it. If Brigantino's former experience here was anything close to what we faced, Saints only knew what we would encounter.

I adjusted the pack on my back, tightening the straps around my middle and across my chest. Not owning many items at this point, we hadn't packed heavy, but there were some things I wasn't willing to leave behind knowing the challenges we faced—including some of the medicines I'd purchased from the apothecary. At least I had *some* of the essentials now.

Finally, we reached the base of Kufataba and a gaping, dark maw of an entrance in the middle of its rocky face. The blackness within was complete, as though the darkest of black velvet had been draped across the opening to obscure anything within from view.

Warnings were etched in the face of the surrounding rock—drawings of fire, headless humans, wild animals with horns and fangs and claws, and dead bodies on the ground, but no *acaffilé*. At least the dead here stayed dead. I swallowed, running a finger over one of the line drawings.

"You must be kidding." Niles stared into the darkness of the cave. "Do you even know what kinds of animals live in such dens?"

"Nothing lives in there," Alesh said. "That is…strong magic."

"Magic?" I didn't miss Quinn's sharp glance to Alesh.

Alesh extended a hand outward as though trying to feel for a wall he couldn't see. His dark brow furrowed, pulling concern into his features.

"You cannot feel it?" he asked.

I felt it. I couldn't put my finger on the exact threat it presented, but I felt *something* emanating from the dark hole in the mountain. If I had any sense whatsoever, I would turn and run back to Irzan right now. Quinn's set jaw and focused gaze pushed any thoughts of running away from my mind, not that it had ever been an option.

I heaved a sigh.

"Let's go then," I said, stepping forward. "No sense in putting it off."

Quinn took the lead, pausing a moment at the cave entrance before moving forward again.

"So eager to meet death," Niles muttered, falling in line behind me.

Quinn's form disappeared into the blackness that was the mouth of the cave as though erased from existence. The thought of losing him was so terrifying that I followed without a moment's hesitation. Where Quinn led, I would follow. Always.

As I stepped into the darkness, a bone-chilling cold swept across my body in a frigid blast that set my teeth chattering, and a second later, it was gone. The very inside of the cave was nearly the same temperature as outside. No longer pitch black, the outline of the walls and floor—and Quinn—were faintly visible.

Behind me, though, was the same magical black curtain that kept me from seeing the world we'd left behind.

Niles arrived, his breath a gasp at the cold shock. Then

Alesh followed a moment behind.

"It's dark," Niles observed.

I could have been wrong, but Niles seemed more talkative since Brigantino was no longer with us to shush him.

"Is it?" Quinn said dryly. "I hadn't noticed."

A ruby glow bloomed from Alesh's staff, providing a dim light that illuminated the space in an ominous gleam.

"I thought the magic was broken," Quinn said.

"I wouldn't try using it for its true intent, but for a little light? Even I can handle that." Alesh sounded almost wounded at Quinn's insinuation.

A moment later, I pulled the talisman from my tunic and lit it with ease, an aqua glow appearing alongside the red.

"Are you sure that's wise, given your magic's recent penchant for killing things without your approval?" Niles asked.

"It's fine," I said. I hoped I was right.

By the light of the two stones, we navigated the twists and turns of the cave, the air growing cooler and less oppressive the farther we descended into Kufataba's depths. Just when I thought the stories about an enchanted forest might be nothing more than Brigantino's fever dreams, the cave dumped us into a mossy forest where sunlight filtered in beams through the lush green leaves above.

I couldn't suppress a gasp of surprise. Even knowing there was an enchanted forest, even knowing we traveled through a magical cave, I still had trouble making sense of what lay before my eyes. Where on Liron was the light coming from? We were *under* a mountain, for Saints' sake.

"Well," Quinn said, eyebrows raised high, taking in the enchantment. "Brigantino didn't exaggerate."

I calmed the talisman, allowing the glow to fade, and placed it back beneath the fabric of my tunic, making sure to avoid brushing the edges of the unwelcome brand that still throbbed painfully. The stone settled into a deceivingly happy hum at my chest once more. If only the talisman would be so happy to be used as more than a lantern.

The air beneath Kufataba was sweet with the scent of flowers I couldn't identify, and strange, fresh greenery new to my eyes. The one word I could think to describe the scene before us was the very word Brigantino had used—enchanted.

Far off, a waterfall fell from a dizzyingly high cliff that shouldn't have existed. Birdsong echoed in a perfect musical cacophony only nature could provide, but this wasn't *natural* at all. There was nothing natural about this. This was magic.

"So how long before we start arguing which path to take?" Niles didn't mince words.

Before we reached Kufataba, Quinn had told us in detail about the first challenge Brigantino faced long ago. Knowing it was only a matter of time before we faced challenges meant to keep us from succeeding made the current surroundings a bit less awe-inspiring.

"The sooner, the better, I suppose." Quinn adjusted his own pack. "Let's go."

I walked beside Quinn, following a worn path through the forest, Alesh and Niles behind us. Despite the ominous challenges that waited some unknown distance ahead, I took in the beauty of the forest.

A bright yellow bird with a wide swath of navy plumage on his wings and tail swooped across the path and landed in one of the nearby trees. The bird was larger than any I'd seen before, its slender orange beak making quick work of the plump, purple berry clasped within it.

In the fern-like fronds on the floor of the forest, an insect buzzed, pausing to collect nectar from the tiny, bright pink, cup-like flowers at the tips of each frond. With its long iridescent body and enormous eyes and wings, it drew my attention. How did such a strange looking creature ever come to be?

"I'm sure you'd love to stop and study every plant and being in the forest, Reina," Quinn said. "But we must move if we plan to make it through the heart of this mountain before the eclipse."

"Sorry," I muttered, realizing that in my observations I had slowed us all. I fell back into line with the others, casting one last glance to the humming insect and the flowers. Specimen cups. I should have thought to travel with specimen cups.

I almost laughed at my own foolishness. As if I could have known I'd be traveling a mystical forest beneath a mountain.

The afternoon wore on—or maybe it was evening—who could tell in this place? Did the *sun* set beneath the mountain? Or was it perpetual day always and forever? I guessed we would find out eventually.

And we did. When *eventually* finally came and

we rested our weary legs in the darkness of the night beneath the mountain, Quinn rubbed the calves and feet I'd unceremoniously draped across his lap. A moan of satisfaction escaped my lips.

"Saints, that's good." Prompted by mild guilt, I said, "I'll rub yours, too, if you want."

Quinn shook his head, as I knew he would. Stubborn man.

A fire crackled at the center of our camp, bringing a small ring of light to the surrounding dark. The sky was filled to the brim with stars I've never seen, constellations I've never known, and no sign of either Stellon or Andra. Without the moons, the sky should have seemed darker. Instead, glittering pinpricks of light strewn by millions across the sky shined brighter than ever, twinkling invitingly.

The birds quieted after dark, but something almost human-sounding howled in the distance every now and again, raising the hairs on my arms. I hoped I'd never have the chance to meet it.

Niles pulled his little book out once more and read by the firelight, though he cast a disapproving glance over its cover every now and again to where Quinn and I sat. And Alesh…

Alesh was the only one of us who seemed utterly indefatigable. He practiced with his staff, stepping and twirling in a hypnotic dance, blocking against invisible enemies, swinging the staff downward, then arcing it back up again.

Following my gaze, Quinn commented, "He's twice our age. Does the man know no weariness?"

I held back a laugh. "One could say the same of you."

Quinn's lips pressed into a line.

"You don't believe me?" I asked.

He sighed, his shoulders slumping just a little.

"I feel more tired than ever," he said quietly. "I fear all of this has aged me decades. Can you remember a year ago, what you were doing? Where you were?"

"I…"

I almost answered that I'd been with him. That we were together.

But a year ago, our world was full of war and the fear of a man who had tried to take the throne of Liron for his own. A year ago, I hadn't suspected I'd *ever* leave Barnham. A year ago, I hadn't yet known about the talisman that had grown to become an extension of my own body.

I closed my eyes, letting the firelight flicker behind closed lids, sliding into my memories. A year ago…

"I was Healer," I said. "Nothing more. Barnham was home. The cottage was mine. Aeros yelled at me if I didn't feed her before the goats in the morning, and the goats yelled at me no matter what. I ground dried sunflower seeds and seleniac into powder and mixed them with briarmint oil to make a tincture for Lara Jemie's headaches. Or maybe I was collecting blood nettles and birch bark. A year ago, things were…normal."

I didn't like the wistful tone that crept into my voice.

"You feel it, too."

"We've both been through so much in the last seven months."

Quinn didn't reply, but his warm hands steadily worked a knot in my calf. I sighed as the muscle released.

"Where were *you* a year ago?" I asked.

As he thought, he switched calves, moving my right leg aside and working on the left. A year ago, I would have died before letting my legs get massaged in public by a man, even Quinn. I glanced to Niles and Alesh. Not exactly very public.

Quinn finally responded. "I was still working for the Order, but I'd just gotten notice to return to Barnham. A year ago, I was on a ship."

It was interesting the way I referred to Barnham as home, but Quinn just called it Barnham.

"I hope your experience on the ocean was better than ours on the Retryant Sea."

His mouth twisted sideways. "Not exactly."

"Really?"

"But at least there was no Chaos Wielder to deal with then."

"Would you like to know where I was a year ago?" Niles asked, intruding on our private moment.

"Not particularly," Quinn answered.

I shifted, tucking my feet beneath me and turned toward Niles.

Niles ignored Quinn. "I was on a field with a thousand other Resistance soldiers, waiting to be sliced open by someone from the King's Army. There were three-thousand of them. I still don't know how I walked from that field in one piece."

Quinn snorted, as though he had plenty to say about how

Niles had been spared.

Alesh thrust his staff downwards one last time, then returned to the fire, barely winded despite his exertion.

"You talk about death often," he said to Niles. "Always surprised you are still here. Why do you think it is that you are still here?"

Niles shrugged. "Luck, I guess."

"I think no." Alesh raised a hand in the air. "I think you are stronger than you believe."

I almost had to physically restrain Quinn from commenting. I took one of his hands and clenched it between mine, willing him to stay silent. I wanted to hear what Alesh had to say, even if Quinn and I didn't feel the same.

Like Quinn, I'd seen the kind of cowardice Niles had shown in the past, but I'd also seen Niles do noble things, even if Quinn insisted Niles acted only for his own benefit.

Niles snorted in disbelief. "These two will be the first in line to reassure you that there's no good reason for me to still be alive. In fact, before the most recent prophecy, they would have delighted in watching me hang by the neck."

"That's not true," I shot back quickly. Maybe too quickly. It didn't matter how much I once disliked Niles, how much I *still* disliked him. I didn't want to see him killed even so.

"Ah, Moreina, always so diplomatic. All right. I'll concede. You might have been content with me rotting in a cell for the rest of my days, perhaps, but D'Arturio? He's always wanted me gone."

Quinn said nothing.

Alesh took advantage of the moment to speak his mind

again. "Sometimes the most persistent weed yields the most beautiful flower."

I narrowed my eyes at Alesh and viewed him sideways, tilting my head.

"Did you just…call Niles a flower?"

Quinn snorted. "A beautiful one, too."

Alesh's eyes sparkled in the firelight. "Something like that."

"Fantastic." Niles stood and stretched. "Well, I'm turning in unless one of you would like to tie me up as the good Captain enjoyed doing. No? No takers? All right, then. Sleep tight." He stood and shook his head, muttering beneath his breath while climbing into his bedroll.

"I miss Brigantino," Quinn muttered.

Three days of traveling through the enchanted forest beneath the mountain was enough to fray my nerves. And I wasn't alone.

Quinn had begun braiding long strands of dried grass into a thin rope and he flipped it back and forth every now and again, then tugged on the ends to determine its sturdiness.

"What are you doing?" I asked.

He glanced upward briefly, then turned his attention back to his rope.

"You'll see," he answered cryptically.

It wasn't like Quinn to relax enough to allow himself a distraction while walking. He wasn't watching and worrying, plotting and planning where to go next. I squinted at him. Why wasn't he on guard for a predator, or the undead, or the first challenge we had yet to encounter?

"This is madness," Niles said as the path began to wind back upon itself. "We should turn back."

"You'd like that, wouldn't you?" Quinn pulled a long strand through another loop.

"You'd probably like it, too. Get rid of me quicker that way, but—oh—wait, that's right, you still need me because of another prophecy."

"That is enough. You two fight like sand cats."

I didn't know what a sand cat was, but I agreed with Alesh regardless.

"No one is happy about where we're headed," I said gently. "Or why we're headed there. Let's just take it easy."

Niles made a noncommittal sound that might have signaled agreement…or could have been telling me to go throw a stone or two. Quinn said nothing.

We journeyed on for another hour, the silence broken by birdsong and the buzz of insects even I had grown weary of inspecting. The straps on my pack bit into my shoulders, making me miss not only Aeros, but also the nudromedaries despite their horrid breath. How much longer would we be beneath the mountain? Was three days here equal to three days outside? Did time move the same way? Could we have missed the eclipse and lost any chance at ridding the world of the Chaos Wielder already?

I bit back on panicked thoughts. There was no point in worrying myself further even if we *were* in an enchanted forest inside a magic mountain.

A sudden thump from behind startled me and I turned to face the noise.

I needn't have been alarmed. Niles had dropped his pack to the ground and stood like a petulant child, arms crossed, feet planted wide.

"What now, Ingram?" Quinn said through gritted teeth.

"I'm finished."

"I beg your pardon?" I asked, in disbelief that Niles would dare cross us, given the alternative. Blazes, now *I* wished Brigantino were still with us.

"This is a fool's errand, Moreina. I won't keep at it. For all we know, we've been going in circles since we walked through that cave."

"Have you seen the cave again?" Alesh held his arms wide and gestured to the forest around us. "Have you seen anything other than trees?"

"No." Niles said sullenly.

"We must keep going," Alesh said. "We will know when we have reached our destination."

"We'll know? Are you out of your head? How will we *know?* Will a magical fae being appear to point us on the right path, Shongoman?"

"Enough, Ingram. We'll follow the path because it's the only path there is," Quinn said.

"About that. Didn't Captain Goon say there would be a bunch of paths? Are we even in the right place?"

"Really! How many enchanted forests do you think there are, Niles?" I said.

"On this continent? Who knows!"

"Enough. We travel now," Alesh said.

"What are you going to do, tie me up and drag me along?"

Alesh looked to be contemplating the idea. "Yes," he said, dropping his pack and rooting through it, presumably for rope.

"We're not tying him up," I said sternly to Alesh.

"We don't have a choice on this, Ingram. I don't like it any more than you do. You think I want to keep walking? You think we're not all on edge, knowing we're soon to be faced with tests we're not even sure we can pass?"

Niles looked almost startled at Quinn's admission, and I was nearly as surprised to hear Quinn admit there might be something he couldn't do, a test even he couldn't pass.

"Pick up your pack, strap it on, and let's go."

Any small connection Niles might have felt with Quinn a second ago dissipated quickly, and resentment returned to his face. "Is that an order, Your Highness?"

"Goddammit, Ingram—"

Quinn dropped the rope and his own pack to the ground.

"Enough," I shouted.

Alesh stood ready to insert himself between the two of them, his staff half-raised, rope clutched in his hand.

"What are you going to do?" I said. "Fight right here? Have it out? Kill each other like you've wanted to for years? You do that and we're all dead." I turned to Quinn and stared hard into his dark eyes. "Pull it together. You're better than this."

He shook his head as if to clear it from whatever thoughts

had taken hold.

I turned to Niles. "And you," I said. "You once told me that I was Castilles's only hope, that if *I* died, everyone else did, too, that without me, there was no future." Deep blue eyes cast their gaze downward, as though ashamed to look me in the eye. "Do you remember that?"

He didn't answer, so I repeated myself, a stitch louder. "Do you remember that?"

"Yes," he said. "I do."

"Well, now there's a prophecy that includes all four of us. And if any one of us doesn't make it through this hellscape of a mountain, we're all as good as dead…as is everyone else on Liron. Do you understand?"

Niles gave a slow nod. I turned my eyes to Quinn and Alesh, who both nodded as well.

"Get your packs—all of you—and let's move. And Alesh, we are *not* tying anyone up, so put the rope away."

Quinn bent to grab his pack and a slow smile spread across his lips. He picked up the thin homemade rope he'd been weaving and shook the dirt from it. Then he gave a low chuckle.

"Is something humorous?" I asked.

"Not at all, Reina. I'm just…fairly certain you single-handedly passed the first challenge for us," he said.

"I—"

That's right. The first challenge. It had something to do with challenging our resolve. Brigantino said they had argued over which path to take. Had we not just done the same? Or at least something similar?

"Also," Quinn said with a sideways grin. "Hellscape? A bit dramatic, no?"

"I swear to all the Saints above, Quinn D'Arturio…" But I didn't finish my sentence. I let him smile. I might have even smiled a little bit with him.

CHAPTER TWENTY-FIVE

Stolen Memories
Quinn

Three days. Three whole days for the first challenge to present itself. I cringed internally. The timing didn't bode well for the remaining two challenges. At this rate, we'd be lucky if we made it through the mountain by the end of the week.

Time was not our friend.

I glanced at Reina, proud of her—so proud—and yet trying not to let it show too much. She'd just be embarrassed.

When I finished winding the grass strands into a rope long enough for a necklace, I admired my work. It wasn't gold. It had no jewels. It wasn't pretty on its own. Not even a little.

"Where's the shell?" I asked her.

"The what?"

"The little pink shell you picked up on the beach in Aberly."

It occurred to me she might have discarded it, that perhaps it wasn't something she'd intended to save.

My ears burned with the foolish heat that crept up the back of my neck. How to explain myself out of this one…

Then Reina dug her hand into the pocket of her tunic and produced the tiny shell with the hole at one end, saving me from having to explain anything. I took it and fed the rope through the hole.

She took the necklace in her hand and held it up. A smile spread across her face.

"A necklace," she said with delight, her eyes lighting with the first hint of a smile I'd seen from her in days. "That's what you've been making all this time."

"You saved that shell, and so I thought maybe…" I shrugged.

"I was saving it to make a necklace," she said, finishing my sentence.

I nodded.

She handed the necklace back, then turned her back to me.

"Tie it on?"

I nodded, fumbling with the rope a moment until I managed a knot. It was childish compared to the exquisite talisman she wore beneath her tunic, but it was the kind of gesture I would have made years ago before we were a king and a sorceress. Back when life was much, *much* less complicated.

"You know what this reminds me of?" she asked. She bit her lip.

I shook my head. She turned and smiled at me again, her eyes bright with the memory.

"When you used to make flower crowns for me," she said.

I glowered, pretending to know nothing of it.

"*I* made you flower crowns?" I asked. "Are you quite certain?"

Her shoulders fell a hair. She scowled. It almost made me laugh, that scowl. No pout. Reina would never stoop to a pout.

"Quinn D'Arturio, of course I'm certain! You don't remember the spring I taught you how to make them, then insisted you make me a new one with fresh flowers every day?"

I narrowed my eyes. "Are you sure you've not confused me with another boy from your past?"

Her lips parted. It wasn't difficult to know the moment she realized I was teasing her. She smacked my arm and leaned in to place her lips on mine. Then, all too quickly, her lips were gone. I sighed.

"Come," she said. "Let's go or I'll have you start picking flowers to weave me a Kufataba crown, too."

"I thought I was the king," I muttered playfully, but I strode onward, my heart lighter for the shared memories and for the smile on Reina's face.

Her long hair was tied in a knot at the nape of her neck, and her gaze moved over the forest around us, even though we'd all grown weary of it. She never stopped taking it in. How many remedies was she thinking about while examining the plants we passed? The capacity of her mind where medicine was concerned was inconceivable. Then again, she wasn't limited to medicine, was she?

Reina had succeeded in the first challenge where I would

have failed.

And I couldn't say why I would have failed. I knew what kind of challenge to expect for our first test…and yet, I'd still fallen deep into it and sprung the trap. Was my distaste for Ingram so strong that I could be goaded so easily? The thought was unnerving.

I'd been taught not to react to that kind of set up, so why had I?

A peculiar fog had overtaken my brain in the moments before I'd lost the ability to think rationally. I swallowed. At least we would know what to expect for the second challenge, whenever it chose to present itself to us. Now I had some sort of warning as to what would come. The next time I felt that fog…well, I'd know not to make any rash decisions.

As it turned out, we didn't have to wait long before the second challenge presented itself. In half a day, we reached the edge of the forest to find ourselves on the sandy shore of a wide lake. The sand slipped into the water, then dropped off after a few feet, the deeper water appearing an abyss of unsettling blackness.

I peered left and right along the shoreline, searching for where the path continued, but in both cases, the forest led straight to the edge of the lake, tangled vines and overgrown underbrush making any progress through it impossible.

"We're going to have to swim, aren't we?" Ingram said, the usual disdain dripping from his voice.

The thought had crossed my mind, but there was no way to swim the lake with cumbersome packs unless we built some sort of raft to carry them. And if we were going to build a raft, we might as well take the time to build one big enough to carry the four of us.

"I do not swim," Alesh said, pointing to the water.

"Not at all?" Reina asked.

Alesh turned to her, his mouth twisted into an amused smile.

"I have not had the opportunity," he said with a tilt of his head.

In the desert of the Southern Plains, it wasn't likely Alesh had ever encountered so much water. His awe at the size of the Retryant Sea was proof enough of that. It seemed knowing of the sea's existence and witnessing its massive size firsthand were two different matters.

"It doesn't matter," I said roughly. "We can't swim it."

"Then what do you suggest?" Ingram asked.

"Look!"

Reina pointed to a spot on the sand where words appeared as though written by magic—and I suppose they *were* written by magic since there was clearly no one here to write them.

> *To pass the test,*
> *a fee required.*
> *A memory you must give,*
> *Deep fear or desire.*
> *The choice is yours,*
> *but choose with care.*
> *For the memory becomes ours,*
> *Once laid bare.*

"The second test."

It wasn't a question, and even though I'd prepared the others for what the second test would hold, I wasn't sure if I was ready to face it myself. Memories. What kind of memories were considered payment?

I'd been reminiscing enough lately, more than enough. Maybe losing a memory of the Order wouldn't be so bad after all. And yet, losing a memory…would it change who I was? Fundamentally, deep inside, the memories we created *shaped* who we became. Would I be different if even one of those memories existed in my mind no longer?

There was equal fear written across the faces of the others. The true cost of the second challenge was higher than we'd considered. And yet, not paying it wasn't an option.

"All right," I said. "Let's get this over with."

I stepped forward. I couldn't expect anyone else to give up a memory if I didn't do so myself, I couldn't expect my subjects to follow if I wasn't willing to lead.

Not that the three with me were *subjects*, necessarily.

"How do you suppose it works?" Reina asked.

I didn't know the answer, but the magic of Kufataba—whatever it was—answered for me. I stepped toward the sand. The black water grew brighter, turning deep blue, then almost white as though a sun bubbled from the depths to occupy a space beneath the water's surface. The water above the small sandy ledge rippled in invitation.

Reina put a hand to my arm, but I didn't turn to meet her eyes. Now was no time for hesitation. I stepped forward into the water, letting the lake lap at my boots, the water seeping into minuscule cracks in the sole, numbing my feet with the cold.

I expected the lake to take a memory. I didn't expect the memory to be visible to everyone else, but the lake itself transformed into a giant viewing screen where my story was laid bare for all to see.

I didn't have a choice as to what memory I could give up despite what the words in the sand had said. I wasn't given the opportunity to shuffle through and choose one at will. Instead, the spirit of the lake—or the mountain—flipped through my memories like a bookkeeper shuffling pages, searching, peering into each one for the information it desired.

The memories swept through my mind in a jumble so jarring it was difficult to discern one from the next. The emotions flew right along with them. Pain, despair, hope, love, confusion, anger, fear—so many emotions at once. So many emotions I had spent years bottling up and locking away to keep from interfering with my place in the Order. It was all I could do to hold back the confused tears my eyes wanted to set loose.

I dropped to my knees in the water. A ragged gasp escaped Reina's lips behind me, but I was unable to comfort or reassure her. As the magic tore through scenes of my life with the force of hurricane winds, I could do nothing but fight to remain conscious. My pants soaked through with lake water, numbing the rest of my legs, but there was nothing I could do. I was no longer in control of my own body, let alone my mind.

I didn't want to give up a memory. I didn't want Reina to see what I had done, what I had become, but Brigantino's warning flashed through my mind. Give up one memory willingly or lose them all. I unleashed a yell in a voice I hardly recognized as my own and just when I thought I couldn't withstand another moment, I fell into a vision of the past projected on the lake's surface.

Oh, no. Not this one. *Take one from the Order!* I pleaded to no avail. The lake did not respond. *Don't take—*

"Withdraw."

Father looked from the letters he was reading at his office desk, startled to see me standing in the room with him. He'd gained weight since I left last year, his face a little rounder, his clothes tighter at his waist. My mother's doing, I supposed.

Were it not for the reason I was here, I might have smiled at the surprise in his eyes, at the fact that my training had paid off, and at how I now moved undetected. It'd been a long year. At least some part of it was worth it.

"Quinn! What on Liron are you doing here, my boy?"

He stood and moved to hug me, but I shook my head and held up a hand to keep him at a distance. He looked confused—almost wounded—but he didn't need to feel the fresh lacerations beneath the shirt on my back. I couldn't let him know. He'd blame himself. My father always had.

"I can't stay," I said. "I need to get back to my post. I'm just here to withdraw my proposal."

"Your—"

"For Reina's Choosing."

Sudden understanding crossed his face.

"You got my letter."

I nodded. If I knew Reina at all, the last thing she needed right now was another person trying to make decisions for her. I didn't need to add to her pain. After her mother...well, she'd had enough. Another suitor squabbling for her hand when she desperately wanted her freedom was just one more burden.

I wanted to believe she'd be happier with me than with anyone else who might offer, but the truth was that she'd be happiest without a husband or a family to tie her down. She'd been dreaming of being Healer for too long. I couldn't ruin it for her. Not now. Not while she was still grieving.

"Quinn, you've been waiting for this for—"

"I know," I interrupted. I didn't want to give him the chance to talk me out of what was best for Reina. I brought my eyes to his, schooling my face to erase the regrets I held deep inside. "Look, perhaps I've changed my mind, all right?" I lied.

"Oh."

Father looked almost crestfullen. Maybe he'd been looking forward to gaining a daughter-in-law more than I realized.

"The Order is the best thing that's happened to me. I have no desire to rush back to Barnham for a betrothal right now." I took a breath before adding, "And maybe not ever."

He nodded in response, the shock still setting in.

"I have to get back." I turned to leave. "I'm not even supposed to be here."

He nodded again. "You're sure?"

I swallowed. Was I sure? No. The only thing I was sure about was that my own plans had gone to hell and I wasn't going to muck up someone else's life because of it. Especially not Reina's. She deserved better.

So much better.

I gave a firm nod anyway. "I'm sure. But—" I shouldn't ask it. I shouldn't. I had no right to interfere. "Can you see to it she's happy with whatever outcome you choose for her?"

There. I said the words.

"Of course. You know I love her as much as you do," he replied, his words a sharp dagger twisting in my chest. He wasn't stupid. He knew I still loved her. "I won't see her unhappy."

I nodded in response. Then I disappeared from the room—out the front door this time—and made my way across the dark streets, then through darker meadows and forests surrounding the town I knew and loved. I paused when I reached the hillside overlooking Reina's cottage.

Warm light glowed behind the shutters. She was there now, awake, with her nose stuck in a book. Or maybe... maybe she was crying, numb with shock. She'd just lost her mother after all.

I let myself take two whole steps toward the cottage before I stopped, reining myself in.

I'd given her up. That was the whole reason I'd come. To give her up.

I nodded like the ghost I'd become and turned back to the road that would take me to South Trellington. My future was elsewhere. And Reina was not a part of it.

I gasped, inhaling a giant lungful of air as though I hadn't breathed in an hour. I fell forward onto my hands in the shallow water, trying to pull together my thoughts, wrap my mind around what had just happened.

I—lost something. There was a thought in my head… and now it was gone. What was it? Blazes, what *was* it? I squeezed my eyes shut.

"Quinn." Reina joined my side in the water, a light hand on my back. "Quinn, can you stand?"

For a moment, I forgot how to speak. My tongue stuck to the roof of my mouth and my voice refused to cooperate. I coughed, then forced words from my lips.

"Aye. I'm fine."

The weakness of my voice said otherwise, but I ignored it and stood, eager to get Reina out of the water.

I didn't want her to experience what I had just gone through. I didn't want her to know the pain of—

Of what?

I couldn't remember what had been so painful moments before. How was that possible? Even knowing the memory was the payment required, I stood in dumb shock that somehow I couldn't recall what had just happened.

As I pulled Reina back from the water's edge, I croaked, "What was it? What did it take from me?"

Emotion flooded her eyes.

"Oh, Quinn."

She put a hand to my unshaven jaw. Was I mistaken, or did her lip tremble? Oh, Saints, what had she seen?

"Was it something from the Order? How bad? What did you see?"

I rifled through the memories of my time in the Order, trying to remember the horrible things I'd seen and done, trying to determine if she'd now seen them, too, but I couldn't find anything missing. All the horrors, all the things I would have preferred not to remember—they were all still there, locked away in the corners of my mind. I almost breathed a sigh of relief. She hadn't seen them. At least…she hadn't seen the worst ones. Had she?

How could I know what was missing if it was, indeed, missing?

"Say something!" I said, my mind racing to the worst conclusions.

Brigantino said the magic would steal a memory. He didn't say the memory would be visible for everyone else to see. What I lost, Reina, Alesh, and Niles gained.

"It's all right," Reina said. "It's fine. We'll talk later."

The water rippled and a portion of a walkway rose from its depths, droplets sluicing off its surface, sliding back into the lake below. The walkway extended a quarter of the way across the lake. I had no doubt that if there were three in our party, it would have extended a third of the way across, five and it would have extended a fifth of the way.

"I will go," Alesh said, eyebrows drawn in determination.

He'd gone pale beneath his deeply bronzed skin. Whatever was taken from me was enough to worry him, no matter how much he might pretend otherwise.

He stepped forward until the water lapped at the ankles

of his worn travel boots, leaning on his staff as the magic swept through him. I watched with equal intensity both the lake with its flickering projections of his memory and the fight in his body against the emotion and pain.

Through it all, Alesh remained standing. He squeezed his eyes shut against whatever it was that spun through his mind and elicited a broken gasp when the magic settled on one memory to take. The lake rippled again, and a desert scene unfolded before us.

It's a difficult thing, living someone else's memories. It's hearing their thoughts, feeling their emotions, existing *as* them for that moment in time. As the lake began to expose Alesh's memory, Reina grabbed my hand and squeezed. I squeezed back, hoping I could offer comfort.

There was another man in the image, and it was he, not the young Alesh in the scene, who held the staff. The shongoman who passed before his time, though he looked remarkably like Alesh now. My eyes flicked to Alesh, eyes shut, standing pained in the water.

Of course. Alesh's father.

In the scene, the teenage Alesh lay propped on pillows within a tent, withered and drawn. His eyes fluttered open every now and then, but mostly they remained closed, and his chest rose and fell in rapid, shallow breaths. Another man approached from the corner of the scene—the yagaman—delivering last rites in a language I didn't comprehend, but somehow understood through the emotion of the memory.

When the yagaman finished speaking, the tear-stained shongoman stepped forward and I understood then what he was about to do, that he stood poised to relieve his son of the burden of dying. A choice no father should have to make. I sucked in a breath.

He lifted his staff and touched his palm to his son's hand. Young Alesh grew pale beneath his father's hand, his breath shallower than before, the pain already melting from his features, his expression already relaxing into peace.

Suddenly, the shongoman ripped his hand from Alesh's, shook his head, and called out. As he screamed out his grief, his eyes grew hard with anger, and the veins in his neck bulged. In the image, the younger Alesh didn't move, but tears flowed freely from the eyes of the Alesh who stood before me.

Abruptly, the shongoman laid the staff the length of younger Alesh's body, wrapping his son's hands around its shaft, then covering Alesh's hands with his own. He bowed his head, leaned his body over his son's, and began an unfamiliar incantation. I didn't know the words, couldn't even guess at their meaning.

The yagaman tried to stop him, coming back into the scene, clutching the shongoman's shoulder, begging him to stop.

Soon enough, it was clear what was happening. The shongoman aged quickly once he recited the incantation. With every repetition, he aged further, but the health and youth he yielded didn't disappear. Instead, it melted into Alesh's own flesh, the ruby in the staff glowing like an ember, helping father to heal his son, even at his own expense.

Balance. This was what Alesh talked about. Death wasn't

a *bad* power to have, provided one kept the balance. Alesh's father had given up his own life to ensure his son lived.

Younger Alesh sat up suddenly, his cheeks no longer sunken, his eyes no longer closed, but taking in everything around him, including the dying old man across his lap. He screamed.

The scene vanished in the lake, replaced by rippling water and white light once more. Alesh opened his eyes and wiped the tears from his cheeks. As he took in his surroundings, he drew his eyebrows in confusion.

I extended a hand to help him back to the dry shoreline. He turned in the water and another large piece of the walkway emerged from beneath the water. Unsurprisingly, the walkway now extended halfway across the lake.

"I'm not doing it," Ingram said—the first words he'd spoken since we figured out what needed to be done. "I won't."

"You will," I growled, taking a step forward. I didn't come this far to be foiled by a weasel who owed his very life to the woman who stood beside me. No.

"I—"

Reina put a hand to Ingram's arm, silencing him.

"I'll go first," she said, her voice barely more than a whisper.

I clenched my fists at my sides and tried to take a deep breath, my body unwilling to cooperate. Reliving my own horrible memories should have been enough. To see Reina suffer…

Please don't make her relive what Bruenner did to her.

Please don't make her relive what Bruenner did.

She stepped forward into the water and closed her eyes in anticipation of what was to come.

The magic decided quickly for Reina. Maybe it recognized her gift and decided to spare her from reliving so many memories. Maybe it saw the good in Reina's soul and took pity on her. Or maybe it simply found what it wanted right away. The lake rippled and projected her memories for all to see. I swallowed hard.

"Mama!"

Reina couldn't have been more than six or seven years old, her rounded cheeks pink with exertion. Seeing her the way I remembered from our childhood was a punch to the gut. As I viewed the scene, my muscles clenched. She flew through the front door of the cottage, sliding across the floor in stockinged feet and crashing into her mother's workbench. Several glass vials teetered at the edge, then fell to the floor, shattering into pieces. Reina's eyes grew wide with an unspoken apology. She bit her lip to keep the tears from coming.

"Oh, Reina." Her mother slid the remaining vials away from the edge of the bench even though the damage had already been done. "Always in a hurry."

She rose to get a broom and dustpan and handed the pan to Reina who took it dutifully and held it to the floor so her mother could sweep up the spilled contents of the bottles. When she was done sweeping, she took the pan from Reina and emptied it into the wastebasket, then kissed the top of Reina's head. She sat once more and cupped Reina's cheeks in her hands.

"All right, my love. Now what were you in such a hurry to tell me?"

"I love you!" Little Reina blurted.

Her mother laughed, a warm sound that rose deep in her throat, then she kissed the top of Reina's head again.

"And I love *you*, Little Me."

"Little Me?" Reina pulled free from her mother's grasp and gazed upward with large, round eyes. "That's silly!"

"Oh? And why is that silly?"

"I'm not *you*! I'm *me*."

Her mother bit back a smile, playing serious with young Reina.

"And what are you, if not a little bit of me?"

Little Reina put her hands on her hips, planted her feet wide, and stood tall—as tall as her tiny self could. She flipped her unruly dark hair with its single white streak behind her shoulder with a toss of her head.

"I. Am. Me!"

"That you are, my love. That you are." She placed her hands together on her lap and leaned forward. "Come now, would you like to see how to make a nightlight from glow beetles?"

"Yes!"

Reina's face lit as though a lantern had been turned on high behind her eager eyes.

Her mother stood.

"Then come sit, Little Me. Let's make some magic!"

She pulled a stool beside her and Reina scrambled upon

it, a smile plastered on rosebud lips, her eyes fixed on her mother's face. The love. The pure love from the memory was overwhelming. It wasn't guilt as in Alesh's memory, or whatever horror was taken from my own mind. It was pure, undiluted love.

The memory faded and Reina gasped, emerging once again in the present, confusion in her eyes. She looked from me to Alesh to Niles and back again.

"It's all right," I said, helping her from the water.

She put a hand to her chest and gripped the neckline of her tunic, holding tight, her breath coming in gasps. Her wide eyes darted every which way, trying to find something familiar.

"Reina." I bent to place my face even with hers. "Reina, look at me."

I held the sides of her face, not unlike how her own mother had in the memory we'd just seen. I continued to hold her until her dark, panicked eyes met my own and her breathing slowed.

"You're safe," I said.

"Something's missing."

"Nothing is missing," I reassured her. "We're all here. The magic of the lake took a single memory. No more."

"No, Quinn. I-I can't remember. There was something important to me, something I…needed. I feel…different. I'm not me!"

I rubbed a thumb along her cheek.

"The lake took a memory of your mother. I'll share it with you again. We'll talk deep into the night and you'll have it back. I promise."

I hadn't anticipated what it might feel like to lose a memory so cherished. I hadn't imagined the hole that would be left behind. I'd heard Reina's mother call her Little Me long ago when we camped in the field behind the cottage and built rock towers in the stream. I knew she half-loved and half-hated the endearment, but I never imagined what it might cost to lose the memory of earning that name, of gaining what was an essential part of her identity.

She swallowed, worried eyes once again searching the ground as though she might find the memory right here beside us.

"I promise. Understand?" I said again, moving to hug her.

She didn't answer, but she nodded into my chest and sniffed, and I kissed the top of her head.

I turned to Ingram.

"Your turn."

CHAPTER TWENTY-SIX

Past Revealed
Reina

I hid my shaking hands in the pockets of my tunic, hoping Quinn couldn't see how the lake had affected me, how much it had taken. I knew when I stepped into the waters that I was to lose something vital. I'd watched both Quinn and Alesh have memories yanked from their minds, and I saw how each of them had been affected. I knew it wouldn't be easy.

And yet, somehow, I expected something different. I couldn't begin to imagine what I'd lost even though Quinn told me it was a memory of my mother. Just knowing the lake took from me the one kind of memory I could never replace made my face burn with anger. Why hadn't it taken a memory I could have lived without? Why hadn't it taken something I'd rather never have known to begin with?

As another section of walkway rose from the water, I kept my eyes glued to Quinn. I needed to center on him, his gravity. I would always find myself in Quinn.

Quinn was home.

Focusing on him, I forced my breath to even and my galloping heart to slow. If he said it would be all right, it would.

It would.

Which was all well and good except it looked as though he might have to throw Niles into the lake. Niles had gone white as a sheet, a sheen of perspiration on his face, his pupils dilated wide in terror.

"I can't do that," he said. "I can't. Do you know what it will do?"

I remembered well the stories Quinn told me, the things Niles had done, the innocent people murdered under his orders. How many times? How many terrible memories could he provide? How many horrifying scenes? I didn't want to know.

I almost wanted to tell Niles *not* to go into the water, not to burden the rest of us with the memories he owned, but the walkway across the lake wasn't going to raise itself without payment, and Niles had to pay his dues.

"Ingram, get in the water."

Niles shook his head and stepped back.

It was all the incentive Quinn needed. He lunged at Niles, grappling with him until he managed to maintain control, twisting one of Niles's arms behind his back, tweaking the pressure just right so Niles didn't have a choice but to move where Quinn directed.

"You don't know what you're doing!" Niles cried hoarsely. "You don't understand."

"I understand all too well." Quinn's voice was hard.

Alesh watched with sympathetic eyes. A part of me felt bad for Niles, who hadn't been given a choice in this journey, but a bigger part of me remembered who he was just a few months ago, the things he'd done. I kept my mouth clamped and watched Quinn force him into the water.

He let go only when it was clear the lake had taken possession of Niles's memories and that Niles was paralyzed until the lake allowed him to move once more.

Quinn looked to me, probably expecting to see judgment on my face, but I offered only sympathy and maybe an apology that he'd had to go to such lengths to get Niles in the water. This once, I understood what Quinn had said so many times before. Sometimes, we were given no choice.

The magic of the lake took control of Niles's mind. At its mercy, he loosed a long, keening whimper. In watching, I relived how it sifted through my memories and made itself at home in my head, how it hadn't been a threatening presence but had done nothing to make me feel at ease either.

I shuddered.

The surface of the water rippled, reflecting the pale blue of the false sky overhead before projecting Niles's memory.

"So, that's it, then? You're leaving?"

The raspy voice belonged to a woman with unkempt chestnut hair and a wrinkled, saffron-yellow dress that looked to have been worn far too long. She lounged in a worn armchair on the other side of the room, but the noxious fumes rolling from her breath were still nauseating.

A teenage Niles stared back at her.

"What would you have me do?" he asked. "I can take care of you this way, Mum."

She cackled and tossed a foot over the arm of the chair, then leaned back and stretched.

"You'll be killed in a month."

Niles's eyebrows drew together as though he hadn't thought of such an outcome.

"The kingdom is at peace, and a soldier's pay is a good one," he said. "I can send home coin. You won't be forced to leave."

But Niles's mother had already stopped paying attention, her eyes glazing over with boredom, scanning the room for something more interesting. They landed on a table covered in plates and dishes presumably from their last meal, though bits of dried food stuck to each piece, and it seemed some of the dishes had been there longer than others. An empty carafe lay on its side beside two glasses used days earlier.

She sat up suddenly. "Be a good boy. Hand me that bottle."

Niles hesitated a moment too long. The tall glass bottle she pointed to also sat on the table, half-full of hateful wine and Niles wanted nothing more than to smash it against the wall. She'd get better if she stopped drinking. He was sure of it.

"What are you waiting for?! If you won't do it, I'll get it myself."

With that she stood on unsteady legs, collapsing into the table, shuffle-stepping forward. She reached for the edge of the thick wooden tabletop, toppling plates and bowls with a clatter and flipping a chair in the process.

Horrified, Niles reached to help her from the floor, but his actions only angered her more.

"Let go! Let me go! I'm fine."

She pulled herself into one of the chairs closest to the bottle, then sighed when at last she had her hands around its slender neck. She caressed it once, this friend in liquid form, all the while Niles watching, hate growing in his chest. I could feel it almost as strongly as I could my own beating heart.

"I'm still going," he said after she drank her fill.

Her head snapped upwards, her gaze pinning him with a lucid ferocity he hadn't expected.

"Go, then," she said with a smile like acid. "Go, little boy. You'll find your death just as your father did, and his father before him."

Niles hardened his features and stood taller at her insults, but the boy deep inside was a well of emotion. So much emotion. Anger, embarrassment, helplessness—all of it swirling beneath the surface in a violent whirlpool.

And yet…more than anything? He wanted to make her proud, to see her smile. He wanted to hear her laugh again. She *had* laughed once. It seemed so long ago.

"We're going to get you the help you need," he said.

At that, she cackled again. "Nothing will fix these legs," she rasped, gesturing to the half-useless limbs.

It wasn't just her legs, though. He'd seen her shake out her hands when she thought he wasn't looking, staring at them as though they belonged to someone else. The numbness and tingling had spread. She just hadn't told him.

He picked up the bag he'd packed and slung it across one shoulder.

"I love you, Mum. I'll find you a cure."

It was a foolish promise from a foolish boy with no power, but whose optimism knew no bounds, even in the worst of times.

Niles had been an optimist.

The revelation was shocking. As long as I'd known him, Niles had been a coward, living in fear of his own destiny, but forever trying to prove to the world he was something… more. Perhaps this was why. It wasn't difficult to imagine how someone who'd held such hope for the future could get turned around when put on the front lines of a battle, the horrors of which he couldn't have begun to imagine.

I love you, too. I love you, too…

Niles's thoughts rang through my head as though I'd thought them myself. It was all he wanted from her—a mother's love, some sign of approval before he headed to Irzan to train with the King's Army. Was it too much to ask?

She opened her mouth, hesitating a fraction of a second and, for that moment, hope welled until his chest nearly burst with the force behind it.

"You're not strong enough. You've never been strong enough. Mark my words, Niles, you'll *die* trying to prove your strength."

His hope shattered into a thousand pieces, replaced with humiliation and anger.

He spared her one hard, cold glance, then nodded and left, his lips pressed into a thin line, the rims of his eyes an angry red from holding back tears he was too old to cry.

I moved my gaze back to Niles, the Niles of now, who slowly opened his eyes in a confused daze. I prepared for him to lunge at Quinn, but he didn't. In fact, he seemed… almost devoid of emotion.

Maybe it was better for Niles to have lost such a horrible memory. Maybe it was good for him to have forgotten how the awful woman he'd called his mother had treated him before he left home.

Niles had told me about his childhood once, but he'd never mentioned that his mother was ill…or that she was inebriated most of the time. No wonder he had sought to drown his own worries and sorrows in the same way. It was all he had known.

I swallowed back a lump in my throat. Niles had become exactly what he detested in his mother, which explained his self-hatred all too well.

As he stepped from the water and the final portion of the walkway rose from the lake, I put a hand to his arm.

"Oh, Niles," I said softly.

His eyebrows drew together, expression darkening. He yanked his arm away from my touch.

"I don't need your sympathy," he bit. "No matter *what* you saw."

I stepped back, not expecting such vitriol from him after what I'd just seen in his mind, but I needed to remind myself that *he* didn't remember what we'd just seen. He probably thought I was ready to judge him for all the mistakes he'd made much later on.

We crossed the long walkway over the bridge in silence, and I couldn't stop thinking about the images the lake had shown me, and the irony that in taking the memory from one person, it gave the memory to their companions. Trustworthy companions could provide the memory back again, but travel with the wrong sort and you might never know what you lost, or what might be used against you.

My gaze fall on Quinn, eyes sharp ahead, jaw set. I would regain my memory again, or at least the knowledge of it. And he would regain his. I would never keep something from him.

I swallowed back a cough. Maybe that wasn't entirely true. The eye-shaped brand still burned on my chest. I *was* hiding something from Quinn. I caught a glimpse of Niles to my right, though I tried not to make my observations known. Niles knew my secret, knew what I'd promised the Chaos Wielder.

And Quinn didn't.

But I wasn't deliberately *hiding* it from him.

I would tell him. I just needed to find the right time, *and* I needed a plan for what I was going to do about my promise to the Chaos Wielder. I wouldn't keep that promise, but how to get out of it…well, I'd have to figure out something. And when I did, I'd share the full story with Quinn.

The water lapped at the walkway languidly, as though it hadn't just viciously ripped an important memory from each of us. I wondered how the walkway had risen and if it would stay above the water for us or disappear again once we crossed.

Please don't let us have to come back this way.

At this point, I didn't know who I was praying to. God? The Saints? Kufataba? All I knew was that I didn't want to lose another part of myself.

Was this why there were no guides beneath Kufataba? Staying too long in the enchanted forest and crossing the bewitched lake time and again would eat away at a person, bit by bit, little by little, until there was nothing left to give.

"What does Kufataba mean?" I asked, eager to break our party's sullen quiet.

Quinn pressed his lips together, probably thinking of a way to avoid explaining it to me. Great. So, it must have meant something like *all who travel here perish* or *you now belong here forever.* Or maybe, *shortcuts for a steep price.*

"It means Death Mountain," Alesh answered for Quinn.

Well.

Quinn shot Alesh a look.

"It doesn't mean anything," Quinn said sharply. "Not really."

Alesh shook his head. "It means Death Mountain because to travel over it is to wish for your own death. Its peak cannot be climbed."

"And beneath its surface has *so much* more appeal," Niles muttered.

"Maybe it is difficult here," Alesh conceded. "But it is not certain death."

"Oh, so only a maybe-death then. Excellent. Just wonderful."

Too bad the lake hadn't taken Niles's memory of sarcasm. He shoved his hands into the pockets of his tunic and began to whistle.

I tried to avoid looking at the lake, at the water that had

once again turned black, making it impossible to gauge the depth. I tried to avoid thinking about what kind of creatures might live in its depths, supposing anything could survive in a lake that stole memories to begin with. And, what would happen if someone fell in? Would the lake absorb all their memories entirely? I shook the thoughts from my head and walked just a little faster.

When we finally made it across the walkway and onto the land on the other side of the lake, Alesh gave an audible sigh of relief, tension releasing from his sagging shoulders. I might have been worried about whether or not we'd have a walkway if we had to come back again, but not knowing how to swim, Alesh was more concerned about whether the walkway would remain standing while we traveled it.

Like the opposite side of the lake, the shoreline was tree-lined, but behind the many trunks and branches, the land on this side was rocky and far drier by comparison, which we discovered as we ventured onward.

I turned at the sound of the walkway sliding back into the black water. As it disappeared from sight, my breath hitched. On some level, I knew the lake would swallow the walkway again. I'd been optimistic to hope it might stay raised.

After what we'd experienced at the lake, no one was interested in conversation. Quiet was for the best as the path became what appeared to be a mountain pass. Niles stopped at one point, looking up into the *sun* above and the peaks that now rose on either side of us.

"How?" he asked, throwing his hands out, then letting them fall to his sides with a slap. "I thought we took the pass under the mountain to *avoid* climbing a mountain. And yet here we are."

Alesh shrugged.

"No one ever said it made sense," Quinn said. "Keep walking."

Despite his words, Quinn's tone wasn't as sharp as he tended to be with Niles. Maybe he'd been affected by living through Niles's memory of his awful mother, too. Perhaps even he realized that Niles's demons haunted far deeper than he'd imagined.

By the time we stopped to eat a quick lunch amidst the boulder field between the two peaks, the *sun* had already made its way across most of the false sky. My bones ached with fatigue, but still we didn't dare stop for more than a few moments. If I thought I was the only one eager to move forward, to get out from beneath the blasted mountain and back to the real world outside, I couldn't have been more wrong. Not even Niles protested when we began our steady ascent once more.

I desperately wanted the mountain to give us a rest before the third challenge. At the same time, all I wanted to do was get the task—whatever it was—over and done with. The sooner we could leave the mountain behind, the less on edge we'd all be.

"I don't like this," Quinn said. The boulders had grown farther apart and the field tapered, then dumped us into a tall, slot canyon between the two mountains, the vertical walls stretching skyward for a hundred feet or more.

The canyon between the walls narrowed as we walked

and I ran a hand against the smooth sandstone beside me, wondering how the walls of the canyon had been carved. As the *sun* set somewhere high outside the canyon, the path grew ominous, the darkness ever oppressive. The walls pressed inward.

"Maybe we should camp outside the canyon before it gets completely dark," I suggested.

In the shadows, Quinn shook his head.

"Too late," he said. "We're in too deep now."

A ruby glow lit behind me—Alesh's staff again. I removed the talisman from beneath the fabric of my shirt and let it light slowly, feeling the glow in my veins as much as in the stone itself.

"If we turn around, though, we can camp outside the canyon and face the third challenge tomorrow instead of today. We'll be refreshed and better equipped to handle it."

"I think it's too late for that."

CHAPTER TWENTY-SEVEN

The One Who Failed
Reina

My gaze trailed to where Quinn pointed, barely making out a series of repeating niches in the smooth rock surface of the canyon walls. At the very top was a cave-like opening.

"The exit," I breathed.

Thank the Saints. We'd be out from beneath Kufataba before nightfall. Or whatever passed for nightfall beneath the mountain. We just…had to climb sixty feet upward along a smooth canyon wall with no safety ropes.

I swallowed.

Alesh dropped his pack, then strapped his staff against his back, winding it between the layers of fabric that made up his tunic. He tilted his head to gaze to the dark opening far above our heads.

"At least we have a path," he said, extending his fingers to touch the hand and footholds carved into the rock.

"Leave the bags," Quinn said.

"But we'll need those supplies," I countered.

"It doesn't matter. We can't climb with full packs. Empty out everything we don't need and leave it here. Consolidate the rest into my pack. I can climb with it."

Giving up any supplies made me uneasy, but Quinn, as always, was right. There was no way to climb with them.

We dumped the contents of the bags onto the ground, sorting what was needed and what we could leave behind before packing a single bag for Quinn to carry.

I caught Niles looking upwards at the daunting canyon wall, taking a shaky breath.

"I've seen you climb," I said, remembering the day he'd impressively climbed a cavern wall to retrieve the talisman.

His gaze turned back to me. "There's a big difference between ten feet to the floor and a hundred."

"It's not a hundred feet," I scolded. "Maybe fifty. Sixty tops. I've seen you climb, Niles. I know you can do it."

Quinn didn't wait for us to sort out which order to climb. He tightened the pack against his shoulders and placed his hands and feet in niche after niche, moving upward.

"The sooner we get there, the sooner we get this over with," Quinn called. As if we needed a reminder that we all wanted to leave Kufataba behind with every fiber of our being.

"You go," I said to Niles. "I'll follow. That way if you fall, you'll land on me."

I was *almost* rewarded with a smile. "Quinn would never allow you to go last," he said.

"I will go last," Alesh offered, though I hadn't realized he'd been paying attention to our hushed conversation.

"There," I said to Niles. "It's settled. If you fall, you've got cushioning all the way down. Now go."

He looked ready to argue, but instead, he took a breath,

and placed an unsteady foot in the first niche.

Waiting until Niles gained some height before I began to climb, I shifted from foot to foot on the ground in anticipation. A ladder, I reasoned with myself. This was nothing more than a very large ladder. There was no reason to panic. I had no reason to worry that I might fall.

Then water began to flow through the base of the slot canyon, a trickle between my boots at first, then quickly gaining in speed and depth. I shot a glance to Alesh, who met my gaze with wide-eyed concern. He urged me forward with a quick flip of his hand, and I no longer hesitated to start climbing.

I gripped the dusty niches tightly, missing the callouses I'd once had from compounding so many medicines. There hadn't been much need for compounding in Irzan, not within the castle walls anyway. As the dry, hard niches bit into my fingers and palms, I cursed my soft hands.

One niche. The next niche. I kept climbing, listening for the sound of rising water below. And was it me or—

"Beware," Quinn shouted from above. "The handholds get smaller the higher you climb."

Fiermi.

Above me, Niles paused in climbing and glanced back over his shoulder.

"Don't!" I said quickly. He squeezed his eyes shut and took a deep breath. "Don't look down, Niles. Just keep going."

But he froze in place, paralyzed by his own fear.

"Niles," I called. "You *must* keep going. The water is

rising in the canyon. We'll all be swept away."

We'd be swept into the boulders at the mouth of the slot canyon…or drowned when caught in an unexpected turn beneath the water. As much as I wanted to know how the canyon walls had been formed earlier, I wished nothing more than to be ignorant of it now. The water below roared ferociously.

"Just…climb over me. Go around me," he said between heavy breaths.

"There's no way to go around you, Niles. You can't stop," I said, my arms burning with the strain of holding tight to the wall. I spared a glance down. Alesh held tight to the wall, but the raging water rose inches from his boots.

Thank goodness Quinn had our only pack and was far above at this point. At least Niles wouldn't slow him. Alesh called something from somewhere below me, but the water drowned out his words.

Then a horrible grinding came from somewhere above. I snapped my head upwards, my eyes glued to Niles's legs. Somewhere over him, something was happening.

"Climb faster," Quinn called. "It's closing! I must have triggered something."

Quinn's words had the desired effect on Niles. He began to climb again, mumbling words under his breath. I followed as closely as I dared without getting kicked in the face, reaching and pulling myself upward, hoping desperately to reach the top before whatever it was sealed our fate in the water below.

I couldn't let myself be separated from Quinn. I wouldn't

allow it.

Gritting my teeth, I heaved onward, my fingers beginning to slip on the ever-narrowing niches. The sweat on my hands had combined with the dust to create a slick coating on my fingers and palms that made each grip more difficult than the last. I pressed the toes of my boots into the divots to keep myself on the side of the canyon wall. With each upward movement, the grinding sound grew louder until I could feel it vibrating in my bones.

"Hurry!" Quinn said, sounding strained.

The grinding slowed, making a different sound now, but it hadn't stopped. Finally, Niles reached the floor of the cave and swung his legs up and over. Muffled curses followed. When I reached the last few handholds—tiny crevices that could hardly be called handholds—I wanted to weep with happiness, but there was no time to let my muscles recover from the strenuous climb.

Instead, I had to fling myself beneath an enormous stone Quinn strained to hold up with his back to keep the mouth of the cavern open, and yet my arms were limp and my legs buckled when I tried. The strain from the climb had fatigued my muscles to the point of failure. I was a newborn foal, fumbling on unfamiliar limbs.

Panting, I crawled forward. Niles, who had already entered the cavern, reached a hand to help me and it was all I could do to collapse on the floor and regain my breath. The top of Alesh's head came into view once he reached the last of the climbing niches, and he struggled to pull himself to the ledge.

Quinn gritted his teeth, face contorted in concentration, but his legs began to give, and the enormous stone pushed downward on his back despite the veins that bulged in his neck from the strain. Niles dove to keep the stone from pressing down entirely, but there wasn't room for Alesh to climb through with both Niles and Quinn attempting to hold it at the same time.

"Move out," Quinn cried hoarsely, his feet slipping.

"No," Niles said. "You're exhausted. You can't hold it. Let me do it!"

"You…can't," Quinn said.

"I *can*."

Niles spoke the words, but they came out a roar, and he pushed into the stone with all his strength, not only stopping it from falling further, but actually pushing it upward. Saints, where had he found the strength?

Quinn had no choice. His muscles failed, and he collapsed. I grabbed his hands and helped drag him, stumbling, into the cavern.

Niles's whole body shook, his eyes trained on a single spot in the dirt. Alesh scrambled beneath the stone, reaching last minute for the staff that had come loose from its bindings and fallen to the ground just outside the opening.

"Let go, Niles," I said, offering a hand to pull him away from opening and the stone's crushing weight.

Niles raised his head to look at me, piercing blue eyes as clear as the day I'd first met him, clear and lucid. Unlike the charm and amusement that had played on his features then, his expression now was all serious, his mouth pressed tight, eyes fighting to convey a message I didn't understand.

"Come on," I said.

Still struggling beneath the weight of the stone, he didn't speak, but I followed his gaze down to his foot, where he'd wedged it between the rock wall and the floor of the cavern in order to get traction to hold up the stone. He pulled his leg slightly, but his foot stayed wedged.

"You're stuck." The hollow words came from my throat, but my voice was hardly more than a whisper.

I bent to his foot, frantically digging at the packed dirt around it with my fingernails, trying in vain to get his foot loose. If he let go of the stone—even if we got him most of the way clear—his leg would be crushed. Niles…would die.

Oh, God! That's what the old woman in the apothecary had seen.

He will not make it.

I swallowed back a sob.

Quinn kneeled beside me, gripping Niles's ankle to wiggle his foot free, but it didn't budge. Niles trembled with the effort of holding the stone.

"There must be something in here we can use to hold the stone up!" Alesh searched the back of the cavern. Desperately, I turned, looking left and right, but the large space was empty of anything useful. There was nothing.

"Reina," Quinn said from his spot on the ground behind me. "Reina, it's no use."

Tears blurred my vision. "No!" I said. "There's *got* to be a way. We're not leaving him."

My nails broke in the hard ground, scraping uselessly

against the packed dirt again, and I let out a sob, a rasping croak I didn't recognize as my own voice. I didn't care if they all heard me come undone.

"Moreina," Niles said, voice soft.

My lips parted. I slumped, something in me breaking. I met his gaze again, a river of tears coursing down my cheeks.

"It's all right," he said, beginning to quiver beneath the weight of the stone. "*The One Who Failed* is serving his purpose."

I bit back another sob. I didn't want Niles to be a failure. I didn't want him to give his life so we could live. He'd had an awful childhood. He'd done terrible things. And then he'd spent years with horrible remorse eating away at him. Why shouldn't he have another chance? Didn't we all deserve a second chance?

"Go," he said, motioning with his head. "Go on. I don't want you to see."

He wobbled a moment, then pushed upward again as though his strength could be renewed by resolution alone.

Quinn stood behind me, pulling my hand, urging me forward into the dimly lit passageway at the back of the cavern. I stumbled, looking back at Niles once again, then slipped my hand from Quinn's and ran to Niles's side.

"Niles," I said urgently, wiping tears from my eyes. "You're strong enough. You've always been strong enough, and your mother? She would be so proud." I put a hand to his cheek. "So proud."

Did he remember his mother? Did he remember who she was and what she really thought of him?

Did it matter?

I'd rather him die knowing he'd done something right, knowing that someone was proud of him. I could give him that, at least. The hope in Niles's eyes—relief, maybe—flared bright. A single tear crested the rim of his eye, plopping onto the rock floor. He nodded once in reply.

I joined Quinn at the opening to the passageway, but now Alesh took up a place beside Niles, whispering words I couldn't hear. Niles heard them, though, and that was all that mattered. An eerie calm came over Niles's face. He nodded, then stopped struggling.

I didn't have a chance to object again. Quinn swung me into his chest, holding me tightly, shielding me from the resounding boom that echoed through the cavern. I jumped at the sound, even expecting it, even knowing it was coming.

Niles was dead.

CHAPTER TWENTY-EIGHT

Payment Due
Quinn

He'd done it. I didn't want to give Ingram credit, but he'd saved Reina *and* Alesh…by giving his own life. I didn't think he had it in him to sacrifice himself, not even after what Reina said. It was one thing to feel remorse, but something else entirely to repent in any meaningful way.

And he had.

Reina told me he'd come to terms with what he'd done, that he knew he had much to make up for, and I hadn't believed her. I mean, I believed he'd said it. I just didn't believe he meant it.

She sniffed quietly into my chest. I stroked her hair, then rested my cheek on the top of her head and closed my eyes, consoling her the best I could, given the circumstances. If I could have just held the blasted stone a little longer, if my body hadn't given out, maybe we could have avoided this entirely. I fought with the rising regret in my chest. Regret gained us nothing. What was done was done. I shoved the regret, the guilt, behind a partition in my mind.

And despite it all, I wasn't sorry Ingram was dead. His death was payment for the many lives he'd claimed.

As she stepped out from my embrace and wiped her eyes and face of the tears she'd shed, Alesh rejoined us, putting a hand to her shoulder.

"It is done," Alesh said. "He felt no pain."

Reina nodded dully.

"Let's get moving," I said, squeezing her hand gently.

The passage walls glowed with a dim cobalt light that appeared to come from within the rock itself. Reina dragged a hand lightly along the walls, but the blue glow did not transfer to her fingers.

"You cannot take a sample with you." I teased a small smile from her lips.

"I'd love to study it," she said quietly, her mind still on other things.

I had no doubt Reina would study anything and everything Liron had to offer if she could get her hands on all of it. Was the construction of her workshop finished? I'd intended it as a surprise for her birthday next month. When completed, it would be six times the size of her cottage with multiple workbenches and more glass jars and bottles than she could possibly count, let alone use. A third of the building was to be encased in glass walls, dedicated as a greenhouse for the plants she used the most, or maybe the ones that were most difficult for her to find.

It took everything in my power not to tell her about it now, not to see her face light up at the idea of so much space to do the very thing she loved the most. But it would have to wait, if only for the fact that we'd just lost Niles. Detest him though I might, Reina had forgiven him. The loss was far too raw to bring up a gift in hopes of lifting her spirits.

We followed the twists and turns of the glowing tunnels beneath the mountain for half an hour. Every time we came upon another turn, I hoped it would be the one that took us to the exit that would release us from this enchanted world.

We'd passed the three challenges—resolve, fortitude, and strength, and still there was no sign of our exit. Kufataba should be finished with us. We should be allowed to leave. *Why* hadn't Kufataba released us yet?

Outwardly, I let no sign of my frustration show. The last thing I needed to do was worry Reina and Alesh, but inside I had to wonder if Kufataba wasn't yet done with our party.

In a way, it was why I wasn't surprised when a solid glowing blue wall stopped us in our tracks.

Reina's sharp intake of breath mirrored my own.

"What is that?" Alesh asked.

"I don't know."

The only answer I could give.

I placed a hand to the surface of it, pressing lightly, but the wall gave no play.

"We did what Kufataba asked," Reina said. "We completed the three tasks Brigantino told us we would have to face. Maybe this is…the exit?"

"It does not feel like an exit," Alesh said, his eyes closed, feeling for the magic as he'd done before.

"What does it feel like?" I asked.

"I do not—"

Choose.

The word spoke itself into my mind, a whisper I might

have thought I'd imagined except for the fact that Alesh flinched and Reina's eyes widened.

I searched for the source of the voice, even knowing it had come from inside my head.

"Choose what?" Reina breathed.

Choose, the voice repeated.

When none of us responded, the voice spoke again.

Choose your sacrifice.

"Sacrifice? Sacrifice!" Reina said in disbelief. "Have we not sacrificed enough already? Did you not see our friend who gave his life but two hours ago? The old woman said he wouldn't make it. And he didn't! That's it. We've given you our sacrifice already!" She turned as she spoke the words, shouting into the space around us, searching for somewhere to release her anger.

The voice did not respond.

"What old woman, Reina?" I asked, my voice so much calmer than I felt.

"The woman at the apothecary. I went back. For the herbs, but also for her sight. She's a seer, like me. She saw it. She saw our success and said *he* wouldn't make it, but she didn't say who. Niles has already been taken from us. We shouldn't have to sacrifice anything else!" Her voice rose, going on about the woman and the apothecary and sacrifices we shouldn't have to make.

A fourth challenge. Brigantino hadn't said anything about a fourth challenge. There were only supposed to be three. Unless...

Unless the memory of the fourth challenge had been

taken from him on his way back through Kufataba the second time.

Choose your sacrifice.

I closed my eyes.

"What must we sacrifice?" I asked aloud.

One who will stay.

Not what. Who.

I almost laughed. Of course we wouldn't complete the journey. Of course one of us would be sacrificed to whatever gods Kufataba worshipped. Of course. Because nothing about any of this could ever be straightforward. My anger died as quickly as it had flared, and my breath quickened.

Maybe this was the way to absolve myself of the mistakes I'd made. Maybe I could redeem myself, forgive myself for the horrible wrongs I'd done. Whether done on behalf of the Order or not, they were still *my* wrongs and only I could take responsibility for them.

"The one who…" Reina's voice trailed off.

Her eyes shifted in realization of what Kufataba was asking and in understanding that I was the only person who was expendable.

"No!" she cried.

I rubbed a hand across the back of my neck, trying to work the knots deep within the muscle. I took a long, deep breath and released it. Then I slipped the pack from my shoulders and set it on the ground.

Here. I am here. Here and now. I tried to repeat the mantra again, but it did no good. Not today.

"It has to be me," I said, blinking slowly, reluctant to

meet Reina's eyes.

Alesh offered no argument. No doubt he'd figured it out before I had to begin with. He wasn't daft.

"No! We sacrificed *enough*." She turned and spun to the glowing wall. It continued to pulse dark shades of blue, indifferent to her anger. She pointed at it as though addressing a child. "Enough! You don't get to take anyone else." Her voice cracked on the last word.

Choose.

I stepped forward, taking hold of Reina's hand, pulling her to me, and embracing her in the last hug I would ever give her. Inhaling, I buried my nose in her hair, breathing in everything that *was* Reina.

"Shh, this is a way I can earn forgiveness for the wrongs I've committed," I told her quietly. I swallowed. "I can finally be free of the things I've done, Reina."

She gripped my arms with a strength someone her size shouldn't possess, then looked up at me, her dark eyes full of unshed tears ready to spill over any moment. Those eyes, eyes that saw into my soul.

"You're the only one who hasn't forgiven yourself. This won't help!"

"It's what…I have to do."

I took in every curve of her face, the way her eyes could go from demanding to pleading in an instant. Then I brushed her hair back and pulled her to me, kissing her forehead, feeling the warmth of her skin beneath my lips.

I was a fool to think the two of us could have a storybook ending. Those kinds of things happened in fairy tales and this was no fairytale. Fairy tales weren't full of war and undead, of pain and sacrifice, and they didn't leave a trail of wounded and broken.

Reina choked back a sob, her body nearly convulsing with the effort. All I could do was hold her tighter, squeeze her until I wasn't sure whose tears were soaking my shirt— hers or mine.

I couldn't remember the last time I'd shed tears. I didn't even remember the last time I felt the urge, but right now? Right now, I couldn't even be sure if the tears I shed were from sorrow or anger.

I was furious.

Not for my own life. I'd come to terms with my own mortality in the Order. But for Reina to lose *again,* and for Alesh and Reina to have to go on to face the Chaos Wielder… it wasn't fair.

"Let it take me instead," Alesh offered half-heartedly.

He knew it wasn't a possibility. Perhaps he'd only said it to show Reina the futility in wishing for things that couldn't be. I kissed the top of Reina's head again, then pressed my cheek against her hair.

"You and Reina are our one chance at defeating the Chaos Wielder. Without the magic of death and the magic of life, chaos will go unchallenged," I said, hating that my voice was nowhere near steady. Blast it! I needed to be stronger.

"But you're the king!" Reina said.

I swallowed. "Kings come and kings go. Castilles will find a new ruler. With Grandmother Elle in charge and you there to oversee things, the two of you will make the right decision. Or…perhaps it's time that Castilles embraced a queen instead."

I cupped her cheek with the words, making my meaning more than clear. My grandmother wouldn't live forever, but she could ensure all her knowledge was passed to Reina. She could groom Reina for the leadership role I knew she was capable of tackling.

Reina shook her head and buried her face into my chest again, fighting back another round of sobs.

Make your choice.

"You can't go," Reina said, her head snapping upwards, her hands gripping my shirt in desperation. "I have things to tell you. You can't leave."

The choice has been made.

The wall transformed into a wavering liquid that remained upright, defying all natural laws of gravity.

"I have things I would like to have told you, too," I told her, thinking of her workshop, of a real proposal, a royal wedding, and all the dreams I'd almost never allowed myself to indulge in. An uncharacteristic wave of gratitude washed over me. It didn't matter how short a time we'd had together. It was our time, a time I'd almost missed entirely. Thank the Saints for small miracles.

"No, Quinn. You don't understand."

I kissed her then—hard, as though I could somehow convey that I understood all the unsaid things, that I knew, and that it no longer mattered. When I pulled back, I bent my forehead to hers, not caring that Alesh was here to witness our goodbye. For all I cared, he no longer existed. At least, not for this moment.

"I love you, Reina. I always have. I always will."

"I love you," she said, her voice so small I almost missed the words.

I didn't hesitate. I stepped backwards into the cobalt liquid wall, never losing sight of Reina, my heart near to bursting with all the things unsaid and all the lives never led.

And then—

CHAPTER TWENTY-NINE

Inviting Death
Reina

The iridescent blue liquid swallowed Quinn's form, coaxing his body into a deadly embrace, and I shrieked. The sound echoed across the small space. I bent, wrapped my arms across my middle, and clutched my sides, crumpling to the floor.

Oh, Saints. Quinn. Not Quinn!

Alesh held me as I fell to my knees and rocked back and forth. I couldn't have lost him, not Quinn. Not my rock, my heart, my home. Not Quinn.

Quinn's loss from my life made Niles's death just a few hours earlier seem as though it had happened years ago, decades ago, eons ago—as though it was something I no longer needed to concern myself with. Quinn was my *only* concern.

Quinn…who was gone. Forever.

I sobbed and let Alesh hold me. I leaned into his warm, comforting presence, allowing myself a moment to forget it all, to grieve for what I had lost and what Quinn had sacrificed, to grieve for a life I'd never have, dreams that would never again be the same.

What I wouldn't give to have the pain of death in my bones now, to know…to truly *know* he was gone. That ache, which had seemed a hindrance all my life, would have been a blessing at this very moment.

I sobbed until I was spent.

Alesh didn't rush me or push to move forward. He simply held me, arms loose around my shoulders, his fatherly presence a comfort when I otherwise had none.

When hiccups overtook the sobs and the tears no longer flowed, I stood shakily, holding tight to Alesh's arm for comfort. I viciously glared at the shimmering liquid wall, but it had disappeared sometime during my breakdown and now only an ominous blackness stood in its place.

Alesh reached for the pack Quinn had carried moments before and rummaged through it until he found a water skin. He handed it to me.

"Drink," he said. "Let the water replenish your tears and your soul."

I drank, but the cool water sliding down my throat did nothing for my soul. My soul was empty now. Hollow.

I wiped my mouth with the back of my hand and handed the water skin back to him. "Let's go," I croaked.

"No," he said, placing a gentle hand on my arm. "We wait. Just another moment." When he realized I was about to protest, he added, "I need time to capture my breath."

"*Catch* your breath."

"Yes, I need time to catch my breath."

His lie was obvious, but done for my benefit, so I took a moment for myself and breathed deeply, trying to remember my purpose, trying to focus on the entire reason Alesh and I were still here.

My head throbbed. I cringed as I swallowed and put a hand to my puffy eyes. They'd be swollen straight into tomorrow. Briarmint and aloe. It's what I would treat myself with if I'd thought to bring it with me.

Maybe if I focused on remedies, I could survive this day. And maybe if I made it through this day, I could make it through tomorrow, too.

"Let's go," I stood on shaky legs.

Alesh regarded me a moment, then nodded and we moved to the blackness before us. I looked to him, waiting for confirmation that the velvet blackness was what I hoped.

"The exit," he confirmed. "The same magic."

Of course it was.

The exit would present itself now that Quinn had given up everything.

Don't think. Don't think! You can't think of him now.

Briarmint. Briarmint and aloe for a headache and swollen eyes.

What else? Something else, Reina.

Lobelia for breath. Yarrow for fever. Tumeria for pain.

Yes. Keep going.

A tincture of harkspun nettle and willow bark for inflammation of the gums. Gingerene to fight nausea. Lavender balm to soothe the nerves. Lobelia for asthma. Psyllium and trelynx for constipation...

On and on, the list kept my mind from coming back to Quinn and prevented me from dwelling on my grief as we made our way from beneath the mountain. When we emerged from the darkness, an unfamiliar terrain greeted us.

As we left Kufataba behind, long, flat grasslands extended miles in every direction with waist-high willowy fronds that tickled my fingertips.

"I have never seen such lands," Alesh said. "You?"

I shook my head.

Fluted pear nectar for rejuvenation. Vinegar for indigestion. Eucalyptus and steam for nasal congestion.

Alesh turned left, then right, then around in a circle.

"What are you doing?" I asked, my voice still hoarse.

His gaze met mine almost reluctantly.

"I think we need the map," he said.

"No."

"We do not have a choice. There is no time. The mountain is behind us, but in front of us?" He gestured to the plains that looked the same in every direction. "There is no road to follow."

I didn't want to open that map again. Not after what I'd *seen*. Not when I knew what it would bring. Not with grief so raw in my breast.

"Be quick," I said, shifting back and forth on my feet, suppressing the panic that welled in my chest.

I turned and closed my eyes, and Alesh opened the map. As the Winds of Chaos kicked up the dirt and grasses on the plain, spinning debris all around us, I held my breath.

Then Alesh folded the map again and dried grass and dirt rained down on us as the winds stopped dead. I swallowed. The damage was done. The Chaos Wielder would once again find us. He would be none too happy knowing just how close we were…or maybe he'd be delighted to find there were only two of us remaining.

Kai leaves, warmed and moistened, for a stye in the eyelid. Seleniac dissolved in honey for a cough. A topical application of vellowroot oil for blemishes of the skin. A tincture of basil and lavender oils for half-headaches.

Alesh tucked the map back into the pack and pointed his staff to the southwest. "This way," he said with a nod.

I followed without a word. There was nothing that needed to be said, nothing worth expending the energy of opening my mouth for conversation's sake. I traveled behind Alesh through the grasslands, passing like a ghost in his wake.

A ghost. I almost laughed. Quinn had spent his time in the Order working as a spy, but he'd always referred to it as being a ghost. Was this how he'd felt? Lost? Broken?

Every passing hour could have been days. Or weeks. It made no difference now. I understood we still needed to find and remove the Chaos Wielder from his position, but I watched myself from afar, living my life separate from my body.

In the evenings, we camped in the open plains after stomping down the grasses for a place to lay our heads, then woke in the mornings, and trekked onward again and again. The days blurred together. I ate when Alesh said it was time to eat and stared at the stars when Alesh said it was time to sleep.

And always, I ran through my lists of remedies. It was the only part of life that made sense anymore.

Lemonbalm for cracked fingers. Bellblaze dissolved in proxide for earache. Pink echlorea for seasonal allergies. White echlorea for hives.

On and on, my list. Always with me.

The list in my head kept me from thinking about more painful things, from remembering what I'd lost, but it also kept me from seeing the viper in the grasses when we stomped down our bedding one night.

The flash of fangs was so quick that I didn't react. Alesh turned when I cried out.

I looked first downward to where the snake had struck, the two small dots of blood soaking my breeches—evidence I was in very real danger—then to the ground for the snake who had disappeared into the higher grass.

"What did it look like?" He dropped his staff and pack to the ground.

I sat in the grass, staring at my leg.

"Reina," Alesh said, sitting beside me and grabbing hold of my shoulders. He forced me to look at him. "What did it look like? The…" He grew frustrated, looking for the word, then motioned a writhing snake with his hands.

I blinked furiously, trying to remember.

"It was…pale green," I said. "With a white stripe down its back."

"Look at me." Alesh pointed to his own eyes to keep me focused. My mind began to slide away again. "Very important. One line or two?"

I opened my mouth, then closed it again, struggling to remember the brief glimpse I'd had when the snake had struck and then slithered away into the shelter of the long grass.

"Two," I said, picturing it again in my mind. A pale green snake with two thin white lines running along the length of its back.

Apparently, this was not the right answer. As he rooted through the pack for supplies, Alesh looked distressed. I hadn't bought antivenin at the apothecary. Not that I owned antivenin for whatever kind of viper this was back home.

"It was poisonous, wasn't it?" I asked, my voice small. There was a tingling in the back of my throat and an unfamiliar metallic taste. Venom.

Alesh nodded distractedly and sorted through the various packets in the bag.

"There's nothing of use in there," I said quietly. "It's over."

He placed the packets down, his shoulders dropping in defeat.

"Are you sure?" he asked. "Are you sure *two* stripes?"

He held up two fingers as though maybe he had misheard my answer.

I nodded.

My leg had begun to swell beneath the knee. Whatever bit me contained more than enough venom to make the entire area of my leg burn with pain, and enough pain that I had grown nauseous.

I swallowed against the building lump in my throat and closed my eyes.

"I'm sorry," I said. I needed to say the words before my

body failed. "This is my fault." My eyes filled with hot tears I couldn't shed. "Niles and Quinn sacrificed their lives so you and I could do what needed to be done, and I…I ruined it all in one minute. He's going to win. The Chaos Wielder will win. Oh, Alesh, I'm *so* sorry!"

I would have sobbed, but the pain robbed me of my tears, a searing burn through my lower leg, now into my thigh.

At least…at least I would join Quinn soon.

Alesh stood. He paced a moment, searching the ground, tapping his hand against his staff. Then his gaze returned to the grasses and the sky, anywhere but at me. That, alone, was telling of his state of mind…and of how abysmal my condition was.

"What…kind of snake was it?" I asked.

I stifled a hysterical giggle that bubbled in my throat, threatening to turn me into a stark, raving lunatic before I died. Had I lost my mind? What difference did it make what kind of snake it was? A venomous one was the answer.

A deadly one.

Alesh bent his head to his staff and closed his eyes.

"Prayers won't help you now," I told him.

Saints help me for thinking such thoughts. God help me for saying it out loud.

Alesh's eyes flew open and he met my gaze, then kneeled beside me and gripped my arm.

"We have one chance."

"Numbing the pain won't stop the poison from flowing through my veins and shutting down my organs," I said, certain his idea was to allow me to die without pain as he'd done for Niles.

"No," Alesh said with a shake of his head before rushing onward again. "We use both magics. Both at once. Yours and mine. We control the life *and* the death within. It will take both."

I stared at him.

"My magic is useless, Alesh."

I couldn't use it without Quinn.

His eyes grew wild with desperation. "No! Your magic is mine and mine has become yours. If we work *together,* we can kill the poison. Grow healthy…healthy…"

"Tissue?"

"Yes! Healthy tissue."

I sucked a breath through my teeth. The pain had traveled to my lower abdomen, slicing into my womb with a ferocity worse than I could have imagined. In no time at all, it would reach my kidneys, my lungs, and my heart. I was dead either way.

A sudden calm swept over me. Shouldn't I feel panicked? Was it wrong I didn't? My heart thumped steadily as though I were about to heal another person and not myself.

I swallowed again and breathed out through pursed lips. Maybe Quinn's hair sewn into my boots would be enough. Maybe. It was my only hope.

"All right."

I spoke the words, all too aware they could very well be my last.

Alesh shoved the pack behind my back so I had something to lean on, and I pulled the talisman from beneath my tunic.

It caught on the seashell necklace Quinn had made for me, but I tucked that beloved treasure into my tunic, away from sight.

In a moment, both the talisman and the staff glowed brightly, and I was thrown into a vision state. Instead of an aqua haze, the world around me had become a deep purple, so dark it was nearly impossible to see at all.

My breathing grew shallow, my chest tight—a sign I didn't like to see in the strongest of my patients, let alone one who'd been bitten by a snake. I pushed past the discomfort, forging deeper into the purple vastness until I became aware that I wasn't the only one within the haze.

Of course Alesh would be here. He used his staff in the same way I used the talisman, but I was still shocked to see someone *within* the haze and not just outside of it.

"First, we kill the poison, cut it off before it can cause damage," he said.

"How?" I barely managed to get the word out.

I hadn't dealt with death before. I didn't understand how to close off veins, how to stop the venom from moving closer and closer to my heart.

"The same as life," he answered. "Only different order. I cannot do this part, not with our magic confused. You must do it. I will tell you what to do."

I gave a weak nod.

"Feel the dark of the poison. It will be black in your blood. Search for it inside your body."

I focused on his words, desperately trying to find the darkness in my veins, but finding only rich, red blood.

"It's not working! It's no good," I said with a shake of my head.

I couldn't see or feel anything that shouldn't be there, even when I *knew* it was there.

"Look harder!"

I closed my eyes tighter, concentrated, and dove deeper into my body, searching for a darkness, *any* darkness.

"It's there!" I squeaked as my consciousness floated through a wave so black it almost knocked me over. I braced myself as it washed over me.

"Good, now stop the flow."

I looked for a way to stop the blackness from flowing, but I couldn't stop it without also stopping the blood mixed in with it.

"Close off the flow. Close it. Entirely. Pinch it."

A piercing pain shot through my abdomen again and I fought against the nausea, fought to stay engaged with the talisman and within the purple haze.

"I will create a new path for the good blood with *your* power. You must isolate the poison with *my* power."

He meant to cut off the vein entirely. I didn't know if it could be done, but I focused all my energy on a spot downstream from the blackness until the edge of the vein crumpled in on itself, dying instantly.

Such a move might have killed me in a larger vein or artery, and yet even as I sealed the vein, I could feel Alesh creating a new path, a new vein for the blood.

"Close the other end," he said, a new vein swiftly forming from elements within my body.

I destroyed the vein just after his newly created segment, encapsulating the poison in a tiny piece of a vein no longer connected to anything. I thought I would feel relief, but pain was all that came.

"Do it again," he said. "There is still more. The poison has divided itself into different paths."

I panted, searching for the blackness again. It was easier to find this time, easier to seal off as well. We repeated the process twice more, until I felt as though my entire body had been trampled by horses and dragged across the ground.

When I finally withdrew from my shared vision with Alesh, I was coated in a sheen of perspiration and the pain had taken over every organ and every muscle. Swallowing was excruciating. Moving was out of the question.

I was dying. We'd done what we needed to, but too late.

Alesh kneeled beside me and placed a hand to my shoulder.

"It is done," he said.

"I'm sorry," I croaked. "We tried."

He narrowed his eyes at me questioningly.

"We have done it," he said. "You will live."

It didn't *feel* like I would live. I tried to shake my head, but the pain that radiated from my neck into my temples made for a feeble attempt and my head rolled to one side instead.

"Something's...wrong," I panted.

He shook his head, kind lines appearing from the corners of his eyes as he gave a tight smile.

"Sleep," he said.

Sleep was death, but sleep was a release from the pain.

Quinn, I'm coming.

And so, I let death come.

CHAPTER THIRTY

Chaos Found
Reina

Death was more painful than I expected.

As I cracked my eyelids open, I was prepared for my head to split in two. Thank God the stars shone overhead and not the sun, and thank the Saints both moons were near setting. I blinked at the sky. So many stars, so many unfamiliar stars. Nothing here was right.

Squinting, I raised my arm to my temple, surprised that it took immense effort to move it and also at the ache still lingering there. My entire body burned, right down to the smallest toes on my feet.

Which meant…I was alive.

I turned my head to Alesh, who sat crouched beside me, lightly dozing by leaning on his staff in a position that looked uncomfortable. I was alive. I wanted to feel relief—and I *did*—but another part of me, a much bigger part of me was swallowed by grief and anger—oh, so much anger. I'd almost been with Quinn.

It was a selfish thought, a foolish one. I knew how important this blasted prophecy was. I knew what Alesh and I were up against, and I knew he had no chance of succeeding without me, but dammit all to hell, how I wanted to be with Quinn!

I remained still, staring at the twinkling stars until the morning light chased them from the sky, the sun warmed my cheeks, and a light breeze ruffled the grasses like a giant silver-green ocean. When Alesh stirred, I turned my head to face him and attempted to stretch fingers and toes, grateful to find the pain had abated.

Alesh grinned wide when he met my eyes, his own eyes lighting up with relief.

"You are alive," he said.

I nodded and the pain in my neck intensified, causing me to cringe.

"That part is normal," he said. "There is always pain in the body after changing what is inside."

"Not with life," I said.

Alesh raised a finger in the air. "Ah, but you are not working with life now. I am."

I pushed myself to sit upright, ignoring the ache in my bones. Not the ache of death. I didn't have that anymore, not since my power had transferred from life to death. No, my body ached from Alesh asking it to create new tissue while I destroyed already existing tissue.

"Alesh," I said. "What happens to the veins I cut off, the capsules with poison in them?"

The smile slipped from his face.

"It is too difficult for you to handle," he said. "I will have to do it."

I eyed him.

"When we rid the world of the chaos and my power is mine again and yours is yours. Then, I will take care of the poison."

"Those pieces of vein that contain the poison won't last forever," I said, well-aware that my body would eventually try to attack and destroy the tissue that served no purpose. Once that happened, the poison would be released and be absorbed into my bloodstream a second time. I was a walking bomb with no idea of when my fuse might be lit.

Alesh nodded gravely. "It will last long enough. It must."

His words brought no comfort. I got to my feet, unsteadily reaching out to take his arm as I stood, every muscle in my body screaming as though I'd run ten miles and then slept six hours afterwards.

"How long until the eclipse" I asked.

I'd lost track of time long ago. If nothing else, the snakebite had brought me back to the present, back to my body, and refocused on what needed to be done.

"The eclipse." Alesh scratched his head and counted on his fingers. "We have thirty-five days."

I stared into the distant plains, wondering how far we had yet to travel, how long until the Chaos Wielder played his next trick. Rubbing my fingers against the smooth stone of the talisman, I replayed the scene from my vision and the Chaos Wielder's demand for the stone. I'd seen myself handing it over. Why would I? How did I escape that future?

How could I prevent it from happening?

Alesh had set a snail's pace for my benefit. For once, I didn't have it in me to push forward faster. It took all my energy and focus to put one foot in front of the other. At least the soreness abated the longer I walked.

Traveling the plains was nerve-wracking. Unlike the forest where one had any number of places to hide, or the mountains where one could camouflage, the plains were flat—so, so flat. Endless miles of grassland stretched in every direction and Kufataba's silhouette paled in the distance behind us.

Here, anyone could see us coming.

Which is why it made no sense when a teenage girl appeared behind us with no warning. In these wide-open spaces, we should have seen her long ago. Alesh took on a defensive stance immediately, but I stood with my hand at my sides, knowing full well there was no way to prevent the confrontation to come.

It wasn't difficult to guess who the girl was since there was no one else she could possibly be. She was maybe twelve or thirteen, her painted face a perfect oval, petite chin jutted outward as though proud she had snuck up on us. Amusement played in her deep-set pale eyes, leaving little doubt that this was the Chaos Wielder. Whose form had he stolen this time? I didn't recall seeing this girl during our journey.

Her dark hair was slicked back into a tight bun and covered by a black, beaded headdress dripping with gleaming white pearls. Atop the headdress, a jewel-studded crown that looked to be worth more than all the gold in Irzan sat delicately on her head.

I took a fortifying breath. I'd *seen* this before, seen *her* before.

"You again," I said.

"Now what kind of greeting is that?" the girl said.

"And who are you supposed to be this time?" I asked.

Her lips stretched across her teeth in a smile. The same smile the sailor had given, the same smile that belonged to the little girl outside the desert town, the same grin the fake Adan Iyer had given.

She cocked her head and eyed me as though contemplating how easy it would be to bring me to my knees, and the gems in her crown sparkled with the movement.

No, not a crown.

My eyes focused on the intricately bejeweled metal.

A diadem.

The realization shook me, and I let my gaze roam over her completely. This wasn't a form she had taken. This was… this was the Chaos Wielder *herself*. The Chaos Wielder was not only a child, but she was…a *she*.

"Coming to you as *me*," she said. "I figured you'd had enough of the games, so here I am."

I narrowed my eyes, focusing on the diadem again—the source of her power. If we could relieve her of it...

"Why now?" I said. "Why not show your true self earlier?"

She shrugged, the same confounded smirk still glued to her lips.

"Chaos is funny, Life Bringer. I've learned so much more since I first took control. In the beginning, I had to take on the form of others as I knew no other way. Now, I simply ride the Winds of Chaos wherever I need to go. I'm getting stronger."

Since she took control.

She was new. Whoever was the Chaos Wielder before her had kept chaos in order, which is why we'd seen no evidence of it sooner.

"Whoever trained you did not do so well, I think," Alesh said, brows drawn downward.

Annoyance flashed in her eyes. "Could you do better, old man?"

"At keeping chaos under my control? Certainly."

She gave a tinkling laugh.

"I don't want chaos under *control*," she said. "Where's the fun in that?"

"You call this fun?" I said. "People are *dying* from your antics!"

"And why shouldn't they?" she said, her pale eyes boring into mine. "People die anyway. That's what we do. We live. And then we die."

She brushed an imaginary speck of dirt from the skirt of her long cream-colored gown. The manner of dress wasn't what I'd seen so far in the Southern Plains. I itched to ask Alesh if he knew where people would dress in this style, if he could guess where she might be from. And why target the north for her devastation?

Questions. Quinn wanted to ask questions. That hadn't

changed just because he was…no longer here.

I couldn't say *dead*. Not yet.

"Why the north?" I said, meeting her pale eyes straight on, reading their truth.

She shook her head, giving me a confused stare.

"Why start with chaos in the north?"

She shrugged. "I stirred up trouble in many places. Chaos knows no reason and has no boundaries. North, south, east, west. Heaven, Hell, or Liron. It makes no difference to me."

"Who was Wielder before you?"

"My, my. Many questions, my dear Life Bringer. I already answered one. Now I have a question for you. We'll play it like a game, yes?"

I looked on, wary of what she might ask, my fingers itching to use the talisman I no longer could control well. I didn't dare. I had no doubt she would turn my own magic against me. No matter how strong I once was with the talisman, her ability to stir up chaos was too risky.

"Very well then. I'll take your silence to mean you wish to play."

I did not wish to play.

"Did you like my surprise?"

My brows drew together in confusion. I racked my brain for what she could possibly be referring to.

"The snake, silly!"

My lips parted in shock. "You…"

"With a Gohmi viper?! Are you out of your head? Do you know how painful a death that is?" Alesh cried.

Another sly smile.

"She's not dead, I see."

"No," I said, my throat dry. "I did *not* like your surprise. My turn to ask a question. What is the purpose of all of this? Why lure us here?"

"Because you have something I want. You both do. Offer me the necklace, Life Bringer. You made a promise."

This was it. The moment I'd seen, the moment I'd tried so hard to find a way out of.

"I made that promise before you killed the sailor whose body you used to visit," I said, shaking my head and stalling. "You don't deserve the necklace now."

Fury lit in her eyes.

"You would *dare* cross me?" she shrieked. "You took an oath! The sailor's life meant nothing."

A savage wind knocked me from my feet. I fell hard onto my rear, the breath knocked out of me. With that, the mark I'd hidden from view for so long burned as though I'd been freshly branded again. I crawled to my knees, nearly blinded by the sudden pain over my heart. Alesh came forward, putting a hand on my shoulder, trying to help, but I pushed him away. I did this to myself. I didn't want the Chaos Wielder to take out her wrath on him.

I put my hand to my neck, feeling the talisman's chain warm from the heat of my body, knowing I couldn't access its power in any way. Then my fingers brushed the rope necklace Quinn had made for me and I reached into my tunic, fingers gripped tightly around the little pink shell.

"Take my necklace," I said. I pulled the shell on the rope over my head. "I promised you I would offer it. Here it is, my offering!"

I held the rope necklace Quinn had made, the shell dangling from the ugly rope constructed from Kufataba grass. The only piece of Quinn I had left…and I willingly offered it away.

The alternative was unthinkable.

Quinn would want this.

She howled with rage, setting the pearls on her headdress swinging.

Alesh attacked at that moment, not with his staff, but with full-on magic, letting loose everything he could think to throw at her. Grasses grew in waves, the blades closest to the Chaos Wielder wrapping themselves around her wrists and ankles at the same time the blades all around us grew to twice our height to conceal us.

"Come!" he said, extending a hand to me. "We must go!"

Wind gusted wildly, blowing the grasses open wide in all directions, exposing us as easily as Alesh had concealed us. The Chaos Wielder ripped free of the flimsy shackles, pulling the blades up by their roots, giant chunks of dirt falling from the strands. She flung grass in every direction.

"You cannot escape me!" she boomed in a voice bigger than the young girl should have had.

With a wave of one hand, she set fire to the grass. The flames spread as though led forward by oil, feasting on the dry grassland. I sent a panicked look to Alesh. How could we fight fire? Life and death were no good to battle something that was never alive to begin with.

We raced across the grasslands, trying to escape the

spreading fire, all the while hearing the Chaos Wielder's giggles above the crackling of flames. She danced through it all, robes twirling through the flames without setting ablaze.

Alesh skidded to a halt and turned to avoid the flames in front of us. Coughing, I followed. A second turn, then a third.

She's herding us, guiding us where she wants us to go.

Sure enough we turned again when we were met with another wall of flame. I threw an arm to my head, trying to block out the smoke and flames to focus on where she was leading us and where we might be able to break free.

"Had enough yet?" she taunted.

My lungs burned with smoke and tears welled in my eyes, forcing me to blink to see at all.

I was tempted to jump through a wall of flame to escape her maze, but…what if she'd built more than a wall and all I did was jump into the middle of a blazing inferno?

"Use the magic," Alesh yelled back to me. We navigated another turn. "You have to use the magic."

"I can't!"

"There is no choice!"

"How? How can I kill her?"

"Stop her heart. You must reach in and stop it from beating."

He wanted me to kill the Chaos Wielder. Saints, did I have it in me to kill a twelve-year-old girl? Even if the twelve-year-old girl was a raging, murdering lunatic?

I reached into the power of the talisman—the power of death—pulling myself into the dark haze even while running from flames. Part of me was terrified it wouldn't work, that she would know I was using the power against her, but when no retribution came within a moment of tapping into the talisman's power, I dove deeper.

Her heart was easy enough to locate in her chest, it's wild, rhythmic beating proof of her excitement. She enjoyed watching us run for our lives. That, alone, should have been enough for me to stop her heart dead, but I didn't.

I couldn't.

But we weren't going to die because I couldn't kill a child. I used the power of death and reached deep into the earth, shriveling the roots of all the burning grass. It wasn't difficult to do since the grass itself was already so fragile. Then I reached deeper still until the earth began to crumble, sucking enormous chunks of grass into gaping holes that appeared from nowhere. Large pieces of dirt and grass fell into the deep chasms I'd opened.

I pulled Alesh to a stop on ground I'd safely avoided destroying. I didn't have to ask for his help. Already he had tapped the power of his staff, the purple haze enveloping both of us in a cocoon while he worked to grow healthier, stronger roots to stabilize our patch of land.

As he worked, I turned to the Chaos Wielder without warning and shot a dagger of pure dark power into the land below her feet. It crumbled instantly and she fell, her creamy robes staining brown with streaks of mud. She grabbed at the bedrock to keep from sliding into complete oblivion. I hoped the diadem would slide off her head and into the chasm below, but though it was skewed, it stayed tightly wound in the pearls of her headdress.

The air changed suddenly as though her power had been curbed. Something—I couldn't begin to name what—changed. The flames died out almost instantly, leaving charred, smoking black masses everywhere she'd directed her fire to spread.

Her eyes wild, the Chaos Wielder looked at me with fury—or maybe it was disbelief since she had clearly never been bested before and didn't expect to be knocked off her feet now. Then her brow set in determination and she raised a wind stronger than all the hurricanes I'd ever known. I squatted close to the ground, Alesh beside me doing the same, both of us wrapping the long grass through our fingers and around our wrists to keep from being blown from our feet. Through it all, I clung tight to the little seashell still clenched in my fist.

Alesh leaned harder into the power of his staff, the roots of the grass swiftly growing over our boots to keep us grounded, weaving together around our ankles and back again to secure our spot.

The wind stirred up so much dirt that it became difficult to keep my gaze trained on the Chaos Wielder, yet I peered through squinted eyes regardless. She let go of her handhold all at once, but instead of falling into the abyss below, she raised her arms and turned her face upward, then dissolved into the wind, letting it carry her only Saints knew where. If not for the wind and the dirt and the grass flying through the air, I would have opened my mouth in disbelief.

As quickly as she'd appeared, she'd disappeared again.

The wind, however, wasn't so quick to die down. Perhaps it was her way of reminding us her power was greater than either of ours.

"I really do not like that girl," Alesh said when a quiet finally descended.

Standing, I snorted and pulled grass from my hair and clothes.

"You should have killed her. It would have been a mercy."

I closed my eyes in shame and turned my face away. Quinn had believed there were times when killing was merciful, too. It was a sore spot between the two of us. At least, it *had* been.

"I couldn't," I croaked.

Alesh could have just as easily killed her himself, but I didn't bring up this particular point. If he didn't realize life could be used to kill, I'd rather not give him the opportunity the next time we met the Chaos Wielder.

My shoulders dropped with the thought. Dear God, we would meet her again. Her words and actions had made that clear enough. She wouldn't change her mind. Not now, not ever.

Maybe…I should have killed her.

As Alesh healed the land, pulling large pieces back together by entwining and strengthening roots, I tucked Quinn's seashell necklace with its now tattered and broken rope into my pocket, running a finger back and forth across the shell's scalloped edges. Alesh regrew grass through the burned portions, reinforcing the land again and again until it was safe to journey from our spot.

"Let us go," Alesh said, looking tired for perhaps the first time since I'd known him. There were lines on his face that I was sure I hadn't noticed before and a fatigue in his eyes he couldn't hide.

"Alesh," I said after some time picking our way across the grasslands again. "Did you feel a change? Right before she…disappeared, I mean? Did you feel something shift in her power?"

He eyed me, considering his answer.

Finally, he nodded. "There was a change, but I do not know what."

"I think she cracked the stone in her diadem when she fell."

I'd been replaying the scene in my mind since we started walking again and I was certain she'd hit her head on one of the rocks deep below the grass roots when I opened the earth beneath her. I was almost positive that was the same moment I'd felt the shift in her power. If her stone was cracked, her power might now be unreliable…which meant we stood a much better chance.

"If the stone is damaged, her power is limited," Alesh said.

I nodded.

"It did not seem limited when she disappeared in the wind. It did not seem limited when she drifted like ash into the sky." He put his hands to the sky as though miming her disappearance into nothing. "You could have ended it," he said, shaking his head. "But that is in the past. I will teach you how to use the power. We will work."

I opened my mouth to reply, then stopped dead in my tracks, the air suddenly thin, my lungs reluctant to breathe. Alesh was several paces ahead when he realized I'd stopped walking.

"What now?" He threw his arms out, then let them fall again, his staff clunking the ground with a muted thump.

Wide-eyed, I met Alesh's gaze slowly.

"I…used the talisman," I murmured.

"Yes, you did. As you have done many times before. As you did when you helped trap the poison."

Alesh waited, no doubt wondering if I'd lost my mind.

"I can't use it without Quinn."

"The north king is dead."

"I…I might have had enough power to isolate the poison without him here, I could have, but…" I licked my lips, my mind spinning wildly with a hope I almost didn't dare voice. "This? What I just did? I couldn't have used magic on that scale unless…"

My knees trembled, threatening to buckle. I turned back to where we had come, to Kufataba's nearly indistinguishable peak far, far away, almost invisible against the white sky.

I took a shaky breath.

"Quinn is alive."

CHAPTER THIRTY-ONE

A Man with No Name

Surrounded by light, he floated, blissfully unaware of who he was or how he'd come to be. Was he unborn? Hundreds of years old? An immortal entity?

It didn't matter. Nothing mattered but the light. He turned his face—did he have a face?—to its vibrant, warm rays and bathed in it, soaking in the absolute quiet. The light filled his lungs, his heart, his mind, his entire body, until he felt as though he was *the light itself.*

Without the pull of gravity or memory, the peace surrounded him, soothed him, became *him.*

So much peace without memory.

An odd thought, that. In knowing such, it must mean that he'd had memories once…a life once.

Something prickled at the base of his neck, a pinching sensation, easy to ignore at first, but persistent. Soon, the pinching became a stinging until the stinging morphed into a raging torrent of excruciating pain he couldn't seem to free himself of.

And then…then the memories came.

Oh, how they came, each one a fresh hell he was forced

to relive again and again. Each one a reminder of the things he'd done, the liar he'd become. The hypocrite. The deceitful, miserable human. Worse was the hope in his chest that he could have redeemed himself. Hope. What business had he in hoping?

The memories flashed never-ending behind his eyes, eyes now blinded to the warmth of a light that seemed never to have existed at all. Surely this was Hell and he would pay for every wrong he'd committed for the remainder of eternity. He'd always known this might be the price.

He screamed soundlessly into the void, and that, too, was endless.

Endless screaming.

Endless suffering.

Endless horrors.

Forever.

THE END

ACKNOWLEDGMENTS

A giant thank you to all the readers who made The Heart of Death possible. Because of your love for Reina, Quinn, and their cohorts, I was able to dive back into their world and send them on new adventures. (But who am I kidding? They were going on those adventures with or without an audience. So thank you, readers, for giving me the audience to continue telling their tale.)

To my immediate and extended family, I am so grateful for your support. You've always cheered me on and encouraged me to follow my dreams. Every book I write is a new dream made reality, and it's all because of you. Caelyn and Abigail, I hope you never stop dreaming.

To my friends, critique partners, and beta-readers who have cheered me on and helped make my work stronger in any small way, thank you. Jean Grant, Barbara Longo, Jess Rancatore, Vanita Shastry, and Rachel Strayer from your "Huh, what's going on here? I need more details" to your "I knew it!" comments, I appreciate all the time you put into reading and commenting, and into debating and discussing plot, characters, and their motivations with me…again and again. Also, a big thank you to Liz Mann, who *should* have been thanked as a beta reader for A Thousand Years to Wait. Thanks for being so patient in waiting to see your name in the acknowledgments, Liz!

A big thanks to my SCBWI critique group. You've made me a better writer and I sorely miss our in-person monthly meetups. (Go away, Covid.) Thank you, Jay Mehta, Cindy Mock, and Linda Stengle. Your support means the world.

To my Twitter writing friends, there are too many of you to name, but I'll try. Thank you to Lakshmi Iyer, Kristin Jacques, Mariely Lares, David Lins, Shanah McCready, Maggie Moris, Tammy Oja, Maria Stout, Ralph Walker, and so, so many others. I couldn't have continued writing without your encouragement and I'm so happy we can talk craft. I know I've missed naming so many people here, and friends, if your name isn't listed, please know I'm still so thankful for you! Thank you. All of you.

To my friends and coworkers at the library, I am so grateful to have your support on this journey. I couldn't have asked for a better workplace to spend my days or better people to spend them with. A shoutout to workwife Nancy because... well, workwife.

A special thank you to my cover artist, Jess Bieber, who actually *might* possess magic in her ability to visually represent my words in a breathtaking cover time and again. Thank you from the bottom of my heart for gracing me with your artistic enchantments. Lastly, a thank you to my talented editor, Sorchia DuBois. I don't know what I'd do without you.

ABOUT THE AUTHOR

L. Ryan Storms is a writer, photographer, traveler, and dreamer. She's a member of the Eastern Pennsylvania chapter of SCBWI who enjoys working PR & Marketing for her local library. She has written articles featured on the front page of local newspapers, but mostly she writes novels near and dear to her heart. She holds a B.S. in Marine Science from Kutztown University of Pennsylvania and a Master's in Business Administration from Marist College, but writing young adult fantasy has always been her true passion. Her first young adult novel, *A Thousand Years to Wait*, was an award-winning finalist in American Book Fest's 2019 Best Book Awards.

Storms lives in Pennsylvania with her cancer-survivor husband, two children, and a "rescue zoo" featuring two dogs, two cats, chickens, and an ex-racehorse. When she's not writing, reading, or keeping her kids in line, she enjoys hiking, photography, and planning the next big adventure.